The World Out There

The World Out There

a novel

John Talbird

MADVILLE PUBLISHING

Lake Dallas, Texas

FIRST EDITION

The World Out There is a work of fiction. Names, characters, places, and incidents either are the products of the author's imagination or are used fictitiously. Any resemblance to actual events, locales, businesses, companies, or persons, living or dead, is entirely coincidental.

Requests for permission to reprint material from this work should be sent to:

Permissions
Madville Publishing
P.O. Box 358
Lake Dallas, TX 75065

Author Photograph: Melinda Yale
Cover Design: Jacqueline Davis
Cover Art: *All Bantering and Debating*, silkscreen, 2008, Melinda Yale

ISBN: 978-1-948692-36-6 paperback, 978-1-948692-37-3 ebook
Library of Congress Control Number: 2020936689

In Memory of My Mother

1

"Something weird is happening, Mom."

Jan turns from the window, shakes the daydreaming trance from her head. The kitchen is bright and stifling with afternoon air. She cuts the water, dries her hands on a dish towel. A sluggish fly buzzes past, half-dead with heat, not worried about flyswatters. Jan kneels so she is face-to-face with her son. She loves seeing Hank up close like this—it gives her chills to think that someday he will be her height, someday she will have to look up at him. His curly blond hair is out of control. A man thought he was a girl last week in the grocery store. Perhaps she should cut it, but she is afraid of screwing it up. She hates going to the barbershop: those thick men with their cheap cologne and cigarette breath, fat fingers holding scissors too close to his neck, the long wait while she bites her nails and spits the slivers, scowling guy pushing a broom. She puts her fingers through Hank's curls, his serious expression making her smile.

"What do you mean, buddy?"

"It just keeps jumping. My chest." His eyes move slowly downward. The fly buzzes. "That was it. Did you hear it?"

"Yeah. You got the hiccups."

"Will it go away?"

"Sure. Try holding your breath."

He puffs his cheeks, places his fists against his neck as if to hold the air back. The clock on the wall hums. Hank hiccups and giggles, placing a hand on his heart as if to pledge allegiance. "Just a sec," Jan says, filling a glass with tap water, tasting it—room temperature, metallic. "Here. Drink this fast." He does, but after a few swallows, his chest jerks, eyes widen. She smiles. She knows it's nothing, but wants to fix it. "Hey, buddy, try to drink upside down." He frowns and bites his lip. She nods, recognizing the stupidity of her suggestion. "Like this," she says, taking a mouthful from the glass, turning and bending so she is looking at him through her legs. She swallows, smiles upside down, black curly hair pooling on the gray linoleum floor beneath her head. "Got it?"

He giggles and swallows some water, hands the glass back, bends over. The water runs down his face, into his hair and onto the floor. His laughter, jarred by hiccups, is musical in the kitchen. Jan pours the rest down the drain. Through the window, she can see Hank's cat, Smoke, inching through the grass, hunting something she cannot see. She could turn suddenly, yell "boo," scream, scare the hiccups from him. Of course, that's a ridiculous idea.

He looks at her as if to say *What next?*

"They'll go away, buddy. Get your bathing suit on. We need to leave if we're going swimming."

Jan packs a lunch—a couple of peanut butter and jelly sandwiches, potato chips, sodas—and they head down 441 to Lake Walters. The grass on Paynes Prairie looks dry enough to spontaneously combust under the Florida sun. Palmettos poke up from the ground like clumped daggers. The long, green sedge speckled with white flowers stretches for as far as she can see. Wavy lines of heat rise in the air as the road blurs and twists ahead, the dark mirage of water evaporating as they approach. Sweat runs down the side of her face, ribcage, the small of her back. The steering wheel vibrates like a lawnmower handle. Hank runs his fingers through his sweaty hair. Warm wind whips through the open windows, passes out again. Elbow against the armrest, Hank stretches to peer at the speeding scenery. He is wearing his new blue bathing suit, a YMCA T-shirt, black sneakers, the Donald Duck sunglasses his grandmother gave him last spring. Jan touches his hair and gets that feeling: chest contracts, eyes blur, and she tries to swallow, but the feeling is stuck in her throat. Sometimes, she thinks she loves him so much it will kill her.

"How are the hiccups, buddy?"

"Still there."

"What the hell, eh?"

He shrugs and she laughs. Then she flips the blinker and turns onto the dirt road leading to Lake Walters. The old Chevette leaves a cloud of dust, obscuring the road in the rearview. Her tongue is gritty, air smelling of chalk and gasoline.

"Hey, look, buddy."

A brown rabbit crouches in the middle of a freshly mowed field. Its black eyes turn toward the passing car, and then it hops off, seeming to skim the grass. The little automobile struggles, groaning up a steep hill, and then the lake is below, sun glittering on its rippled surface, tiny people running on the beach, splashing in the water. Hank hiccups and Jan presses her foot and the brake goes all the way to the floor.

There is a surge of panic and she stamps again, thinks she has pressed the gas by accident, slams her foot against the other pedal. The car shoots down the hill, toward a family crossing the parking lot. She hits the horn again and again, silly sounds from beneath the hood like a cartoon duck, inappropriate for the frenzy in her chest. She stomps on the brake pedal while Hank says, "Mommy, Mommy, Mommy," too calmly for a four-year-old in a brakeless car. The father yanks his little girl and he and the mother run, dragging the boy across black pavement. Jan jerks the wheel, swerves from the family and other blurred bodies and Hank is saying, "Mommy, Mommy, Mommy," and the Chevette nicks a car—gray, large like a Buick, Oldsmobile maybe, who cares, she can't think about that—there is the deep crunch of metal and tinkle of glass. She jerks the wheel away from a large oak; they run up a hill, green and cushiony with grass. It nudges the front of the car into the air and then they float.

Jan inhales and she and Hank look at each other and, briefly, smile. They hit the water and Jan lets out a big sigh because water is soft and she thinks that they are safe. "That was exciting. Huh, buddy?" Her laughter is shaky and without humor.

"Uh, Mom, water's running in the car."

"Don't worry, it'll be okay. We're just a few feet…" She is

surprised that land is so far away. In fact, her shock paralyzes her, not allowing any movement but the slow scan of eyes as she measures the distance: Ten? Fifteen? Twenty yards? The placid water is marred by rings expanding from the little car, horizon wet and rising to blot out vision. A large, flabby man—sunburn, too-tight T-shirt—moves toward them, struggling against lake, free-styling arms through the air. His eyes are white circles of dismay, tiny teeth framing open mouth. People gather on the beach to gawk. Water is pouring into both windows and their feet slosh in it. Hank stares at Jan, waiting. "Don't panic, buddy. It's going to be fine." She pops off her seatbelt and reaches into water for the button on Hank's.

"Goddamn. What?" It will not unlatch. Jan feels her lips curling into something like a smile but not, the situation too surreal with dream terror to be true. She can see Hank is not scared, he trusts her, waiting. "Don't panic, buddy." She jerks at the seatbelt, punches the button, jabs until her nail breaks. "Goddamn it. Fucking goddamn! Come on!" He hiccups, eyes round with fear. Or maybe shock at her language. "Don't panic, baby. When the water comes up, hold your breath. I'll get you out." He nods once, his cheeks puff and the water is over his head.

Jan is under and Hank looks back with fishlike eyes. She jerks at the strap which is unbudging. But then, with the second pull, shoulder straining as if to break, it comes loose. Sliding Hank free, she shoves him through the open window and his head bumps the frame, knocking an explosion of bubbles from his lips, air rushing crazily toward the light. She hears herself moan beneath the lake, dragging him to the surface. Putting her foot down, she sinks, surprised not to find mud, and swallows warm, gritty lake water. She kicks up, sucking in sweet air. It tastes clean. She can even feel it in her teeth. Hank's eyes are closed, mouth open, lips blue and fragile like wet paper.

Shouting and splashing next to her ear. "Lady, here, let me have him."

"No!" Jan yells, bats the hand away, swallows another mouthful, coughing. Her arm is across Hank's chest as she swims toward shore. A few feet and there is mucky earth beneath her. Hank is in her arms—light, limp, like a doll, no, not like a doll, skin rubbery, tongue gray between even, white baby teeth. Her mind is chaos, a garbled what next: *How do I get him to the hospital with the car gone? Call Ray? He'd threaten to take my son, got him into this mess now get him out. Could I walk? I could…* But when it registers that her son is not breathing, language breaks down, mind screaming atavisms.

The sun and water slide across her eyeballs, blurring everything but dark figures gathering and murmuring, hands to mouths, milling, unsure postures. Sand and spidery shadows, sprouts of grass fly up at Jan's corneas as she drops to her knees on the sand, son in arms. She lifts his neck, stares down his pink throat, pinches his nose, puts her lips against his. Breathing into his mouth, lips gritty with lake, her good air travels through his lungs. She wills the air to exist, become solid, something she can see—not this ghost she inhales through her nose and mouth. An image from grade school comes unbidden: science class, cartoon Os, arrows pointing them in the right direction. Muttering from above, the concerned hum of people with white and wrinkled toes. She pulls away, listens down his throat; there's nothing but the sound of sea. Pinch, breathe, listen. Nothing. Pinch, breathe, listen. And then he coughs, sputters water, squints into her face, the sun. Jan's tears come and her chest squeezes and she knows that this is it—this is going to kill her.

"It's all right, buddy, it's all right. Don't be scared. You're okay. Don't be scared." Putting her hands beneath his head, she pulls him so tightly to her it is as if she could pull him inside her. He is shaking, but no, she is shaking, tears hot and salty.

His voice is warm in the cup of her ear, fills her with joy and some sort of indefinable sadness: "It's all right, Mom, I'm not scared." His words tickle the tiny hairs in her ear and then he hiccups.

It is two in the morning and Jan has insomnia, not uncommon and predictable after the events of the day. She has spent the last hour sitting on a chair in Hank's room, watching him sleep. Twice, she had to touch his chest to make sure he was still breathing. After the second time, when he shifted onto his side and mumbled something unintelligible, she decided to get out of there before she woke him or just made herself crazy.

She cracks ice cubes out of their tray and into a glass, breaks the plastic seal on the bottle of rum she bought the day before. The liquor smells like rubbing alcohol with a sweet tinge. She licks her lips, fills the glass half full, almost takes a swallow, but instead opens a tiny can of pineapple juice and pours it over the rum, yellowish orange diffusing in clear liquor—it looks like the knockout gas movie bad guys use. She stirs it with a finger. Not bad, a bit strong, but okay.

The emergency room doctor looked Hank over, said he was fine. Put his card into Jan's palm, home phone number in pen. *If there are any problems, call me.* And with the adrenaline wearing off, relief running through her like cool air, she asked: "Doctor, he's had these hiccups for over twelve hours. Is that normal?"

The doctor tilted his head, rubbed his chin, smiled, lectured in a voice rich with authority: "…spasm of the diaphragm… involuntary inhalation…sudden closure of the glottis…that sharp, distinctive sound we call the…"

"Yes, yes, but is it *okay?* Is there anything to worry about?"

He kept smiling, staring, and then shook his head as if to say both, *No, there's nothing to worry about* and *You overprotective mothers, you kill me.* But he just said, "Don't worry. Hiccups are completely harmless," and placed a hand on her shoulder and slowly squeezed.

"Well, good, I was just worried. You see…" And then she stopped with a sudden realization: *He's flirting.* It was something in the way he stared into her eyes, the slight upward curve of the lips. He was good-looking: dark hair, young, a few years older than her, tall with wide shoulders. He could have walked off any hospital television show. But the thought of him standing there in her personal space, flirting with her while Hank sat a few feet away on an examination table with his hair frizzed, a plump, gray-headed nurse wrapping a blanket around his shoulders, whispering soft words and kissing his forehead, only hours after Jan brought him back to life with her air: it made her a little sick. There were goose bumps on her arms, a sour taste in her mouth, and her head hurt. She shrugged his hand from her shoulder, turned to Hank and said, "You ready to go, buddy?" He put his arms around her neck and, as she lifted him, it all came back: the sunlight at the lake, that taste of muddy water, his arms flopping at her sides as she stepped through thigh-high water toward land, moving with the slow desperation one feels in dreams, and her eyes stung. It was easy to ignore the rest of the doctor's words as she carried her son from the room: "Uh, Ms. Pender, I was wondering...Ms. Pender?"

The ice clicks against her teeth, so she mixes another. The alcohol is giving her a buzz: she is relaxed, the world does not seem as scary or complicated as it did a few minutes ago, all edges dulled. Sitting on the couch, she tips her head against the wall, closing her eyes. The sweating glass feels good in her hand. *My car is ruined,* she thinks and the sentence conjures an image of her tiny silver Chevette at the bottom of the lake, guppies swimming in and out of the open windows, light filtering down on a calm Hank with ballooned cheeks, crash of bubbles rushing to the surface. How can she ever save enough to afford another car? Will she be able to drive? When she moves her foot to press that pedal on the left, how can she assume the car will stop, that she and her son will not go flying into danger again? Bodies of water, brick walls, the wheels of semis: the world is full of death. Her father will probably buy her another car, but she is thirty-four. When will it stop? When will she not need to be taken care of? She should call Hank's father, tell him what happened, but it is late. The VCR clock reads 2:33. Actually, Ray would probably be up, but he might be out and Jan's not crazy about talking to what's-her-name. The new girlfriend is a decade younger and Jan hates when she catches her on the phone, that coldness, as if that little chick has any right, as if Jan gives a shit about Ray, as if she would consider getting back with him even if he were single and willing.

She considers turning on the stereo, but the thought of deciding which CD to play is overwhelming. She could watch TV. She feels wide awake, but her eyes are tired, feet deadweight on the coffee table. Moths tap the glass doors in double time to the rhythm of her breath.

Jan's eyes open to sunlight streaming through the living room window. "Shit," she mutters, dragging her teeth across her tongue. She spilled the last of her drink on the sofa and the cat is purring and methodically licking the spot. The rum and pineapple juice which seemed so inviting last night is now a sweet-scented stain on the beige couch; it makes her depressed. The clock reads 9:38. She has missed her first class. Putting the glass on a coaster, she goes down the hall to Hank's room, rubbing the sleep from her eyes. "Honey, don't you think it's time to get up?" There is a tightness in her chest as she walks through the weirdly still house, resisting the urge to run.

He is not there.

The sun bleeds around the drawn blinds, throwing soft light on dust motes. She goes to the kitchen, bare feet aching against the carpet and then linoleum, calling, "Buddy? Where are you?" There is a chill on her arms. The kitchen is empty and she stares, body rigid, feet sucked to the floor as if taking root, the only movement her swiveling head, examining each surface: counter with a smear of red, catsup; stove, one eye missing; refrigerator, son's bright abstract art beneath magnet letters, B, J, L; spin of second hand on white clock face. The phone rings, cracking the silence in half, making her jump, snatching a shout. She picks the receiver up on the second ring.

"Hello?"

"What the fuck happened?"

Anger, sudden and liquid, rushes through her chest at the sound of Ray's voice. "I can't talk."

"Yeah, Jan, you can talk. I see in the paper you almost drowned my son."

A breath shivers out before she speaks; she wonders why the phone does not crack in her fist. "Ray, I didn't almost kill him. I saved his life." She chews the inside of her mouth. "He's okay. A doctor at the hospital checked him out and said he was fine. I couldn't help it. The damn brakes went out."

"How did that happen? Jan, when you hear that squeal it means you need new brake pads. It doesn't mean drive until they quit."

"Don't…" Her voice falters—he's right, she had been hearing that squeal for weeks, maybe months, and just hoped it would go away. "Don't lecture me."

"Baby, if you can't handle him, let me take over."

"Ray, you know this has nothing to do with fucking parenting skills." The quiet in her voice frightens her.

"No. I don't know that."

"Ray…don't. Custody is settled. If you try to change things, I'll fight." She hates the pleading in her voice, the hint of whine: "The judge awarded me custody."

"Yeah, I remember. Maybe we should ask Hank? If he wanted to live with me, I don't think I'd care what a judge said. It doesn't seem like you should either."

She tries to ignore the fear crawling across her belly with tiny legs; the clock's second hand hums like mad. Ray sounds so reasonable that Jan wonders where the dread comes from. She looks around the kitchen for something, a weapon perhaps. Black handle of serrated knife leaning in the dish rack. If she sliced the telephone cord, it would spit blood.

And then out the window there he is: Hank crouched in grass—that same spot where Smoke was hunting yesterday—meticulously setting up little green army men, grass so long he has to position each carefully between the blades. His lips move silently as he talks to the plastic men gripping tiny guns and grenades. She stares at the black holes in the phone's mouthpiece. The white handgrip is smeared with her own fingerprints, Hank's too. The kitchen feels dirty.

"Ray, do you have to do this to me now? Can't you just remember when you loved me and not make me feel like complete and utter shit right this minute?"

There is an intake of breath and then nothing. He does not speak for seconds, maybe a full minute and they listen to each other saying nothing.

"Jan…I don't know. I'm sorry. My band played last night, I didn't get much sleep. Then I see this on the front page this morning. My god, what do you expect?"

"Ray, I need to get ready for school."

"I know. Jan…are you okay?"

"We're fine. I've got to go. I'll talk to you soon."

"Can I talk to Hank?"

This reasonable request surprises her and she stares through the window at her son. There is a smudge in the lower corner of the pane which glows gold in the sunlight. Hank's face passes back and forth on the other side of the smudge, clear then blurry. He seems a wisp, something she made up. She has a sudden urge to grab him, get in the car and go. Where? In what car? She bites her tongue.

"Of course. Let me get him."

Saturday afternoon, a little after one, and Jan is late for work. She is a part-time employee at Book Purgatory, a used bookstore. She had considered trying to scrape by on college grants, student loans, food stamps, and the bit Ray gives, but found herself getting bored and lonely on those odd weekends when Hank disappeared with his father. *What now?* she'd think as soon as they pulled off, Hank strapped into the passenger seat of his dad's jeep. She had dates and would hang out in bars with friends, but there was always something off. She had no real connection with those people—friends from school or guys who would ask her out after class. They seemed young. Some of them were.

It is a good job, pays over minimum wage—not much, but over. She works with interesting people—writers and musicians, artists, community activists, people who like to talk about books. But good conversations are rarer than she would have thought. Since working there, she has become intimately familiar with the types of books most people want to read, like historical romances with their covers depicting busty heroines forced backward by handsome Cro-Magnons, true crime books and their black-and-white police photos of carnage. She has had to flip through *Playboy* magazines as the store will not buy these unless they still have their pin-ups. After a long day, her eyes itch from dust and her head hurts from the steady throb of fluorescents. Most of the time is spent counting and pricing and shelving books, many of which she is not even interested in looking at, let alone reading. People's contempt for books has been disheartening. She has seen a man take a pocketful of change for his dead mother's books rather than trade for different ones. She has seen books so moldy they looked as if they had been stored outside with the gardening tools. She has learned to be careful with boxes in a certain spectrum of filthy, because invariably they will eject cockroaches or silverfish. And even though she has had a few engaging conversations about literature in the last few months, she has also had to realize that, despite the perks—cheap books for Hank and her, creative and intelligent coworkers—this is a job, this is retail, and books are "product."

Still, she usually enjoys her job. But at moments like now—running around the house shoving toys and a change of clothes for Hank into his backpack—she would rather not be working. She is taking Hank to his friend Patrick Henry's house and Book Purgatory is the last place she wants to be today. She wants to be with her son, drink a beer with Patrick Henry's mom, Rain, while the boys play in the sandbox or the inflatable pool in the back yard. But Jessica called in sick and William, the manager, said they were desperate. Besides, she and Hank need the money.

"Are you sure you don't mind spending the night at Patrick Henry's house?" Jan asks as she locks the front door.

"No," Hank smiles, "he's my best friend." He is having trouble with his helmet so Jan leans in to help and he hiccups.

"You've still got the hiccups."

"Yeah." He shrugs.

"Do they bother you?"

"No, I'm getting used to them." He smiles and tugs on a hank of her hair.

"Ow, don't do that. Do you hiccup all the time?"

"Not all the time." He wraps his arms around her neck.

Picking him up, she straps him into the child's seat on the back of her bike. "Ugh. Soon, you'll be too heavy for this." He nods. "Soon, you'll be lifting me up." He nods again. She gets that feeling. Her chest contracts and her head throbs. She knows she is overprotective, worry grips her temples sometimes, squeezing her skull like a muscle, like a heart, one beat from splitting, cracking in half—her worry would pour forth like gravy, or hiss like gas. Her body would deflate, insubstantial as a popped balloon; a street sweeper would come along and nudge her into his handled dustpan, dump her in a garbage can.

She pushes the bike, kicks her leg over the frame, and pedals toward Rain and Patrick Henry's house. The sun pounds down and sweat is already breaking out on her neck, arms, and back, behind her knees and on her scalp. But there is also a breeze and the air feels good working in her lungs.

"Pedal faster, Mom. Go fast," Hank shouts from behind, hand coming up to touch her back. She pedals faster.

William takes a smoke while Jan sits on the breakroom couch, waiting for her frozen burrito in the microwave. The emergency door is open, letting in dusk light. William, blowing smoke through the doorway, presses the sole of one of his large, black sneakers flat against the jamb, knee jutting out. Skinny and tall—maybe six-three—he has brown, frizzy hair which projects from his head in an afro and a couple days' growth of stubble on his face and neck. His pale arms are covered in tattoos—black lines and symbols which look like Egyptian hieroglyphics. He wears thick black glasses, the kind that nerds in high school used to wear, but seem to have become fashionable. His intense stare, at first, during Jan's interview, intimidated her. She had been a customer for years and always found him a little frightening. He had that introspective gaze she associated with the intellectual, but the way he clenched his jaw made it seem he carried a subtle anger which might burst forth at any moment. When he spoke, though, he had such a calm, deep voice that she felt at ease.

Jan gets a vibe that maybe William has a crush on her. When she takes her breaks, he often comes back to smoke and talk. Most of the employees are college students in their early twenties and, at first, Jan assumed William was just glad to work with someone who was closer to his age. But, as the weeks wear on, and she sees the way he looks at her, the way he teases, the way he compliments her on her hair or a blouse even when she suspects she looks like shit, she is starting to wonder. It worries her, because he is her boss. Also, she may not be attracted to him. She respects him. She thinks he might be one of the smartest people she knows. He has got a degree in philosophy, but knows his way around literature, art, film, history. He backpacks and can name local animals and plant life. He can fix a carburetor or a lawnmower. He designed and built the bookshelves and the front desk in Book Purgatory. And she feels comfortable talking with him.

Or not, like tonight. The microwave dings and Jan removes the plastic plate, setting the burrito on the sofa's arm to cool. William takes a final drag from his cigarette, flicks it outside, and pulls the big, blue door shut. He sits on the couch, turns on the TV, flipping through channels with the remote. She eats her burrito, occasionally looking at him from the corner of her eye. He is staring at the television, mouth slightly open, tongue tip moving back and forth over his teeth. He pauses on ESPN as a gate pops open and a gigantic bull with a humped back bucks into a muddy pen, black chunks of earth flying. The cowboy does a desperate dance, hat gone, gripping the rope around the animal's chest. "I never would have guessed you for a rodeo fan," Jan teases.

William smiles, but does not look at her. "I'm not."

The cowboy's ass leaves the bull's back and comes down again so hard Jan feels it in her own spine. The bull flings the rag doll man up again and this time the cowboy's hand is jerked from the rope. He flies through the air like a sack without bones or cartilage or anything solid and the bull seems to know exactly where he is as if this part is planned. The animal jerks its head and pierces the cowboy somewhere in his lower stomach. "Oh god," Jan says and William takes a breath. The man's hands grasp the place where the horn went in, and as he hits the dirt, a hoof comes down on his back. Frantic clowns converge to lure the bull away. Jan moves her burrito to the coffee table. Her stomach feels full of fluid. Her voice comes out in a rasp: "That's not only ruined my dinner, but I think my evening."

"Yeah," William shrugs. "If that guy is alive he's not going to have much of a life. But what about the bull? A life devoted to people taunting him, enraging him, riding him for sport." He looks at the floor for a second, then back at Jan. "These macho guys think the world exists for them, that they can do whatever they want."

All she can do is stare, not sure how to take this. *Is he joking?* "You're weird," she says.

Jan waits at the front of the darkened store for William who has gone to drop the day's earnings in the safe. Her mood has not improved since her break.

The night was slow and she flipped through a back issue of some rock-and-roll magazine, read an article about a rock star who had recently killed himself with a shotgun. She felt as if she was putting her foot on the brake, slowing to catch a glimpse of blood-splattered bodies pulled from a crushed car. Having abandoned her dinner, her stomach growled even though she had no appetite. She chomped aggressively on a piece of gum until all the spearmint was gone, until it tasted of rubber and then nothing, and still she chewed. She could feel the frown on her face, but did not care, suddenly resenting all the customers—they were ravenous for serial killers and war stories, rape fantasies. She did not have a smile for any of them. She has heard William say on more than one occasion, "At least they're reading." If that is what they are reading, what is so great about reading?

Outside, the parking lot is nearly empty on this side of the strip mall. At the other end, light shines from the large Publix windows; a guy with long, blond hair lopes through the automatic doors with a 12-pack under an arm. "You coming to the brew pub with us tonight?" William asks while locking the door. This has become a ritual for them on Saturday nights when Jan works: He invites her to come out for beers with him and some other employees, she politely says no.

Tonight, she does not feel polite, will not even look at him. Unlocking her bike, she says, "No, I'm tired. I'm going home."

"You said last week you'd join us tonight."

She shrugs, still not looking at him, pulling a strand of hair from her mouth. "Maybe. But I'm not."

"Are you pissed at me for what I said about the cowboy?"

She keeps her face averted, slides the lock into its holder, ties her tennis shoe. "No, I just have to go home."

"Do you have Hank tonight?"

"No," she sighs, "he's at his friend Patrick Henry's house." She brushes the grit from her knee as she stands.

"He's got a friend named Patrick Henry? The 'give me liberty or give me death' guy?"

William has such a comically puzzled expression—eyebrows pushed together, lips turned downward—that Jan laughs despite herself. "Thanks, I just can't," she says, shaking her head. "I'm sorry; I'm in a foul mood."

"That's even more of a reason to come out with us. If you go home, you're going to be lonely and depressed. You won't be able to sleep no matter how tired you are. You'll probably drink and you know what drinking by yourself is a sign of: alcoholism. You'll start drinking before exams, before work. You'll end up on the street selling your body, drinking cooking sherry and rubbing alcohol. You'll lose your looks: your teeth will fall out, your hair will become thin and greasy, you'll lose weight everywhere but your belly which will sag…"

"Stop, you're grossing me out," she laughs. Despite the absurdity of what he says, his stare is intent, expression serious and worried, lines delivered without a hint of facetiousness. He has got his hands on the handle bars, gently steering the bike out of her grip and toward his beat-up truck. The cars move past on University Avenue and hum in bursts of speed as they head toward the campus; they sound happy, as if fun awaits in that direction.

"All right, just one beer, okay?"

"Sure, just two beers and straight home to bed," that mock-serious expression still there.

Jan smiles over the hood of his truck. Was she really in such a bad mood a few seconds ago? She feels desperate to hang onto this feeling. "Are you flirting?"

He does not smile back. "Maybe."

They stumble into Jan's house, William kicking the door closed behind them. He crouches low so she can reach over his shoulders, head bobbing as they lurch across the living room. He looks funny so she laughs. One beer became two then three and the next thing Jan knew, everyone except William was gone and the bartenders were clicking the lights on and off, yelling, "Go home, go home, you losers." Jan laughs some more.

They go down the hall, William panting. She bumps against the wall, feels him bump against the other. She giggles as they enter her bedroom. There is a click and the light next to the bed comes on. They move across the floor in slow motion. William's sweat smells sour, or maybe it is Jan's. He lurches as if he can barely make it, as if he is stretching for the finish line, and they collapse on the bed with a loud creak of springs. Her head spins and, for a moment, it occurs to her that she might throw up. But then the room is right and she takes a breath, runs the back of a hand across her forehead and it comes away damp and cool.

"I'm a lightweight," she says.

"Yes, you are."

She giggles and squints. "Hey, what's the big idea? Goddamn, turn off that light. What are you trying to do, blind me?"

"Yes, I'm trying to blind you." He sounds drunk or tired as he bends toward the lamp and then she is blinking in the sudden darkness, a red spot dancing from eye to eye, then falling out of sight. In the light from the hallway, William's silhouette glows, glasses glint. He seems to stare down at her, large hand on the bed next to her waist. She puts her hand on his wrist, thinks of sex. It has been over six months—some guy (Dan? Don?) in one of her science classes. She knew quickly, maybe from the beginning, that the attraction was only physical. After a couple of weeks, she never wanted to hear him speak again.

Her voice is husky and startling so she clears her throat and tries again: "I've got a queen-sized bed. If you want to sleep here, you can."

He kisses her forehead. "I better not, but thank you." Untangling the sheet in a ball at the foot of the bed, he spreads it over her, brushes the hair from her eyes, wipes the sweat from her face with his palm which he then wipes on his pants. "Sleep well," he says, kissing her forehead again. She smiles. Her eyes close as William moves through the doorway, body flickering like an apparition in the light. She is in complete darkness even as she hears the dull click of a light switch in the hall.

She dreams:

Returning, he slips under the covers and runs his big hands over her body—under her T-shirt, across the stretch marks on her belly, over her rib cage, breasts. He touches her nipples, twists them, takes them into his mouth and they become hard like pebbles; there is a tension in her belly and lower. He is a shadow bearing down with the weight of a pile of bricks, an anvil—she is hot liquid, melting plastic beneath his body. Arching her back, she is aroused and trying to get away, wants to sink into the mattress, but also his body. He puts his lips against her neck, tongue a gliding thing, mouth working as if to teach the skin. She touches him, terrified of offering more than her fingertips, and wants to say both no and yes. But the sounds that come out are gasps which make no sense and she jerks her head from right to left, eyes shut tight. He fills her and she inhales something foul and black. Her saliva wells with a taste like shame and the goose bumps break out. She is dirty, feels as if she has awakened in a cold, dank place like an open grave. Slipping out from under him, his hands fall away, back to his own body. She runs her hands over herself as if they might be clothes, peering at him through the hair hanging in her face. "How could you?" she says. "I'm really disappointed. Don't you know I'm a mother?"

The light from the street lamp outside, the shadows from the frames dividing the panes of glass, throw black fissures on his face as if his head were cracking open. Although his expression is blank, mannequin-like, his voice is so loud she cringes, fearing the words will shatter her: "You're useless. You don't matter. You take up space. You're a void…"

She has to shut him up, cannot bear to hear his voice filling the room, to know it is leaking out and traveling into her neighbors' ears, that they will be listening at their windows to the sounds coming from that single mother's house, that they will come to save her, see her naked against the wall with her hair in her face, his come running down her leg. She picks up something from the floor—a shoe—and throws it, the move futile and desperate. It bounces off his chest and his eyes widen and fill with tears, mouth open without sound. Then a child's howl fills the room and he runs to the front door, flinging it open and disappearing.

Jan opens her eyes on a corner of the ceiling. The abandoned spider web there bows with the weight of accumulated dust. She thinks she should knock it down, but does not know where her broom is, can barely fathom the complexity of finding it, raising it above her head, directing it to that spot. Rolling over takes forever and it is nauseating, a taste no longer beer in the back of her throat and the cavern of her stomach. Afraid she will vomit on herself or the carpet, she is hyper-aware of everything in the room: blank-screened computer, wadded white sock on the floor, too-bright ray of light piercing broken blind, the little clock next to her bed glowing red in the dimness. She holds it close to her face, shocked at what she reads and only slightly able to comprehend. It's 12:03 p.m. 12:03. 12:03?

"Shit! Shit-goddamn!"

A pounding of feet and then a hairy giant bursts into the room.

"Shit," Jan screams again, slamming against the wall, pulling the sheet up to her chin. "What are you doing here?"

William gapes stupidly, and by the time he is finished speaking she can hear her teeth grinding in the back of her head. "... slept on your couch. I was—I was tired...and—uh, I thought I was too drunk...to drive." There is no reason for her to cover herself; she is still wearing the shorts and T-shirt from the night before. Flinging the sheet off, she sits on the floor to put on her sneakers, smells the stale cigarette and sweat coming off her and swallows, grinds her teeth some more. "What's going on?" he asks, deep voice deafening. She wants to tell him to shut the fuck up, but is busy tying shoes—it is complicated and takes forever.

"I was supposed to pick Hank up two hours ago. I can't believe Rain didn't call."

"The phone rang. Several times."

Jan can only stare. Finally, the words come: "Why didn't you answer?"

William opens and closes his mouth like it is on a broken hinge, and she fights the urge to scream. "I thought you were ignoring it," he says finally.

She jumps up, dials Rain's number; it is busy. Slamming the receiver, she brushes past William, runs down the hall, sneakers slapping floor. Each footstep reverberates in her skull. She knows at any moment she is going to vomit down the front of her shirt. Standing clench-fisted in the foyer, staring at the spot where she keeps her bike, all she can do is scream: "Goddamn! Where's my bike?" She rubs her temples, hysteria creeping like insects across her scalp.

"Relax," William says behind her, "it's still in the back of my truck. I'll drive." She follows him through the door, slams it without looking back. But the engine will not turn over and she grips the dash, biting the inside of her mouth. William's eyes flicker at her, but he keeps his head down as if listening for something. And then the engine catches and they are heading down the road.

"Where to?" he asks.

"Summertree Condominiums. It's on..."

"I *know* where it is."

The windshield is like a magnifying glass, the sun shining through it intense, burning the air out, the world out there large and warped. Jan cranks down the window, but the air rushing in is hot and heavy, blow-dryer air. William's jaw is rigid, neck muscles cords. Jan feels something like hate for him, but is not sure why and needs to look away. The scenery rushes past in a blur, twisting her stomach, vertigo seeping through her. The smell of gasoline is strong, a metallic taste in her mouth and the back of her throat. She stares at the vibrating floor.

"Jan, are you all right?"

Sweat on her upper lip and in her eyes, she wipes her face, turns toward William, but cannot speak.

"We're here, Jan. Which apartment?"

They are passing Rain's apartment. "Stop," she yells, opening the door.

"Shit." William slams on the brakes and the door jerks from her hand. She stumbles, loses balance, falls, skin yielding to hot concrete. Bile mingles with the not-beer taste; she gulps to keep it down.

"Jan, are you okay?" behind her, but she's up and moving across the pavement and then the manicured lawn, breaking through the warm stream of a stuttering sprinkler with its vague scent of sewage.

She goes through the door without knocking. Rain steps into the hallway, clutched dishrag and piercingly blue cup, eyes huge with concern and something else. Her face is makeup-free, cheeks red.

"Where were you? You scared me." Jan shoves past, not wanting to talk, suddenly angry at Rain too.

Hank's here. Standing in the dining room, biting a thumbnail, feet bare, one of them turned sideways, double-jointed ankle the image of a broken bone. His face is red and smeared with tear streaks.

"Oh, honey," Jan says, and the shame in her voice brings tears. She moves to Hank, crouching so they are face to face, putting her arms around him, holding him to her as if this were more serious than it is, as if he were dying. Adult voices murmur above and behind.

"Where were you, Mom?"

Hank's voice moves in Jan's ear like a sweet tune which brings more tears for no reason she can name and she squeezes him tighter. She cannot think of anything to say, so says nothing, running her hand under his shirt, across his warm back, running her fingers through his hair, pulling his cheek to hers, turning his lips to her ear, listening to the silence which seems to rush down on the apartment like a graceful, vicious bird. His breath comes and goes in her ear, but there is not one other sound.

2

William squints at the sunlight coming through Rain's front windows throwing red dots all across his vision, dizzy in the craziness in her cramped, chaotic apartment. He wants to wave his hand through the air, as if to brush away cobwebs from his face although they are in his brain.

Hank is crying. Jan too. Rain seems angry about missing church, but it is hard to follow the string of words past the fifth or sixth: "Where've you been. I've been calling…" "…might not occur to you…" "…you need to think of…" The kid bounces a red ball against the living room wall with maddening regularity, leaving dirt marks on the eggshell white. Their dog—a dirty, gray snouty thing with mange on its rump—worries what looks like a stuffed animal into tiny bits of fabric and fluff and slobber.

Since Jan ignores her, Rain eventually whirls on William although they have never met. Standing in his space, she speaks more quietly now, but with a barely harnessed rage: "Now, *who* are you?" When he cannot think of how to answer this question, she takes a step closer. "You guys smell like a brewery. And cigarettes. You know she's got a kid?" She points at Hank to illustrate. William opens and closes his mouth some more. He wants to say, "You don't smell so hot either," the hint of B.O. coming off her and maybe some sort of herbal remedy or wax. She has got an angry pimple on her forehead above the right eye.

William stares, resists the urge to shove her even though his back is against the wall. He says, "I'm William" as if that explains everything. A chuckle comes from somewhere in his chest and he struggles to keep it down, shrugs, coughs into his fist and mumbles disconnected half-sentences: "Had a few, you know how it is, sorry about it."

Jan, standing, Hank's hand in hers, sniffles and rubs her nose with the back of her other hand. "Do you think you could give us a ride home?" she asks. "William? Please?" Hank stares at the floor as if embarrassed.

"Sure." He laughs nervously. "Yes, I'd love to give you a ride. Come on…Hank?" he says, slapping his thigh. "Want to go for a ride in a noisy truck?" Hank says nothing, but presses his face against his mother's leg.

"Let's go," Jan says, pulling Hank by the hand toward the door.

"Honey," Rain says, putting a hand on Jan's shoulder and a few tears run down Jan's cheeks. "Come here," and they hug. William looks away, at Hank who is looking at the brown shag. The other kid keeps bouncing his ball; perhaps he's autistic, maybe it is therapy. The dog growls wetly at what he is destroying. William sneaks a look at the two women who seem like a grumpy middle-aged lesbian couple. "I was just worried," Rain says, into Jan's hair.

"Uh-huh," Jan says, sniffling into her neck.

William is embarrassed; this seems so overdramatic. He wants to leave so bad it itches.

He says nothing on the trip back to Jan's place, truck grumbling, backfiring once at a light. Jan and Hank huddle on the passenger side whispering to each other, and he catches the stray word or phrase, all tilted upward like questions: "have fun?" "eat for dinner?" But most of it is a low hum as if they are communicating in tones and vibrations. He parks on the black asphalt street in front of her house which is an off-white cinder block ranch, like many in Gainesville. It is the first time he has seen it in daylight, and decides it is perhaps the most dingy, depressing house in the world. Some past tenant or the landlord dumped a path of pebbles leading from the driveway to the front door, but maybe they ran short, or people have tracked them off over the years, the brown dirt peeking through. The grass looks like it has not been cut in weeks. The carport—cluttered with boxes, a few balls, and a kid's bike with a flat tire—seems empty and forbidding without a car, like an open mouth with just a few teeth. Her neighbor's yard is fenced off with chainlink rimmed with fans of palmettos so pointy they seem to prick his eyes just to see them.

He shuts off the engine and the truck hiccups and then is silent. Taking a deep breath to psych himself up, he turns halfway in the seat to look Jan in the eye for the first time that morning. He is surprised at the nervousness there. She is like a B movie actress with a secret, the type of character you know is going to bolt.

"I'm sorry, man," she says, shrugging, stammering, "I don't know what happened." There is a pause and then William shrugs too, rubs his nose. She sighs, coughs what might be an attempt at a chuckle. "Ready to go, buddy?" she asks Hank, opening the door, his fist held tightly in hers. Her smile is so sad that William's chest aches.

Seeing her like that, nervous, vulnerable, even scared maybe, does something to him. He was disgusted with the scene at Rain's, annoyed, wanting very much to get this woman he is a little sorry he has hired out of his truck. But suddenly, all of the anger and disgust are gone, evaporated—no trace. It is so sudden, in fact, it is a bit frightening. And thrilling. He has a sudden urge to touch her cheek. He feels like he is moving through a dream, sun glancing off his eyeballs with underwater rainbow effects, can feel the ridiculous grin on his face, seems to hear every bird distinctly. *Yeah, that's a blue jay. And that's a swallow's twitter. Oh, and that's a great crested flycatcher.*

And then it is gone.

"Why are *you* getting out?" she wants to know, squinting at the sun in her eyes.

Perhaps he overreacts. But there is something about the question, following a hung over morning of driving and yelling, that beer-and-cigarette taste stale in his mouth. There are two fingernails pressing against the back of his eyeballs and, for some reason, every single bird in the world has just stopped singing.

"Don't you want your fucking bike?" he asks with what he thought was going to be a smile on his face, but obviously is not. He even points at it in the bed of his truck as if she might be too stupid to know what a bike is. Lifting it out, he wheels it toward her house, can feel that not-smile on his face contorting, yes, definitely a writhing mass of eyebrow and lip and tooth and eye and nostril. He can feel how unpleasant his face must look, yet is too exhausted to think about changing it. He watches her stare at him, the bike like an absurd, giant toy between them. He feels happy at the moment, but no, that cannot be right, what is coiling his gut? And those two fingernails still poke the backs of his eyeballs.

She says, "Could you, um, watch your language? You know, in front of my son?" There is a weird, surprised smile on her face.

He thinks *We will hug and kiss at any moment.* And then he laughs. He feels amused, but the laugh does not sound like a ha-ha laugh. It is more like a fuck-you laugh. "Why don't you stop over-reacting?" he says. He meant it as a real suggestion, like *Hey, calm down, don't stress out.* But it, too, sounds like, "Fuck you."

Her eyes are open wide. She turns her head slightly, brushes the sticky hair from her face. There is a drop of sweat frozen right next to her left eyelid. "Buddy, go on. I'll be there in a second."

Hank trudges off, shoulders hunched, face red from crying, head turned to watch the mean man who leans the bike toward his mother, offering it. But when he lets it go, it just falls in a clatter of metal and pavement. She puts her hands on her hips. William wants to say sorry, that he did not mean to drop the bike, that he is not sure why they are fighting or whatever it is they are doing, but sentences seem so knotty, his tongue like strange meat, that he just wants to go home and climb into bed with the blinds all drawn. "I need to go," he says in a gravelly voice, turning away.

She grabs his arm, voice deep. "No, wait, don't walk away." Her grip is strong and, unfortunately, pressing against a new tattoo on his right bicep, two arrows pointed in different directions, a technical symbol from an old textbook. Her touch feels like someone gripping the skin over a burn. He has a sudden urge to slap her hand away, but refrains, wants to just stand still for a second and see how this plays out. Her face is close, as if she were standing on her toes. And she is. There is something in her eyes, anger maybe or fear. Or just craziness. They are ambiguously wet at the corners. He freezes, cannot spare a heartbeat or single breath. The birds return to their song. She speaks: "Can we try not to be awkward with each other?"

"What?" William asks. Then, peeling her fingers away, "Could you not touch that? It's a new tattoo."

"Oh," she says, looking at her hand. "Sorry." She shakes her head and goes toward the house. "I can't deal with this," she seems to say, but he is not sure he has heard right.

"What?" he yells after her. She does not answer, going inside. The door makes no sound as it closes.

The next morning, the phone rings while William is drinking black coffee, alternately reading the paper and staring out the window, waiting for the day to begin. "Hey, I'm so sorry," Jan says.

"It's all right," William responds, although it does not feel all right. He is not exactly sure what she is apologizing for, even though he feels he deserves one. He is a little frightened of her, although he can see in his reflection in the mirror on his living room wall that he is also smiling.

"No, it's really not," she says. "You didn't need all that…drama." She giggles. "I'm kind of embarrassed. Okay, very embarrassed. I'm sorry I was mean to you." There is a staticky hum on the line as he waits for what she will say next. "So, are you going to fire me?"

"No," he says, and laughs. "I'm suspending you without pay."

"What?"

"Kidding."

"Oh." There is another pause. William opens his mouth to say *See you at work,* then Jan says, "When do you work?"

"Three."

"Maybe you could come over for lunch. Beforehand?"

"Jan, you don't have to make up for anything. All is forgiven."

"I know. I would just like to…Well, come if you want."

William stares out the window at this fat blue jay sitting on a branch of a pine, its face angled directly at him as if listening. Flann, William's orange tabby, is on the window ledge, a clicking coming from her throat as she regards the bird and imagines killing it. A breeze lifts the Spanish moss hanging from the branch and the bird takes flight. The cat glances at William then as if it is his fault, so he scratches her between her ears, realizing that he does want to have lunch with this nutty girl. "How about one?"

Jan has quite a spread on her dining room table: sliced yellow and red bell peppers, cucumbers, cauliflower, apples, pears, freshly made blue cheese dressing, three kinds of sliced cheese, home-made bread. Coffee, a hint of cinnamon, brews in the kitchen. Hank is drawing on the floor, crayons fanned out neatly around him. The image on the white paper is abstract—heavy in yellows and blues. Light flows in through the sliding glass doors, dust motes floating in a sleepy way.

"What are you drawing?" William asks.

Hank looks up and then back down, bites his lip. "Dunno." He scribbles a blue crayon back and forth, tip held sideways.

Jan smiles at William, flicks a thick strand of hair which has come loose from her ponytail out of her face, wrinkles her nose. "I think you scared him yesterday."

"*I* scared *him?*"

She looks away, makes a "V" with her fingers; *peace* she mouths. Offering him a plate—handmade with red, laughing devils dancing on its edge—she says, "Get some food."

"Cool plate," he says, clears his throat.

"My friend, Rain—the woman who yelled at you yester-day—made it. By the way, she says 'Sorry' too. She loves Book Purgatory and doesn't want to get banned."

William loads his plate with food, although he is not par-ticularly hungry. He is feeling a nervous thrill, a tingle shivering across his skin. He pours a cup of coffee, which he does not need, sits stiffly on the living room's beige couch, white stuffing coming out from its arms. A fat, gray cat sleeps on the other side. "Come get food," Jan calls to Hank in her sleepy voice. She leans back-ward, pressing her hands against her lower back, until it pops. Yawning, she tosses nearly a whole buttered roll into her mouth.

"I'm not hungry," he answers, not looking up from what he is doing. She chews, one hand on her hip, the other holding a blue, handmade coffee mug. William sits perched on the couch which feels too short for him, watches Jan watching her son, feels that he has been invited into something private and solemn. She is wear-ing a faded, gray peasant skirt and a plain white T-shirt. On her feet are pink flip-flops and there's a silver ring on one of her toes.

"You didn't eat much breakfast," she says, sips coffee. Hank draws, biting his bottom lip. William bites into a Granny Smith apple so tart he feels it in his back teeth. "What do you call this one?" she asks.

Hank pauses, tilts his head, looking at her. "'Laughing with Daddy.'" Peering over his shoulder at William, his face reddens and he looks back down.

"Good title," she says. She smiles at William. "Let's go outside?"

William follows her across the dirty and cracked patio to a patch of long grass under an oak in her back yard. "That all you're eating?" William asks.

She bites into the Granny Smith apple. "I'm not hungry."

"You didn't eat much breakfast," he says.

She tilts her head at him like a puzzled animal or someone from another culture who finds him exotic. "You think you're funny?"

"I do," he answers, bites into his own apple, squints at its tartness and then tosses it into the bushes.

"Hey, those don't grow on trees," she says.

"Not true."

"Okay." She laughs, taking another large bite from her apple. He can see the half-chewed flesh and skin in her mouth, between her sharp, slightly crooked teeth. He eats a forkful of potato salad, dips a cherry tomato in dressing. "I love these apples," Jan says in a loud voice, raising it to him like a toast.

They both laugh, she crinkles her nose at him, and they eat and drink. A lawnmower buzzes in the next yard. A tapping comes from above, a woodpecker. It is small, black and white, pausing now and then to pick insects from the bark. Jan raises a hand to shield her eyes from the sun. That strand of hair floats to the side of her face and she frowns and bats it away, catches William watching.

"So, about yesterday…" she says, tossing away her apple core, brushing her palms together.

He raises two fingers, mouths *peace*.

"I know, I know," she laughs. "I'm not apologizing again. I guess I'm just trying to figure out why I freaked. I don't know, you might be bored."

"Well, no," he says, sipping from his coffee. "Why are we drinking coffee? Isn't it like a hundred degrees?"

"Do you want something else?"

He shrugs.

She slaps a mosquito, shrugs too, smiles. "Ray is pretty good about doing his part. Ray is Hank's dad." She chews her lip. "Actually, he's better help now than when we were together." She sighs. "But you know, it's hard to be a mom. I never realized how stressful it could be." She pulls up a handful of grass, tosses it in the air, pulls up another. "When Ray and I were together, back before Hank was born, it didn't seem like we had any problems. I know that's not true. I used to go into these deep depressions. I'd even cut myself sometimes." There are tiny, white crisscrosses on her wrists, almost too light to be seen. William had noticed them before but, of course, never asked. "Ray cheated on me several times; we're lucky we don't have AIDS. Still, our problems seem kind of petty now. We drank and smoked pot, did acid, stayed up all night, slept all day, watched a lot of TV, bought records and books, ate in restaurants. College is fun; you're an adult, but not really."

"I didn't think your college years were over." He smiles, finishing his coffee and wiping the sweat from the back of his neck.

"It's different now. Now I want to finish. Get a real job. No offense."

"None taken."

She puts a blade of grass between her teeth, lies back to stare at the sky. "I stopped doing drugs and drinking when I got pregnant and realized I wasn't going to get an abortion. I can remember Ray saying to me in the delivery room: 'Come on, baby, breathe. When this is all over, I'll buy you a margarita.'" She laughs. "I hadn't had a drink in nine months. I'd see him with a beer in the back yard and I would just want to come out here and slap him. I admit it: I love to drink." She laughs, tosses a handful of grass at William.

"Me too."

"I had sort of prided myself that I wasn't a drunk anymore though. Then, the other night I get fucked up and oversleep, forget to pick up my kid."

"You probably only drank three, maybe four, pints of beer over several hours. Why don't you give yourself a break?"

She shakes her head, all the play gone. Turning, she peers toward the back hedge where the neighbor's lawnmower gets louder and quieter as he passes and moves away, circling toward the center of his yard. "It's too soon after the wreck."

"You saved his life." William wants to touch her, maybe just her wrist, but doesn't.

She smiles. "That's true. After almost killing him."

William sits alone on a blistering afternoon in Dynasty Theatres watching *Miller's Crossing*, crunching buttered popcorn and sipping a gigantic cola. He goes to movies by himself a lot, most often like this, in the middle of the day when it is hot outside. At first, he worried that people would wonder what was wrong with him, sitting alone in the dark. But then he realized that no one was looking at him, and if they were, they could just fuck off.

On the screen, a mob kingpin, veined head wet with sweat, screams furiously and slams one of his hired thugs in the face with a coal shovel. At that exact moment, the absurdly loud clang of metal against face reverberating through the theater, William bites down on an unpopped kernel. He can feel the tooth crack, can visualize the fissure running to the root. It is a wisdom tooth—the one on the upper right side. It had grown in straight, but he has gone and cracked it in half. The pain is like wet electricity shooting from his tooth to his temples, squirming along his jaw. The whole action takes less than a second to happen, is so sudden he yells "fuck" without thinking and the few other viewers swivel to look. He waves them off as if to say, *I'm okay, you go on without me.*

He is not okay. The pain from that tooth is like the sound of squeaking Styrofoam, a sound he can feel in his mouth, physical but psychological too. William crouches low in his seat, movie flickering against the screen, projector threading film in a booth above, those six other viewers following the action while he rocks and cradles his head as if it might come off in his hands.

After calling in to work for two days, William finally comes into the bookstore on the third. The bell on the door dings and he feels it in the base of his skull. Everyone—customers, the few employees at the front of the store—seems to stare at him. His face is swollen and his mouth won't close anymore. He is sweating from the heat wave and no air-conditioning in his truck and the fever which sprang up during the night as he watched old horror movies without sound because each time a woman screamed he could feel it in his tooth.

He tries to walk with purpose, wants to slip past the front desk and the employees to his office without a word, thinks that if he can just get to that seat behind his desk, he will be okay. He will lay his sweating cheek against the blotter, maybe punch some numbers into the adding machine if he can stand the sound, and then go back home. The employees—Jessica, Erik, Jan—watch him as he passes, trying to act officiously. Business is slow. Kitschy disco plays on the stereo. Maybe he should not go back to the office. Maybe he should lean over the toilet instead. He would like to rest his face against a cool toilet seat about now. He has been doing that a lot.

Jan grabs his wrist as he tries to pass and he is so surprised that he just stares at her hand.

"What happened to you?" No one else speaks, even customers, as if they all want to know.

William wants to tell her to mind her own business, but instead, sounding like Elmer Fudd, says, "I bwoke a toof."

Someone giggles, Jessica. There's a worry line across Jan's forehead. She lets his wrist go. "Have you been to your dentist?"

He blushes, says, "I don't have a dentist." He says to Jessica and Erik in the Elmer Fudd voice, "Don't you two have work?" and neither laugh this time. Jessica abruptly rings up the customer, a guy with wild, blond hair and a belly which strains the buttons on his thrift store shirt, a guy who stares at William like he knows him. Erik walks off with a stack of romances with battered spines. Jan seems to be waiting for something. "I've got to get to work," William says.

Jan rolls her eyes. "Jesus, William, you can't just ignore it. The pain won't go away." *Leave me alone*, flashes through his mind, but nothing comes out. "I'll call my dentist," she says.

"You have a dentist?"

"Everyone has a dentist." She presses numbers which she has apparently memorized into the black phone on the cinderblock wall.

"I don't," Jessica says, pulling on the waistline of her tight, black jeans.

"Me neither," says William.

"Everybody but losers," Jan says, turning her back on them and twisting the phone cord around an index finger.

"Oh, we're losers," says Jessica. "Not all of us grew up with a silver spoon in our mouths, missy." She winks at William, stage whispers to him, "She was probably a cheerleader in high school."

Jan speaks into the phone, "Yes, this is Jan Pender. I'd like to make an appointment. It's an emergency…"

Jessica steps closer, looking up at William's mouth, absent-mindedly playing with her new nose ring.

William ignores her for a second, trying to hear what Jan is saying into the phone, then turns suddenly on her. "*What?*" he barks, taking a step closer so that she bumps against the counter.

"Nothing!" She turns and rips the strand of receipt hanging to the gray carpeting, shoving it into the overflowing wastebasket, mumbling, "Sheesh, such a grouch. *Why is everyone looking at me? Blah, blah, blah,*" she says, face a parody of complaint. William wonders for a second why he even hired her. She is a smart ass and has admitted, in so many words, that she cannot stand to read. But she is really patient with the customers, even the pushier ones, even the crazy ones like the guy everyone calls "Enema Man."

He has the urge to say *You're fired* just to see her expression, but Jan puts her hand on his arm, says, "I got you in."

Jan's dentist is a square-shaped guy with hands too large, it would seem, to fit inside anyone's mouth. It is late in the afternoon and William lies in a reclining chair, the pain finally dulling from the shots he has just had in the back of his jaw. His eyes open and close slowly because of the good feeling of the gas. The dentist, doing a bad John Wayne imitation says, "Hold on there, pardner, and we'll have this all taken care of." It seems just minutes later when the dentist and his tiny, pretty assistant are helping William to sit and then stand, although more than an hour has passed while they picked the fragments of broken tooth from the back of his jaw. His mouth is packed with cotton already turning red as they lead him wobbling to the waiting room where Jan sits, a dog-eared magazine spread across her thighs. She drops it on an end table and stands, cocking an eyebrow, smiling that sardonic smile. "You look *great*. Really handsome."

"Shut up," he tries to say, the words garbled.

"Ready to go?"

William's consciousness is frayed as Jan drives his truck. Slightly nauseated, he rests his cheek against the window, eyes closed, opening them now and then to tell Jan where to turn. The afternoon sunlight heats his eyelids. The gearshift is tricky and the truck keeps stalling out on Jan at traffic lights. William feels as if his brain is encased in Jell-O as he and Jan climb the concrete steps to his apartment, her hand on his elbow, the other on the small of his back. Then he is supine on his hard, brown couch, one hand flung across his eyes. Jan unfolds the fuzzy, yellow blanket hanging over the back of the couch and drapes it over him. "Should you sleep with that cotton shoved in your mouth?"

William mumbles something, uncovers his eyes which are closed.

"Do you need anything before I go?" She is whispering for some reason.

"No." William pokes the gauze into the corner of his mouth to avoid choking in his sleep, stretches his jaw. "You're a good mom, I bet."

She says nothing for a time and William lies there, waiting for sleep. Then he hears a suck of breath, sudden, and more silence. A tickle of worry, he opens his eyes. She is leaning forward, face in her hands, hair spilling across her shoulders which shake, bottom lip quivering. He tries to sit, rocks in place two or three times, but she puts her hand on his chest, shaking her head. "Stop. No, it's nothing," she says.

"What? What? Nothing?" He is still trying to sit.

"It. *It's* nothing. Okay?" She is not crying now, though her eyes are damp and red. She pushes him gently back into the pillow. "A social worker called." She sighs. "Shit, don't worry about it. I'm sorry I brought it up. Why don't you go to sleep? You must be tired."

"I'm not." His eyes flutter with exhaustion and pain killers. "Tell me." He can only speak in monosyllables, wants to spit the gauze from his mouth. "Tell me," he says again.

"It's nothing." She presses her head to the white, plaster wall, brushes the hair from her eyes, picks a damp strand from her face, runs the back of a hand against her nose. "A woman called from..." and she pauses, inhales, and pulls a tissue from the box on the coffee table. "...Child Protective Services, a social worker." She blows her nose, takes a deep breath, and wipes her eyes. "She made an appointment to come out to the house next week."

"Why?" William's eyes close—the shots, gas, the prescription pills doing their work.

Flann, standing on the coffee table, bumps her skull against Jan's knee, so she scratches the cat's head, stares out the window. The sun is coloring everything in the room a brilliant shade of orange. "I don't know. I'm assuming they think I tried to kill my son. You know, that I drove the car into the lake on purpose?"

"That's crazy." William's eyes close again and then he slips under, into a vague dream of Jan wiping his face with a damp, warm cloth. When he awakes, it is after three in the morning and Jan is gone. Flann licks his cheek, tongue like damp sandpaper.

It is after closing. Jan counts down the register to one hundred bucks while William adds the day's trade slips. Book Purgatory has to report book trades to the IRS even though no cash exchanges hands. Although he's manager, he's never thought to ask the owner, Andrea, why this is. She might not know; for a successful business person Andrea does not know a lot of things. William's not thinking about trades or the IRS or Andrea though really. He is having trouble thinking about anything. The store is dark except for one dim bulb overhead, and the street lamp in the parking lot sputters, deciding when to die as it has for months. The Butthole Surfers tape that was playing loudly at closing time (customers find it annoying and seem to exit quicker when William puts it on and cranks it up) has played through, leaving Dolby hiss. He stops adding, jabs the clear button, rips the receipt and tosses it at the wastebasket, misses, adds again, messes up, starts over. He hits the total button with his fist, rips the receipt, glances at Jan. She will not look at him, chews her lip with concentration. She has not spoken of her breakdown at his apartment a few weeks earlier. Whenever he is near, she has put an apple in her mouth or bent quickly to price the children's books or earnestly examined whatever reading matter happened to be close, whether Derrida or *Nasty Girls* magazine. She might even eagerly say "Can I help you?" to any customer in shouting distance, even once Enema Man who seemed frightened and stalked off to the sci-fi section, muttering something about Allen wrenches.

Without deciding to, William abruptly asks, "So, what happened with that social worker?" He can feel his heart race, hands clammy and shaking.

She glances up like she has forgotten he was there. "Nothing, I guess." She speaks quickly, looking down and up and then down again. She jabs the adding machine faster. "She just talked to Hank in his room for about fifteen minutes. Asked me a few questions: How do I discipline Hank, what kind of meals I make, where he is going to school in the fall, stuff like that. She wanted to look at the kitchen, I guess to see if I had crack pipes lying around or just threw the trash on the floor. I didn't cry once." She giggles and stabs more numbers into the machine and, after a few seconds, rips the tape and rubber-bands it to a stack of money. She pulls a deposit slip from the drawer and notices William who is watching her. "Yeah? What?"

He taps his fingers against the Plexiglas countertop. "I don't know." He grins, then looks down at the floor. "I guess I'd like to think we're more than just boss and employee. You know?"

"Oh." Her head bobs backward as if the idea might be solid and coming right at her. "Okay." She bends to fill in the deposit slip.

"I mean, you know, *friends*," William says quickly. She nods, pen working furiously on the slip. "I just want to help, you know?" She is chewing her lip, really seems to be biting into it. "Jan, could you look at me, do you think?"

She looks up. "Gosh, William. What do you want me to say?"

He takes a step back. A bum the employees call "New Shoes" because, despite his grungy clothes and unshaven and unbathed appearance, he is always in clean, white sneakers, walks past the store windows and taps a filthy fingernail against the glass. William waves, shrugs. "I don't know." They finish the closing routine in silence.

After locking up, she says "Bye" without looking at William, and goes straight to the bike rack. He trudges across the parking lot to his truck, works the key into its ancient lock. Startled at the squeal of her brakes right next to him, he shouts.

"Sorry," she chuckles. She reaches behind her head and pulls her hair back into a ponytail. The street light is behind her and her dark eyes are black in the shadows, cheeks bruised by shadow. William's door creaks open and he thinks that she should put some oil on her brakes, but says nothing. "Hey, I don't know if I pissed you off in there," she says, thumbing towards the store with its red fluorescent "CLOSED" sign glowing. William gets in, looks at Jan through the glass. With a goofy grin, she mouths words at him, moves her fist in a circular motion. He rolls his window down. "Are people going to the bar tonight?"

He stares for a long moment and finally says, "No."

She looks at the ground then, and he can see that she knows he is lying. He wants to take it back, ask her to come along. But there is a lump in his chest and it hurts him too much to speak. She looks into his eyes then and says, "Really, I'm sorry if I hurt your feelings." Her lips move as if she is struggling for the words. She says, "Forget about it, William." She licks her lips and looks at the pavement and then back at him again. "I can be a bitch."

"See you later," he says, starting his engine. As he pulls onto University, he can see her in the rearview mirror, still straddling her bike in the parking lot.

3

Usually, William parks near the back of the lot in the Westabout strip mall so customers can have spaces closer to the door. In his four years of managing Book Purgatory, he has waged a never-ending battle with employees about parking further away so little old ladies can have the closer spots. The employees—who are, for the most part, able-bodied college students—act as if it is an affront to have to walk the extra yards. But no one is here and no one is likely to be here, so he parks right in front of the door.

His tires bump against the curb and he cuts the engine. The truck shudders and then is still, engine ticking as William stares at the darkened windows of the store, the shadows of bookshelves, the comic book bins, the stationary overhead fan. He flicks his keys and lets the metal beaded chain quit swinging before he gets out. It is eleven o'clock and not only is Book Purgatory closed and empty an hour later than usual, but so are all of the other businesses—the lunch diner, Laundromat, the drug store, the grocery store. There is one lone car on the other side of the parking lot and even though the street that runs past the strip mall, University Avenue, is one of the city's thoroughfares, no one drives past. He puts his key in the lock, hears the bolt click back ominously in the silence and, as if to maximize his last-man-on-earth anxiety, a wadded sheet of newspaper rolls past in the dirty breeze.

Inside, he goes behind the counter and presses "PLAY" on the answering machine.

The opening book buyer's shaky voice comes from the speaker:

"William? It's me, Christy. William, I'm scared. I don't think I'm coming in today. I mean, I'm *not* coming in. I've packed a bag and I'm going to Ocala to stay with my parents for a while." William waits, listening to the tape hum. He reaches for the STOP button and then she says, "I might not be back. I'm sorry." And then there is the click of phone and the machine shuts off.

It has been a week since the first murders. The first day of fall classes was much like the previous ones William could remember in his decades of living in Gainesville: thousands of people appearing as if from out of the ground, University and all the other main streets packed with bumper-to-bumper traffic and the air smelling of exhaust, grocery stores full of kids stocking up on mac-and-cheese, canned soup, and beer. The bookstore was busier than it had been all summer, crowded with students searching for cheap, used copies of their required reading and wanting to sell their old textbooks of McInformation. There was an intensity to this first day of classes though which William had never seen before. People looked like their backs were tensed, as if a bouffant-headed woman standing in line at the coffee shop might pull a gun from her purse, or maybe the man with the salt-and-pepper beard and wire-framed glasses might suddenly bite the nose off his waiter's face.

That morning, two college girls had been discovered butchered. That is not what the papers said. The papers said that two coeds were found dead in their apartment. That "foul play" was suspected. That their names were being withheld until next-of-kin were notified. But information like this gets around in a town of 80,000, especially when over 30,000 of that population are college students. The girls had been bound and gagged with duct tape which had been removed, suggesting the killer was familiar with police procedures and knew tape would have been a source for fingerprints. They were raped and mutilated. The killer had carved intricate designs into their flesh. Their bodies were positioned intertwined on a bed as if they were lovers. Two days later, another girl was discovered in her apartment. Her head was left on a bookshelf. By the weekend, the fourth and fifth bodies were found, a young man and woman who lived together. The man was stabbed to death in bed, arms sliced to ribbons, probably in the act of defending himself; the woman's body was left in the

37

hallway. These two had not been mutilated and it was suspected that the killer had been interrupted. The young woman's parents were trying to get in touch with her because of the reported murders and there had been no answer. They were not worried—her roommate, a childhood friend, was a big guy, over six feet tall, had played football in high school. They just wanted to be sure, so they called the apartment manager, asked him to check. When he opened the girl's door, he saw her lying in the hall, blood ballooning from her midsection, pooling on the carpet. There was a black bag on the floor next to her head. When the police arrived five minutes later, the bag was gone.

William feels a chill run across his chest, goosebumps rising, and he looks slowly around the store, dark, still, and empty. He expects something to come charging at him from down an aisle, something waiting for him to lower his guard.

The rest of the scheduled employees call to say they are not coming in either. None bother to offer excuses; all of them, men and women, admit that they are afraid. Over the course of the day, the store has only about twenty customers anyway, all of whom make some comment, usually oblique, about the murders: "Scary times," "I remember when you could leave your house unlocked," "I'm getting me a gun." Mid-afternoon, Andrea calls to tell William to close at five, that the store will operate on abbreviated hours until the town gets back to normal.

Late in the day, store empty, William props his feet on the counter to listen to NPR. A report about the Gainesville murders is on, but the announcer has nothing to say that William does not already know. He is appalled by how brief the piece is, followed by reports on tax increases, rebels fighting in a North African country, and a sentimental essay about childhood.

Jan pulls up on her bike and parks in the rack in front of the store. She is wearing a man's white T-shirt, ratty blue jeans rolled above her ankles, and white flip-flops. She takes off her helmet and her dark brown hair falls past her shoulder in a frizzy mess. Instead of locking up, she carries the heavy Kryptonite lock into the store with her. Her smile is large, kind of friendly, but there is an intensity behind it as if she has just drunk a pot of coffee after staying up all night. Her eyes are wider than usual and there are dark pouches beneath them. She chews her bottom lip and wrinkles her nose as if it itches, but she cannot be bothered to scratch. Gripping the lock so tightly her knuckles are white, she says, "Hi!" nearly a shout full of false cheeriness. "Wow, it's slow, huh? The murders?"

Wary, William just stares; they have not spoken much in the past month.

She does not seem to notice. Speaking quickly, she says, "I went to my afternoon class and there was no one there, not even the professor. No note saying class was canceled, nothing. It was creepy, like everyone had left town because of some natural disaster which I hadn't heard about." She leans on the counter, traces random patterns on the scarred Plexiglas sheet covering it. A stale scent comes off her.

"There is a disaster. What would you call this? You're not even supposed to work today. Why are you here?"

She shrugs and squints out the large windows at the sun streaming in, filling the air with rays of light and stretching shadows. At this time of day, William usually lowers the blinds, but since there are no customers, he has not bothered. "People are stupid to let one guy terrorize them," she says.

"They're not stupid, they're scared. Aren't you scared?"

She shrugs again, looks around the store as if it is new to her, and when she looks at William again her eyes water as if she might bawl. "I'm so fucking terrified, William," she says in a hoarse voice, looking as if she is trying to smile. "I haven't slept in two days." She pulls back a sob, says, "Ray took Hank."

"Where?"

"Crescent Beach. Rain's husband, Art, is a lawyer, and one of his clients said he could use his beach house until this," she smiles and arches an eyebrow, "*disaster* is over. The original plan was that Hank and I would stay there with everyone else."

"Cozy."

She taps her knuckles against the counter and shakes her head. "Art's like a child. He doesn't seem to buy that Ray and I aren't getting back together."

"Why didn't you go?"

She looks at the carpet, then up at the clock. "Clock's fast." Shaking her head as if to clear it, she says, "Ray and I fought. He called this morning to say he had rented a room at a hotel down

39

the beach from the house for Hank and me. I asked why. He said because he thought we'd be *more comfortable*." She pauses, tilts her head at William. "Ray has *no* money. I knew what was going on. His girlfriend was going and didn't want us there. 'Fine,' I said, 'I'm not going.' He said, 'Do what you want, but I'm getting my son.'" She spreads her hands, then brings them together in a loud clap that makes William flinch. "That's how he gets: *My son!* '*My* son!' Fucking idiot." She wipes her face roughly with both hands and when she removes them all trace of tears are gone, cheeks and eyes puffy with fatigue. "Like I'd let Hank stay here with this shit going on."

"You should have gone with them."

"You're probably right, I should have. But I didn't, so it's too late to cry about that." There is silence for a moment. One car, a Trans Am, speeds by on University, motor revving. William and Jan watch it out of sight; she even takes a step toward the doors to chart its progress. With her fingers just barely touching the window, she says quietly, "I'm afraid I'm never going to see my son again."

"You're afraid Ray won't bring him back?"

She looks at the ceiling and shrugs. "Dunno. I don't know what I'm afraid of." That weird, false smile reappears suddenly. "Anyway, the real reason I rode over here through these dangerous streets is to ask you for a favor. Now," she says, raising a palm, traffic-cop style, "don't hesitate to say no. Please. Please, please, please. Nosiree, my feelings won't be hurt." She looks at the counter, at the clock, letting her gaze roam freely. "I've called a few friends, you know, couldn't get anyone. And, well, I'd ride my bike, but it's starting to get dark and…You know." She makes a razor-across-the-throat gesture and nods toward the windows where, true enough, the sun is shining at the horizon and turning the buildings and oaks in the shopping center golden orange.

William says, "Jan, just ask your favor."

"Right. Right, my favor." She takes a deep breath as if it were a particularly big favor. "Would you be willing to take me to Target so I can buy clippers?"

"Clippers?"

"You know, for hair?" She gestures at her hair as if to demonstrate what that is, but he just stares blankly. "Haven't you been watching the news? The guy's victims are all petite brunettes with shoulder-length hair." She gestures at her hair again. "Long, brown hair. I'm little. I don't want to be this sicko's next victim."

"You're going to cut your hair."

It seems horrible to him. Her best feature is her hair, curly and out of control. Even in a ponytail, strands escape. She is always brushing it away from her eyes and it is a constant impulse for William: just reach out and touch it, take the loose strands and tuck them behind an ear.

"Yes," he says, finally. "I'd be happy to take you."

There are people at Target, but not a lot. The shelves in the food section are strangely bare, as if the heat wave has become a snowstorm and people are stocking up. After wandering the aisles for a while, they discover the clippers. Jan examines them all carefully, taking a few off their wire hooks to read the print on the back, then chooses a medium-priced one. As William turns toward the registers, she puts a hand on his bicep. It is on that same tattoo she touched over a month ago, but it has healed since then. He notices her nails are raw and bitten, even the fingertips look chewed-on. She sees him noticing this and pulls away, rubbing her hands together nervously, then jamming them into her armpits, tapping her toe as if to music.

"Just a sec." She smiles, a quick bark of nervous laugh. "I want to get something else. Come with." She pulls his arm, leads him to the next aisle where, after a few seconds, she finds the color she wants, platinum blond. "Better be safe." She winks.

The guy in front of them in the checkout line grips an old crowbar. On the conveyor belt he has a gallon of water and two six-volt batteries. The cashier, a skinny blonde with bad teeth, gestures at the crowbar, paint peeling off it. "I need to get me one of them," she says.

"Whew, don't I know it," he answers, shaking his head. They both stare out the front windows at the strip of horizon glowing a dull red.

William parks at the curb at Jan's house and pulls her bike from the bed. "I've got it," she says, grinning, taking the handlebars and wrinkling her nose at him. All the blinds are raised and her house seems to glisten with white as if every light were on. The sun is so low in the sky that their shadows stretch toward the end of the street like spindly cartoon characters. The crickets are chirping and Jan slaps at a mosquito on her neck. Then, she says, "Do you want to come in for a glass of wine?" She speaks too quickly, glance grazing William's and skittering away. "I could make us dinner and we could cut my hair off." She looks down at the bag in her hands and the smile slips, disappears. "You've probably got plans." She nods. "Some other time, 'kay?"

He laughs softly. "No, I don't have plans. I think everyone I know has left town."

"Me too." She chuckles, eyes widening. The crickets scream like faulty brakes on a car. "Let's go inside. It's creepy out here."

She boils pasta, defrosts leftover sauce she finds in the freezer, also makes garlic bread and a green salad, opens a bottle of merlot. The sauce has jalapenos in it and when William touches his scalp, his hand comes away damp. He drinks too quickly and by the end of dinner his head spins. She piles the dishes in the sink and shakes her head and guides him away when he makes a move to wash up. Hurrying quietly around the house, she checks windows and doors which are already locked and then comes back with a wooden child's baseball bat in her hand. Winking, she says, "Just in case." Pouring more wine into both glasses, she opens the razor, scans the directions. William waits in the silence except for the humming of the kitchen clock, its white face unmarred by numbers, just twelve shiny slices of metal. He lifts the glass to his lips and the rim clicks against his teeth.

Jan says, "I guess a half inch should do."

"A half inch," he says, glass still at his lips.

She slides a black, plastic guard on the end of the razor and puts a chair in the middle of the kitchen floor like a stage prop. She sits, lets the hair fall across her face. "You do it."

"Me?"

"You do it," she says again, then drums her bare feet against the linoleum, giggling, eyes sparkling under the fluorescent lights running along the ceiling. "You do it, you do it." And then she is quiet, a mock serious expression. "Please. Really, please, William."

The quiet look, her sudden stillness takes his words away and he licks his lips, unable to generate saliva. He says, "I've never cut hair before."

"You just run the razor along my head until the hair is the same length. I'll be very still. You can plug in over there." She points to a wall socket next to the stove range.

When William switches on the razor, there is a violent metal pop and then a quiet hum. "Ready?"

She grins and takes a deep breath, closes her eyes. "Ready."

William places a hand against her head to hold it still and she puts a hand over his, the silver ring on her finger rubbing against the back of his hand. Her hair curls around his fingers, cool against the skin, stray thought of faucet water running on yard work hands. The hair falls to the floor. William watches it fall with a feeling just short of pain, hair clumping like clods of earth on the linoleum with the lightness of city haze. Running the razor across her scalp, he discovers her head isn't round, but slightly oblong, thrusting up at the back of the crown, ears sticking out too much without hair. A mixture of horror and wonder ripples through him: *She's not perfect. She's odd.*

When he is done, he runs his fingers lightly over her scalp to make sure the hair is even. He can feel the contours of her skull on his fingertips, the slight pulse at her temple. Her hair is like cool carpet against his fingers and, for some reason, its touch brings back lazy Saturdays watching cowboy movies with his father on the living room floor. He breathes in, air like a shiver down his spine, and wishes his father, now dead, could meet Jan, though he is not sure what they would think of each other.

She puts her hand over his to still it and looks up at him, whispers, "I'm afraid to look."

"You should," William answers, whispering too. "You look great."

She skips, literally skips, into the nearby bathroom and the light clicks on, throws a dull glow over the threshold. He sweeps clumps of hair into a pile with a broom he discovers in a corner. There is a sudden squeal and he drops the broom and takes several steps toward the doorway. Jan meets him, hands covering her mouth, eyes wide.

"I look like a freak," she says.

"No, you don't." He puts his hands on her shoulders. "It's a good look. It's cute."

She looks at him sideways.

"In fact, I was thinking about shaving my own head."

"That's a great idea!" she says.

As soon as she smiles, he knows it is decided. Sitting in the chair, he says, "Use the quarter-inch on me."

William's hair, bristly as a brush, makes the razor whine and Jan grunts as she forces it over his scalp. After a few seconds, she gives up, leaves the room, and then returns with a large pair of scissors. "Ah-ha," she says, snipping them in front of his face.

"Be careful with those."

"Don't tell me you've got castration anxiety." She steps behind him. "Hold still, smart boy." She grips his neck firmly, and snips off some of the length. Forcing her fingers through the curls, she steps on a footstool occasionally to reach the top, switches from the scissors to razor and back again. William feels the warmth coming from her as she circles, arms, elbows, breasts casually pushing against his body. When it is over, she blows against the back of his neck to remove the stray hairs and he closes his eyes, wants to reach back and take her hands in his. She steps in front of him, and her eyes widen. "You look pretty good with short hair, champ."

"Champ?"

She gestures toward the bathroom. "Go look." When he makes no move, she nods again, with more emphasis, until he goes. "There's a mirror on the back of the toilet," she calls. "Make sure I got the back even." He raises the mirror and turns his back on the one over the sink, can hear the light *shhhh* of the broom against linoleum. He touches his hair lightly, as if it were not his, as if he was afraid of startling whoever it belongs to.

In the doorway with the box of dye, she says, "Step two."

There is a tiny piece of paper inside which folds out into a gigantic sheet with diagrams and instructions so detailed they are more confusing than helpful. There is a plastic, cylindrical bottle full of white, creamy liquid which Jan mixes with the dye which is bright yellow and in a smaller tube. The bathroom is suffused with a pungent smell like paint stripper. Dizzy, William leans against the hallway wall to watch. Chewing on her lip and seemingly unfazed by the scent, Jan screws the spout on the large bottle and shakes it, grinning at William. "Industrial chemicals in my hair? Why not?" She puts on the pair of clear, plastic gloves—more like Saran Wrap in the shape of hands than gloves—and applies the dye, squirting the liquid into her hair with one hand, massaging her scalp with the other. Clenching her eyes, she leans against the sink which is quickly splashed with dots of yellow, the tiled floor also speckled. Even when her head is soaked, she keeps squirting until all the dye is gone, buzzed hair plastered to her scalp, skull like a bright, yellow dot. "Oh—my—god," she says when she opens her eyes again. "Oh well." She shrugs and wraps a fuzzy white towel around her head like a turban and says, "Let's finish that wine."

They sit on the couch in the living room, listening to a Van Morrison CD. The song playing has a steadily opening and closing high hat throughout; it hypnotizes William so that his eyes droop. They don't speak and the cat slinks into the room and rubs against William's leg. He reaches slowly for it, but then it is gone. The song ends and, before the next one can come on, Jan disappears down the hall and, a few seconds later, the shower cuts on. William puts his glass on the coffee table, lies on the floor, propping his head on a pillow. He runs his fingers over his short hair.

Sometime after, he feels a gentle push against his shoulder. The pressure is tentative and, although he is aware of it, it is not enough to pull him from sleep. There is another, just a little firmer, and he opens his eyes. Jan is sitting cross-legged on the carpet in a bathrobe and gray, baggy pajama bottoms. Her hair is sticking up in tiny spikes, a startling blond.

"My god," he says, voice slow with sleep. "You look great."

"It does look good, doesn't it?" She smiles, blushing slightly. "You can touch it if you want. It *feels* great." William runs his fingers through her hair and she closes her eyes, rocking gently, and he closes his too. After a few seconds, she gets up and drapes a blanket over him. His eyes flicker open just as a big pillow lands on the floor next to his face. She lies facing him and his eyes close and he feels himself smile and her hand against his hair. He touches hers too.

The next morning, he takes a shower and washes the itchy remnants of his long, kinky hair down the drain. Jan makes egg sandwiches on bagels and strong black coffee. When he comes into the kitchen with a copy of the latest issue of *US Weekly* from the basket next to the toilet, she says, "You're not supposed to know I read crap like that." They sit at her 1950s-era kitchen table in plastic-padded, floral chairs, and he flips through the magazine and she stares out the window at nothing, one foot on the chair with her toes curled over the edge. Sipping coffee, a vague smile on her lips, he wants to touch her new, spiky hair again, but in the light of day he is afraid.

When he gets to the store and sees that it is still closed, he will remember that Gainesville is being terrorized. He had felt so safe and happy.

Business is even slower. After an hour, William pulls the TV from the break room and plugs it in at the front desk. He does not have to watch long before he sees coverage of the murders, but not much new. The same still photos of victims, same images of crime scenes with police keeping crowds back, same students wailing for the camera as they realize that their friends have been killed. This time, though, he is offered more background about the victims. His eyes sting as it is driven home how young these kids are, none of them even drinking age. The shot moves in on a photo of the one male victim, Anthony Gonzalez, wearing football pads and jersey, smiling at the camera. He is a swarthy kid with longish black hair, one off-white tooth in the front of his mouth. He stands 6'2", the announcer informs William with her hyper-serious voice, exactly William's height. He is stockier though, pumped from playing football, probably a tough guy. He had been home, inside a locked apartment. And now, all that is left is a photo on the afternoon news. Just a smile, the barest fuzz of moustache which will never grow. William feels a chill on the back of his neck as if something metallic were slowly being pressed, almost tenderly, against it.

Jan calls at the end of that uneventful desk shift and asks him to sleep at her house. "You know? So we don't have to be alone? I'll take Hank's bed and you can have mine." She speaks too quickly, tripping over nervous words, but sounding too, somehow nonchalant as if she wants to feign indifference. William says yes, wanting also to feign nonchalance although his heart beats so loudly he can hear it coming from his throat.

They drink lemonade and eat stir fry as the sun goes down, filling her living room with yellow light. They watch sitcoms and laugh harder than the idiotic, formulaic half-hours deserve. They sleep in the same bed though they do not have sex. Jan puts her fingers through William's hair and says, "I like your new haircut," words warm and damp against his lips.

"Me too," he says, meaning both of theirs.

She kisses him slowly then, the ginger taste from her tongue on his teeth. He does not want it to end, feels that the simplicity of the world can be discovered in that kiss, nothing matters but that moment and he is greedy for it to continue. It breaks his heart a little when she pulls away and says, "We need to go slow."

"Yes, of course," he says, whatever that means. Anything she wants.

"I like you, William, but things are complicated with me now, and I'm not ready to have sex." She kisses his neck and he puts his fingers in her short hair and runs them against her ears, tracing the lobe, kisses her eyes closed while her arms slide around his waist and he is hit with the sudden knowledge of how wrong it will be if they are not together for the rest of their lives.

A few years later William, idly flipping through a book of poems, will read the line, "The truest aphrodisiac is our certain knowledge that we will die" and he will remember this week. They do not "go slow."

They work together the next day at the bookstore. And, during one of those moments when it is empty of customers, she comes behind the chair where he is sitting, pricing a stack of true crime paperbacks, and kisses the back of his neck. After a lunch of hamburgers and fries, he kisses her greasy lips and his fingers graze her ass. At one point, the day's last customer, a rotund regular with coke-bottle glasses, heads out the front door with a grocery bag of sci-fi paperbacks and comics, calling "Y'all be careful," over his shoulder, and Jan stretches up on her tiptoes to bite William's earlobe.

At five, they are in William's truck, tires squealing as they race to Jan's house, and she is leaning against him, tongue in his ear, hand on his crotch. They press against each other in the kitchen and he touches her nipples and then her hand is inside his jeans. They drop their pants and he perches on that same chair he sat in to have his hair cut two nights earlier while she fucks him, panting into his mouth, fingers pressing down his tongue, his fingers in her short hair already slick with sweat, she saying "God, god, god," he squeezing her ass so hard he is afraid he will hurt her, but unable to stop, shirts drenched with late summer sweat as an oscillating fan blows humid air against them, and William thinks that, yes, they both might be coming, but yes, he is definitely coming and then she is sobbing or laughing into his shirt collar. "Yes," he whispers against her neck, kissing her ear, feeling her suddenly small and without energy, like a fading dream.

Each morning, they awake, not into the tail end of a heat wave, but a spring day. Blazingly yellow daffodils bloom out of season in the rich brown earth outside the bedroom window, bulbs like both sexes, sunlight flickering rainbow light across Jan and William's faces. Bees carry pollen from anther to stigma, and birds chatter at each other, occasionally skidding their swift shadows across the ground. Jan and William run through a box of condoms in days, have sex often and everywhere: In the kitchen. On the couch. On the living room carpet. In the bathtub. On her bed. One evening, after dinner, the sun not all the way down, sky streaked with swaths of red cirrus, they finish a bottle of merlot on the grass in her back yard and fuck there. The box elder and birch above filter dappled light onto their faces and limbs as he comes, she beneath and biting his neck, her slick thighs pressed to his sides. They breathe slowly, then sigh, scent of earth sweet like decay, a decomposing clump of Spanish moss near their shiny faces. Tired with fucking, William runs fingers across her face, feels the sweat on her scalp, wants to touch that moss which shifts like hair in the cool breeze. He doesn't because he knows it will be full of red bugs. And, after a while, they slip into their shorts, gather their glasses and the empty bottle and drift in to stare at the TV in the dark, to lose themselves in the stagnant stages of sitcoms, live studio audiences offering easy laughter and comfort.

Without speaking, without even consciously deciding to, William and Jan have stopped watching the news. Those faces seem frozen with discontent, the expectations of youth in their expressions morphing into a constant state of want. Jan and William sense they are fucking on those kids' dead bodies, rolling in sheets of their photos, and only the bare essentials of life—eating and drinking, sleeping, laughing, breathing, shitting and pissing, and more fucking—can make them not think of it.

The police pounce on several suspects during this week of sex and waiting, but there is one name uttered with growing frequency on the evening news. Although Jan and William are avoiding news in favor of sitcoms and sex, it is impossible to avoid it all, those "late-breaking" stories interrupting shows on every channel. Near the end of the week, that blond, now-familiar talking head appears and says in her somber voice, "This just in: The Gainesville police chief says he believes they have their primary suspect…"

The guy, Eddie Skein, *looks* like a serial killer. The footage, handcuffed and led by gruff cops through a crowd of shouting reporters and cameramen with high-powered lights, reveals a huge and stocky man wearing glasses which don't rest right on his bulbous nose. His cheeks are chubby, giving his eyes a pig-like squint, and his frizzy red hair is a mess, one tail of his flannel shirt untucked, pale glimpse of belly. The bewildered expression on his face is chilling.

"That's him," Jan says the first time they see him on the news.

William stares at her, room dark except for electric guttering TV light, and she turns her gaze to him and smiles hopefully, reaching for his hand. Glancing at the floor, William watches his pale bare toe, digging at the shallow carpet and feels Jan lean into him.

He is uneasy. Skein seems to fit the stereotype of someone sick enough to commit these crimes: abused by a father, suffering with mental problems, probably schizophrenia. Who knows? He is poor, has never had a proper diagnosis. He has a history: arrested for causing public scenes, threatening strangers, swinging into sudden, inexplicable rages. All week people have been calling the police with tips on people who "aren't quite right." One of these, Skein was arrested, but not for murder. While under surveillance, he went into one of his rages and hit his grandmother who he shared a trailer with off Millhopper Road. The cops took this attack as an opportunity to arrest him, and they convinced Skein's grandmother to press charges. Skein had slapped his grandmother before, but when cops tell us to do something, many of us do.

Granted, people shouldn't slap their grandmothers. But an angry slap to a coldly calculated series of murders and rapes, executed with a precision that had left no clues, seems like a big jump to William. And when the police get a search warrant and rip apart Skein's trailer and find no evidence, William doubts his guilt even more.

Apparently, his views aren't shared by many. It is as if Gainesville has taken a collective sigh of relief. Monday, only three weeks after the first murders, the people who have left town return. And like a replay of the first day of classes, there is more traffic, girls in shorts and tank tops, hippies on bikes and punks on skateboards, people loaded with uncracked texts. William can almost hear a shaky laugh passing from mouth to mouth, as if everyone in town has just missed stepping off a curb into the path of a bus. *Wow, that was a close one.*

Jan and William sit at her kitchen table over bowls of cold cereal turning soggy. The fan near the window oscillates and Jan closes her eyes as the breeze hits her lids, opens them and stares at the window hazy with morning glare. "I don't understand," she says, tapping the bell of her spoon against the table, eyebrows rising and dropping quickly. "The murders have stopped. Not a death in two weeks." She spreads her hands as if offering him something.

"Think about it," William says, voice quiet in all that stillness except the whir of fan, plastic click as it reaches the end of its rotation. "If you were a serial killer, wouldn't you be relieved if the cops were saying 'We've got our man,' and it wasn't you? Wouldn't you think it's time to head to another town? Or at least stop killing for a while?"

"Well, gee, I'm not a serial killer. I have a little trouble knowing *what* I'd do."

William tugs on his bottom lip. He knows that at any moment he will hear the sound of Ray's jeep as he brings Hank home.

Jan nods at William's granola. "If you're finished, do you mind clearing out? I haven't seen my son in two weeks and I'd like some time with him."

William sighs, slowly, like maybe he is deflating. He wants to get up and walk out without a change of expression, rev his engine in the driveway and squeal his tires as he drives away, no glance in the rearview mirror. The morning is hot, and he can feel the plastic padding of the chair sticking to his legs, sucking through his shirt and holding fast his back. Jan widens her eyes as if to say *Well?* but he makes no move.

4

Ray pulls his Sportster into the Westabout parking lot, shuts off the engine, kicks down the stand and throws his leg over the seat. Unstrapping his helmet, he ambles across the pavement to Book Purgatory. Hank waves at him from inside, Jan clutching him by the other hand, her eyes dark. Ray pushes through the glass door into chaos. On the front desk, there are filthy open boxes overflowing with books. Spiderweb filament hangs from the corner of a battered hardback in William's hand, some flutter from a ripped strip of cardboard. A clump of dust, fat as a snowflake, floats in the air, buffeted by the overhead fans, then spins away. An NPR newscaster's soporific voice comes from the speakers hanging on the white-washed walls. A customer yells, "Where are the funny books?" another says, "Could I get some help? Could I *please* get some help?" One of Jan's co-workers—a skinny, cute chick with a pierced nostril and olive-black hair—cups her mouth and yells in a mannish voice, "Burkholder! Your order's ready. Burkholder!" A fat oaf in overalls comes through the door behind Ray, says jovially, "Now, these here books, them's valuable. I wanna know for each-a-one how much you gimme." His lower lip protrudes with tobacco, black flecks of it on his yellow teeth.

"What a great place to work," Ray says, smiling at Jan. "So calm and relaxing. You must love to read."

"You're late," she says. "*Again…*" And then her lips move silently like she wants to add an obscenity, but finally just offering, "*Ray.*" The name sounds vaguely curse-like anyway. His smile shifts and he looks down at his son.

"Ready for fun?"

Hank hops in place in his Chuck Taylors, says, "Yeah, yeah, yeah."

"You rode the motorcycle?" Jan asks.

He raises his palm at her. "Please. The other helmet's on the bike."

"Jan? Are you working?" William calls from behind the desk as he jabs numbers into an adding machine. "I can give you $9.75 in trade credit or $2.95 in cash," he tells a guy in a backwards ball cap with sunken pimple-speckled cheeks.

"For all them books?" the guy whines.

Ray grabs Hank's weekend bag. "Let's go, bro."

He takes Hank's other hand, tugging gently, but Jan does not let hers go, says, "Wait-a-second." She crouches to kiss her son's cheek, musses his hair. "What are you doing this weekend?"

"Jan?" William calls.

"Just a *second.*" She waves a hand at him without looking.

"I think you need to go," Ray says, gently tugging.

"Wait!" Jan pulls back.

Hank giggles and bobs between them, says, "Whoa!"

Ray rolls his eyes. "We're going on a road trip. Want to go on a road trip, pardner?" he asks Hank.

"Yes! I love road trips."

"You do?" Jan asks. "Do you even know what a road trip is?" Hank nods and grins. "*Where* are you going?"

"Somewhere. Down the road." Ray moves his hand through the air like a car over hills.

"Could you be more specific?"

"I'll tell you when I know. Come on, pard, your ma has got work to do." Ray lifts his son, smoothly pulling his hand from Jan's. He groans, "Damn, you're heavier than a sack of potatoes." Hank giggles. "Better get to work, honey."

Ray pulls open the door, but can't help but glance back at Jan once more. It has been two months since the murders and the blond is mixed with dark brown now. She almost looks like herself again despite the short hair. The fearful intensity that was in her face after the killings, after the car wreck, only there in some moments, like

53

now, as she rotates her head back and forth, watching father and son leave, but also her coworkers and the chaos at the desk. She is wearing a blue work shirt, jeans, and has brand-new white sneakers on her feet. For a second, Ray sees the future they might have had, not fighting, he temporarily leaving with their son, saying "See you soon," she smiling, blowing kisses, watching his motorcycle carry Hank home to dinner. Dusk sun shines against her tanned skin and he blinks at the two teen girls with mouths full of braces pushing past him, chorusing "Excuse you!" and then bursting into giggles. He carries Hank across the sidewalk, thinks he might hear Jan yell, "Call me if you need anything." But maybe she is saying something else, not even speaking to him. Or maybe it is some other woman talking to someone else. In any case, he does not answer.

At the apartment, Lily is where Ray left her, on the couch, remote clutched loosely in hand, eyes glassy, blond hair tangled about her face which is puffy with sleep. She is wrapped in a blue blanket and on the coffee table is the detritus of her day: ashtray overflowing with butts, soggy takeout soda cup, balled cheeseburger wrapper. Ray tosses Hank's bag in a chair and gently nudges his bong back from the edge of the table. The bowl is still warm and the air smells of dope. "Look who's here," he says to Lily.

"Hey, Hank," she says, stretching her arms over her head, yawning, blanket falling, revealing that she's wearing only a tank top and panties.

"Hi," Hank responds, blushing. She has been living with Ray for over six months, but he still seems shy around her.

"Why don't you get dressed?" Ray asks, slapping her feet gently, and sitting down on the couch so she has to bend her knees.

"I don't wanna!" she whines.

"Can I turn up the volume?" Hank asks.

"You like *Runny and Lowe?*" she asks.

Hank nods as she passes the remote to him. He ups the volume, sitting cross-legged a few feet in front of the large-screen TV. Ray glances at the screen, thinks, for about the hundredth time, that the cartoons Lily spends so much time watching are inane, not like the Warner Brothers ones he was brought up on. Also, not for the first time, Ray remembers that his son is just thirteen years younger than Lily, nearly the same age difference he shares with her.

The phone rings. Ray rubs his eyes while a fat blue thing, a cat maybe, eats a globular mass with hairs protruding from it. Hank and Lily giggle and share a fond glance. After the third ring, Ray answers. "Yeah?"

"Dude, it's Reese."

"S'up?" Ray says.

"We got a gig. Can you play?"

"When?"

"Tonight."

Ray watches Hank watching TV. A dog or albino midget screams at the blue thing to shut up. "Man, I've got my kid tonight." Lily frowns at Ray, but Hank continues to stare at the screen. Maybe his back tenses, but maybe this is Ray's imagination. "Where is it?"

"Calhoun's. Can't you get Jan to take him? We've got the door, plus free beer."

"I don't know…"

"Well, just so you know, the other guys said they'd do it." There is a pause. "We might do it without you."

"What?"

Reese quickly responds, "Now wait, I knew you'd get pissed. But when you didn't make it to practice the last two times, we played without you and it didn't sound bad."

"Right. I suppose Randy played lead."

"He's better than you think."

"And he sang?" Lily is kneading Ray's thigh with her toes; he pushes her feet away.

"Yeah. Me too," Reese says. "You shouldn't be pissed. You've been skipping a lot of practice and we don't want to miss out just cause you're not around. We understand you're a dad, but we need this gig. You can play with us if you want, the choice is yours."

"Yeah, yeah. What time do I need to be there?"

"Cool, man. The guys and I'll move the equipment. Just show up around eight with your guitar."

"Don't worry, I'll be there."

"I knew—"

Ray hangs up. Hank is watching him. "I thought we were going on a road trip."

"We are. Tomorrow morning."

Hank looks doubtful, but just turns back to the TV.

Lily taps Ray firmly with her foot. "Road trip?" She mouths the word *asshole* slowly so he gets it.

"Yeah."

"Where?"

"I don't know. The beach. We'll go surfing." He shrugs at her glare. "What? You're invited."

"What was *that* about?" she asks, tapping her foot against the phone, tipping it off the coffee table where it dings loudly against the carpet. There is a tone until Ray puts it back on coffee table and hangs it up.

"I need to talk to you in the kitchen, Lily."

"Talk to me here, asshole."

Ray tilts his head at her, smiles, can see he has already won this battle. She is *acting* mad. "Want a Coke, Hank?"

"Yeah, Dad," Hank says without turning from the screen.

"Me too. Go get a couple from the fridge. And put ice in cups."

"You sure?"

"Sure, I'm sure. You're a big boy. Use the step stool."

"Okay, Dad, I'll be right back." He runs into the kitchen.

"Hank, can I have one too?" Lily calls after him.

He runs back. "Sure, Lily. Do you want ice in a cup too?"

"Yes, please." She smiles at him, as he leaves the room. "That's the first time he's ever called me by my name," she says, grabbing Ray by the arm.

"Right." Ray nods. "He likes you. This is a perfect opportunity…"

"Fuck off." She falls back into the pillow. The sound of the refrigerator coming open and closing is followed by the click of a cabinet latch.

"Come on, honey," Ray says, leaning into Lily. There is a hollow thunk in the kitchen. "Hank?"

"Dropped a can," he yells, running back into the living room.

"Did you make a mess?" Ray asks.

"No. It was closed."

"Need help?"

"No, I can do it."

"Good boy." Hank runs off and Ray watches Lily who is making a show of pouting. "I'm going to take you both to the beach tomorrow. I'll buy you an ice cream cone."

"Like I said, 'Fuck off.' I've got work tomorrow. And I have an exam on Monday."

"Study tonight. I'll buy you guys pizza. You can rent a movie. He goes to bed early and is the most low-maintenance kid in the entire world."

"What do *I* get out of this?" She is still pouting, but a smile peeks through.

"What do you want?" He nuzzles her neck, squeezes her breast.

"That tickles, dick." She giggles into his ear, biting his neck, but he pulls back, hates when she gives him a hickey, senses that she is marking him.

"Dad," Hank says, breathless, voice low with concentration. "I need help." He is barely holding the three plastic cups of soda in his little hands.

"Sure thing, pal." Ray takes two of the cups.

"I can't reach the freezer, Dad, but the Cokes seem pretty cold so I don't think they need ice."

Ray sips from his cup. "You're right, man. No ice for me. What do you think, Lily?"

"It's perfect, Hank," she says, sipping, caresses his cheek. "Thanks."

Hank blushes again. "You're welcome. It was no big deal."

There is a Mingus song on the jukebox in Calhoun's. Ray leans against the wall next to Reese who sucks on a cigarette, watching the smoke mingling with air already cloudy with it. Three chubby-to-fat guys slouch at the bar, arguing about communism while the bartender scans through channels until he finds a cartoon program. "Shut up, you guys, shut up! I can't take any more!" He puts fingers to his temples and peers at the screen. A woman with a smoker's cough and sleep-deprived eyes, shouts at the bartender, who, gimpy like a barkeep from an old black-and-white film, lurches toward the other end of the bar. He pulls a beer from a cooler, uncaps it, and tosses the cap somewhere. Reese watches a young girl with a dark tan and straight black hair leave the restroom. She reaches into the pocket of her tight jeans and struggles out a lighter, tosses it in the air and fails to catch it. Crouching to retrieve it, she glances over her shoulder at Reese, then Ray. Perhaps winking, she stands and joins her young friends at a table in the corner.

"You know that chick?" Reese asks, a slight sound of annoyance in his throat. Ray shrugs. He has seen her in the record store where he works, does not remember her name.

Randy comes through the Old Western-style swinging doors at the front, gives a cartoonish double-take. "You made it!" he shouts at Ray, blowing kisses with both hands, the veins in his arms standing out, a black barbed wire tattoo rimming his neck, a purplish veiny color. Ray swings a hand, a lazy wave or gesture of irritation. Randy immediately stalks to the bar, puts a bill on it and gets a long-necked beer. "Baby, baby," he yells, doing a weird little hop-dance toward the brunette in tight jeans. Her Zippo is on the table, next to her long fingers, a cigarette smoldering among others in the ashtray and she laughs when Randy tries to kiss her.

Jon fiddles obsessively with his drum hardware on stage. Ray knows he will worry his equipment—readjusting a cymbal stand, putting his ear to his snare while he tunes it, tapping a mike—right up until Combustion plays. Jon is very tall with a beer gut and chicken legs and he looks a little ridiculous in his skater shorts. He wears black socks with white sneakers and runs his fingers through his mass of kinky, sweaty hair. It is not unusual for him to vomit before a show.

"I hope you're not pissed at what I said," Reese says.

Ray takes a cigarette from the pack in Reese's shirt pocket and wiggles his fingers at the bass player until he hands over his plastic lighter. Ray does not smoke anymore, except for when he is nervous, though he is not sure why he is nervous now, having played in bars for nearly twenty years. He inhales, the first puff like burning dirt in his lungs.

"Are we going to fucking play, or what?" says Jon, pacing the carpeted stage.

Reese glances out at the bar, slowly filling with people. "Hold on, precious. Let a few people show. Drink a beer, smoke a joint."

Randy laughs uproariously and the youngsters at the table laugh too, although Zippo girl is looking across the bar at Ray, a slight smile on her lips. She spins the lighter on the table, stops it with a finger, spins again.

More and more, Ray wonders what he is doing: when he realizes he is flirting with a chick who is probably more than ten years his junior, when he looks around and his eyes itch at the smoky dimness and there is that tickle at the back of his throat. He will awake sometimes in the middle of the night, lurching for breath, and Lily will roll over and stroke his chest, say, "It's okay, hon, you're having a dream," in that light Alabama accent he only hears when she is half-awake. He knows that tomorrow, there will be ringing in his ears which will be maddening by nighttime when it is quiet and he cannot sleep, staring at the cathode light of the barely audible TV, a glass of whiskey wet and cold in his hand. Sometimes he can see it so clearly: sitting in a deep chair, still wearing the suit and tie he wore to work that morning, a dog lying on his bare feet waiting for whatever it is that dogs wait for. Jan, in beige dress, ironing a shirt in the next room, eyes barely slits as if she were being lulled into sleep by the peace of their lives. Hank, in denim overalls on the floor near her feet, licks one of those huge lollipops, the kind with swirled colors. When he tries to look through the window of this house, though, it is hazy out there in the world and his head throbs with the effort of trying to see.

"When do you think we should start?" Reese asks, but Ray is walking toward the table where the girl spins her Zippo.

"When are you going to play?" asks the girl whose name turns out to be Kristina. She is still spinning that lighter and has to lean close to be heard over the jukebox which is now playing CCR. She smells of clove cigarettes, sweat, and just a hint of peppermint. Her breath is warm on Ray's ear.

Reese points at his wrist and nods at the stage. Randy tunes his guitar and his amp squeals. Several people groan, but Randy just grins, tosses a pick which skitters across the wooden floor. No one moves to pick it up. "Check, check," Reese says to the mike.

"Check." Jon is tapping his snare, opening and closing his high-hat. "Ray?" Reese says, "Any time."

"Now, I guess," Ray says to Kristina. She puts her hand on his wrist.

"Don't you have a girlfriend?" she asks, still spinning that lighter.

Ray looks at her fingers around his wrist, nails painted purple, or perhaps blue, it is hard to tell in this light. "Yeah."

The guys at the bar are yelling louder, but it's impossible to understand them now with all the racket. "Name's Lily, right?"

"You know her?"

Kristina smiles and her teeth glow. "No. Where is she?"

"Busy."

"Want to hang out? After?"

Ray bobs his head, a noncommittal expression, and pats her hand, turning and moving toward the stage.

The first set is a little rough. It is hard for Ray to concentrate although he has had only two beers and it has been hours since he smoked dope. He used to think about girls while he played, gaze at them as he soloed or sang. It was exciting to openly stare, even at the ones with boyfriends. He does that now, glances around the bar, but feels grumpy, lets his gaze rest at that table in the corner where Kristina talks with some skinny, tanned guy with a Prince Valiant haircut.

The end of the song arrives so suddenly it surprises him and he plucks out a superfluous note. Randy shakes his head and Reese leans close, says, "Where are you, man?"

Randy announces, "This next one is an original. It's called 'Crash Pad.'" The song title sounds strikingly familiar, but Ray cannot place it. Jon clicks the four-count and Ray is a second behind everyone, recognizing the tune as he hears it, stepping to the microphone. He wrote this song, he realizes, opening his mouth and hoping the words come.

Ray sits with Kristina and her friends—she has just introduced them and he has already forgotten every one of their names. "You guys sound pretty good tonight," she says, exhaling smoke at the ceiling.

"We're a little off," he says. "You mind?" He takes a cigarette from her pack.

"I can't tell. I loved that last song you played. Did you write it?"

He clears his throat, lights up with her Zippo. "No." The TV over the bar is now playing a football game. "It's an old Zeppelin song."

"My dad has some of their records."

The team that is not Pittsburgh throws a touchdown. The wide receiver spikes the ball and the camera pans across ecstatic fans.

"You wanna get high?" she asks, leaning close. Ray scans the stage. Jon fiddles with his drum set. Reese, a sour expression on his face, gestures at Ray, mouths *Come here.*

"Yeah, I'll get high. But I've got to come right back."

"Absolutely," she says, grabbing him by the hand and leading him out.

The nights are getting cool and Ray rolls down the sleeves of his flannel shirt as they walk down 13th toward University. He assumes they are going to Kristina's car, but, without even looking around, she pulls a joint from her jean jacket, flicks her wrist to light the Zippo, and inhales deeply, the lighter disappearing as quickly as it appeared. The gesture smacks of practice—repeated enough times in the privacy of an apartment to appear natural.

Ray scans the traffic for black-and-whites. "Do you think we should just smoke out here in the open?"

She shrugs, hands the joint to him, and not to feel like a wimp, he takes it and inhales, handing it back quickly. "Why does it matter?" She takes another, eyes squinting with the smoke coming from the corners of her glossed lips, hands it back. "If a cop shows, swallow it. Or," she shrugs, "don't. Who cares? It's just a joint. What are they going to do? Give us a ticket? Good luck, I don't even have my I.D., do you?"

"Yeah, I do." He takes another drag, a deeper one, holding back the hiccup of a cough somewhere in his chest. It is good pot. He can feel it both in his skull and the heels of his feet.

"Come on, pretty boy." She drags him by the hand down University, takes the joint from his fingers and slides her palm around his waist. "How old are you?"

"How old are *you?*" He laughs.

"Hey, let's go in Wooly Bear." She laces her fingers in his.

"I work there," he says, pulling back.

"I know, silly boy. You don't have to punch the clock. Come on." She darts into the street, between cars, and some honk. He follows when it is safe, but then holds back at the door, steps into the shadows. Pinching the joint, she sticks it into the cigarette pack in her jacket pocket, then pushes through the door and walks confidently up to the front desk like she owns the place, hands on her hips, tilting her head at the manager, the only employee at the record store older than Ray. Ray watches Billy's grin widen at Kristina, quickly scanning her up and down as she leans on her heels, flicking her black hair across her shoulders, tossing that Zippo in the air. She laughs at something he says, and he nods slowly, opens the drawer beneath the cash register and hands her a couple tickets. Pushing herself up on the counter, she leans across and kisses his cheek. He tries to grab her wrist, but she is skipping backward across the dingy gray carpeting, raising the tickets and laughing. Ray smiles although he feels something ticking in his jaw. He needs to pee or maybe just sit on the curb and yank on his hair. He is paranoid all of a sudden. Turning, he heads to the intersection so he can cross over University and get back to the club.

Kristina runs up, grabbing his elbow, laughing. "Where you off to?" For a second, Ray looks at her like he does not recognize her. "What?" she says, but the walk signal has clicked and Ray crosses, Kristina hurrying to keep up. "What's going on?" She laughs, lips only slightly curved as if she is starting to get annoyed.

"What are those tickets to?"

"Fine."

"Fine, what?" He stops in the middle of the street and turns to her.

She laughs and puts her hands to her cheeks. "Fine, *the band.* Don't you work in a record store?" She pulls him the rest of the way to the curb.

"I know Fine," he says, and she laughs harder and he feels that smile which is not quite mirthful stiffen there on his face. "Why did Billy give you comp tickets?"

"Why not? When you're a cute girl, you get lots of free things. I don't have a date yet, if you're curious."

"I've got a girlfriend." He's heading toward Calhoun's again.

This time, Kristina doesn't follow, just yells after him. "It's not like I'm asking you to fuck me, you stuck-up asshole." He waves his hand toward her without looking, and she shouts, "You're welcome for the joint!"

As he goes up the brick stairs in front of the bar, he can hear the strains of live music drifting out the open doors. It is "Winter Eyes," one of Randy's better originals. Ray stands at those swinging doors, listening, fingers absently running along his lips (yes, it is good dope; he feels almost dizzy with it). Randy is singing the lead, a part Ray usually does. Reese was right, Randy is good. His voice has a harshness to it, but it is a good harsh, makes Ray want to kick a hole in a car window. He turns and walks off quickly, before he has to hear Randy play his solo.

The passing headlights flick across Ray's vision and he wonders if there was something other than pot in that joint, and then he is across University and heading down 12th, walking with no destination. He hears the strains of music from a porch, someone yells, "Hey, man," and a car drives slowly past, leaving behind the aggressive thud of bass. He lurches up a hill into a shadowy neighborhood near the railroad tracks, drifting beneath a stone archway toward a house with the outside light on and its front door wide open. There is live music, punk rock, coming from inside and the guitars and drums are like a serrated knife in his consciousness. People spill out the door, chattering dulled sounds lost in the screaming music coming from the living room where a lamp without a shade fractures shadows all across the wall, and people stand with bottles of beer and nod. Some pogo. Ray recognizes Troy Stalin's dyed black hair sprayed into points as he screams into the microphone, the black mascara on his face streaming with sweat. Ray struggles to remember the band name: SOS? SOL? Some acronym, something he could not possibly remember at this moment. A girl with a ring pierced through her eyebrow puts a bottle of cheap beer in Ray's hand and he soundlessly says thanks. "No problem, Ray!" she shouts, although he has no idea who she is. He falls against the scarred wall and tries to regain his balance, tries to sip the beer because he is afraid of getting any more fucked up. The sweat on his face is starting to cool and he smiles, relieved, able to tolerate the noise the band is making with their shitty instruments and shittier sound system.

This is the first place that Ray and Combustion ever played, over five years ago. Not really a bar, it is not clear who, if anyone, actually lives here. Ever since Ray can remember, people have called it Petty's Past Pad, a reference to Tom Petty who supposedly lived here when he was in Gainesville prior to moving with his band to California and making it.

Ray remembers the energy of Tom Petty's "American Girl," back before punk happened. The jangly guitar, thumping drums. He was a senior in high school and as soon as he heard it, he tried to copy the sound. Ray's dad wasn't impressed with rock—jangly or not—and wanted to know where Ray planned on going to college. "University of Florida," he said without thinking, tuning his guitar on the edge of his bed. He lit a cigarette, inhaled.

"Give me one of those," his dad said, and Ray flicked the pack so that one cigarette stuck out. His dad lit up and tossed the plastic lighter back on the bed, then watched him tune for a second longer and said, "Well, you better get applied. Talk to your guidance counselor. If you don't go to school, you gotta work at the store." Ray's dad owned a sporting goods store.

"I know, I know." But his dad was already down the hall, saying something to his little sister: "Will you clean up this mess? My god, you kids live like animals…"

Ray feels ill, walks down the hallway, stepping side to side to avoid loiterers smoking, drinking and flirting. They gaze at him, bored. He has seen many of them in the record store, knows a few names, but most are strangers, people he would guess he has never seen before, but maybe not. The air is full of smoke and rock-and-roll chatter. Stumbling into an alcove, he is suddenly surrounded by people in coats and ties, cocktail dresses, as if he has walked through a rip in the fabric of reality and emerged into a high society social gathering in another place and time. But no, there are dented cans on the floor and a broken lava lamp oozes mysterious green sludge onto the shag. A swarthy guy nuzzles a thin chick in gown with a slit up the thigh, running his hand up her leg, while she sleepily, laughingly wards him off. A petite girl with a bleached pageboy and pillbox hat, runs her fingers in front of her eyes and asks no one, "How long do tracers last?" A few of the well-dressed crowd sit on the floor and some guy with movie star teeth and slicked-back hair says, "Speak! Memory!" and everyone laughs. Shawn Waverly, a painter who has lived in Gainesville even longer than Ray, leans against the wall, pinning a wet-lipped girl with big hips into a corner. Probably no more than eighteen, she blinks nervously, but seems more muddled than scared. Shawn is somewhat of a local celebrity, a guy who gets written up in the liberal weekly, who sells paintings to professionals with disposable income. His paintings, flat folk art illustrations, are loosely autobiographical and vaguely disturbing and deviant—weirdos fondling amputated cat paws, pregnant women making love to snakes. Ray knows that being a local celeb in Gainesville does not mean a whole lot and this makes him both depressed and slightly angry.

Shawn turns briefly from the girl. "Hey, Ray," he slurs in a sleepy voice, "I was just telling Michelle, here, that Janis Joplin sucked after her first album. Tell her." Ray snaps his fingers ambiguously at Shawn then continues down the hall toward the bathroom. "Tell her!" Shawn implores.

The bathroom door is off its hinges, the moldy blue shower curtain ripped from its rings and bunched over the tub's drain, sprinkled with green fragments of beer bottle. Ray sets his beer on the filthy sink lip and presses his palm against the wall, zipping down with the other hand. Concentrating, he stares at the kitschy Cold War-era poster that warns of workplace bathrooms breeding Bolsheviks, lets his gaze drift across the miscellaneous compact discs staple-gunned to the ripped floral wallpaper. "Ah," he says, as the flow comes. The well-dressed guy with slicked-back hair sticks his head into the room, says, "A 5/4 rhythm. That's a very useful tempo—it's the same one Christmas songs are played in," and then disappears. Ray feels someone in the doorway again, someone other than the rhythm expert. One of the women from the other room—dark gray dress, a silver necklace glittering against her fair skin, brown hair falling across shoulders—stands so closely behind Ray he can feel the heat off her body. She is tall, with severe lips and a pinched nose, looks over his shoulder at his penis, says, "Looks like you'll have to start over."

Ray looks down and is surprised to see that his dick is engorged, semi-erect, getting more so. It seems huge in his hand, or his hand is suddenly small. The walls breathe. "I don't think I can."

In a lockless room, Ray fucks the woman from behind, dress hiked around her waist, panties in a ball at their feet. He grips her thin waist, and she leans into the wall, pressing her palm against another kitschy poster, a print of a woman with a head-scarf and clinched bicep beneath the inscription, "We Can Do It!" Ray's partner, who isn't as tall as he at first thought, perches delicately on spiked heels, balancing like a ballerina of fucking, sucking breaths in rhythm, exhalations silent. The only light in the room comes from the television where a soft-core sex scene takes place: dark-haired man and woman writhing in blue light, genitals hidden with convenient sheet fold or thrust knee or glid-ing fingers. They breathe, "Oooh, ahhh," above light porno piano and a ballad crooner's anguished Spanish. Beneath these sounds is the chaos which probably signals the end of the punk band's set. There is a discordant, jangling buzz within this menagerie of guitar and bass and drum and cymbal and animal screaming which Ray suspects is one of the lead guitarist's pickups coming loose, metal screws vibrating within the wooden body of its gui-tar. Within that sound, the woman grunts, "Huh...huh...huh," back a pale blue beneath him. A drop of sweat balances on his eyelash, fragments the room kaleidoscopically, and then falls.

SOS/SOL's set over, people—scruffy post-punkers and over-dressed slummers—float around in vague stasis, perhaps looking to pair up. Ray staggers through the crowd filling hallways with smoke and talk, pushes into a relatively clear space, yes, the thor-oughly modern kitchen, pulls open a dented dishwasher to find a somewhat clean glass and drains it twice of tepid tap water, wip-ing the sweat from his face and looking around the space for any-one he knows. A head-phoned, pigtailed girl in a micro-miniskirt nods to the rhythm of her gum-chewing, pulls a strand of pink from her mouth, reinserts, chews. A guy with the shakes is talking to her, or just to the side of her face, encouraged by her nodding. The only other two people in the room are a young, earnest guy in an untucked, white button-down and jeans, wire-frame glasses. "So, you don't always know where you're going when writing your books?" he asks a grizzled guy with Mohawk and goatee in a sleeveless T-shirt.

"Fuck that shit," the guy says, taking a slug of iced caramel-colored liquor and gritting his teeth. "I'm like Charlie Parker. I improvise."

Ray recognizes the guy as Gainesville's lone famous writer, Harold Leath, a Southern gothic novelist who is occasionally jailed for public disturbances. The guy looks at Ray and says, "Your fly is down."

Ray turns his back to the others, zips up. He pushes through the screen door into the back yard and leans against the white-washed wall there, dusty surface grit on his hand, breathing hard, waiting to see if he will throw up. From where he stands, he can see Leath and his protégé through the glazed-glass slatted window which is cranked open despite the night's cool. Leath takes another drag of whiskey, says, "A character has to do just what he *has* to do. I like to let him go, let him ramble a bit. I can't tell him what to do, you know? He's the one that has to decide." The writer's young companion nods, a dimple appearing in his chin, mouth coming open, but Ray doesn't wait to hear what he will say. He turns and crashes into the brush behind the house, branches swiping his face, tripping and going down on a thorny vine, getting up and crawling, moving toward a light—a neighbor's porch or lone headlight or a miracle. He falls again, and this time does not move.

At some point, Ray realizes he is walking again. He stops, stares at the closed door of Calhoun's. Stepping closer to the glass, he can peer over the swinging doors into the bar.

It is bare and dark except for the gimpy bartender who pushes a mop in a lethargic rectangle of light. Ray raps the glass, but the bartender keeps pushing, lips pursed as if whistling. Clicking his watch against the glass, Ray shouts, "Hey!" This time, the bartender looks up, yells, "We're closed!" points at his watchless wrist.

Ray looks down at his watch, steps away from the door and holds it up to the street light. Somewhere over the course of the evening, he has broken it, face cracked, digital light extinguished.

He steps back to the door, puts his hands around his mouth and yells through the glass, "I need my stuff!"

The bartender gestures helplessly at the empty stage and then seems to forget Ray, returning to his mopping.

Ray shuffles to his Jeep, trying to pull his keys from his jeans as he walks, failing, then stopping beneath a streetlight to get the bunch of metal from his pocket. A light spray of rain falls, passing Ray's cheeks and eyes on the way down. He has to touch his cheeks to know that he is wet. The key goes easily into the lock, the engine turns over without problem and, even though a patrol car pulls behind him on 34th and even though its lights come on, when he pulls to the side, the cop drives past. Ray laughs softly, putting his forehead into the steering wheel, pressing until he feels that the fingergrips might dent his skull.

Still chuckling as he steps up the concrete stairway to the second floor of his complex, he moves the apartment key toward its lock and then pauses. The door is open slightly, television on, zany cartoon sounds coming from the living room. He stands there, suddenly sober, mind swift with images: those still faces of the girls on the evening news, the murders from two months earlier. That early-morning rush to move Lily and Hank to the Crescent Beach house, that unexpected week of fun although there was a blade of fear in his ribcage when he thought of Jan still stubbornly in Gainesville. Eddie Skein is in jail now. The serial killings have stopped. Life is normal.

All of these thoughts take no more than a second to race through Ray's head, then he is pushing the door open. That 24-hour cartoon channel Lily perpetually watches is on, too loud, the only light in the room. He flicks the switch although, for some reason, the thought of more light gives him a slight feeling of nausea. Broken glass glitters on the carpet, iridescent with the reflection of Ray's flannel shirt, jeans, disarrayed hair, the wide blues and blacks and whites of his eyes as he moves into the room. The mirror over the couch—an antique, one of the remains of his grandmother's antebellum life before her son placed her in a convalescent home to await death—is shattered, fragments hanging on like jagged teeth in the oak frame and speckling the yellow couch and gray carpet.

Ray goes down the hallway, flicks on the light, more glass crunching beneath his boots. "Lily?" he calls, tentative. He flicks on the bedroom light. More glass, the mirror over the dresser also shattered, the wall behind it pale and wide as a cartoon monkey's mouth. The bathroom light is on and Ray feels very frightened, hesitates, wants to turn and leave, but instead moves toward the rectangle of light. He pushes at the door, says, "Lily?" quietly. The mirror over the sink, too, is smashed, Ray's fragmented movements reflected back at him a million times as he steps into the room. There is a steady, slow drip from the bathtub faucet. Ray's practice amp sits in the middle of the tub, ragged crack running up both sides of the baize fiberglass, a spiderweb of smaller fractures branching out from the point of impact. Speckles of water glisten on the amp and on the tile behind it there is a message in red lipstick: "FUCKER! THINK YOU CAN GO + FUCK ANY BITCH? FINE! SICK OF YR SHIT. I HOPE YOU DIE!!!"

Ray treads on the remains of his shattered dishes and cups to get a beer from the fridge. In the living room, he leans against the wall since it seems too dangerous to sit anywhere with all of that broken glass. On TV, a fat cartoon woman in golden tiara hypnotizes the people at a dinner party. As soon as the crowd's eyes swirl with cartoon hypnotism, the woman says, "Now masturbate!" The swirling-eyed folk, tongues lolling and cartoon slobber flying through the air, rub between their legs, massage breasts, animal noises vibrating the speaker in the TV.

Something nags at Ray, pushes from a corner of his skull, a finger pressing a nail into his brain. He can see Lily beckoning, that flirty, lazy smile, playful wink. She says, "You like *Runny and Lowe?*" Hank nods…

"Hank!" Ray drops the beer to the floor where it foams over the carpet. Without knowing where he is going he heads back through the front door, slamming it behind him. After running down the stairs to his Jeep, he has to go back to get his keys which dangle from the lock.

He drives to the Student Ghetto where Lily's best friend Jill lives, leaves his Jeep running in the driveway behind Lily's VW Bug and pounds on the door until Jill opens. Jill is smoking a cigarette in a holder, hair up in points. She is wearing a black slip over her jeans and a T-shirt with a skull on it, and loosely holds a cocktail glass, an olive floating in clear liquor. "Hey, fuck-o," she says like this is a term of endearment. Light stereo jazz tinkles in the next room.

"Let me speak to Lily," Ray says, putting his palm against the door as Jill tries to force it closed.

"She's not here, you ass."

"Lily, where's Hank?" Ray says, going into the living room. Jill's hairy little brown dog yips at Ray's feet, darts forward to nip at his trousers, scampers away, barks some more. Lily lounges on a cigarette-burned couch rescued from a curb. The walls are covered with band flyers—not one, Ray has noticed before, of Combustion's. An end table ashtray is as packed as possible with butts and ashes, and several beer cans on the floor are sprinkled with gray flakes too. Jill's yappy dog upends one of these and dirty liquid seeps across the floor. No one seems to mind.

Lily sips from her own cocktail glass, makes a luxurious show of taking an olive off its plastic toothpick between her teeth. "How should I know? He's your kid, dick weed." She smiles sweetly. "I suppose you've been home. Reese called to see if you'd shown up. It seems you stepped out after your first set with some tart."

"I went to get high…" Ray says and Jill interrupts:

"Our Raymond has love for sale." She holds her glass like a heroine from a 1930s movie.

"What does that even mean?" Ray asks, then slaps the side of his head and answers his own question. "Who cares? Listen, Lily, you need to tell me where Hank is."

"You'd think a dad could keep track of his own kid, don't you, Jill?" Lily asks.

"Certainly. I mean, it's a total tragedy."

The dog barks.

"Listen, Lily, nothing happened between me and that girl. We just got high."

"Could you guys knock it off?" A woman in a pink robe and fluffy slippers is standing in the hallway. It's Jill's roommate, Ray forgets her name—she has an annoying, whiny voice. "I've got work tomorrow, you know?" She rubs her eyes with her fists like a child, then perks up. "What are you guys drinking?"

"Martinis, dear," says Jill as if this were the grandest of parties.
"Bombay Sapphire?"

"Are there any others?" Jill calls, a trill of laughter.

"Can I have one?"

"Yes, of course. When we get rid of this cocksucker we'll have
a grand old time. Snuggles, bite his dick off if he gets out of
hand," Jill calls, Ray assumes, to the dog as she moves toward the
kitchen.

"Fine, I'll just look around," Ray says, going down the hall
where the girl came from. No one seems to care except for the
dog which follows him, barking incessantly. It is a quick search.
The house is small with two bedrooms, an unmade twin bed in
each surrounded by clumps of clothes and more band flyers. The
shabby bathroom smells of wet towels.

"Lily, listen," Ray says, coming back to the room. She and
the robed woman are sharing a good laugh, arms stretched along
the back of the sofa. The dog's barking has, like the jazz, become
background noise. "Just answer yes or no: Did you take Hank to
Jan's?"

Lily sighs, and the smile leaves her face. She almost looks sad.
Slowly, she opens her mouth and says, "Yes or no." Both women
laugh uproariously at this.

"Listen, you cunt, I'm not fooling," Ray says, grabbing her
by the shoulders and slamming her against the back of the couch.

There is a light snick at his left ear, and then a prick of pain.
Ray lets Lily go and steps back quickly. Jill is back, the smile still
there but different somehow. Her martini and cigarette are gone,
one hand on her hip, the other holding a knife.

"Is that a switchblade?" he asks, incredulous. When he pulls
his hand from his neck, his fingers are smeared with blood.

"You know, it's been fun, Ray, but you need to get the fuck
out of here."

"I just want…"

"Yeah, yeah, you want." Jill jabs the knife at him. "Go."

The dog follows him to the door, barking all the way.

In front of Jan's house, Ray listens to the Jeep engine tick. The
first birds are singing and there is a hint of pink on the horizon.

Running his palms across the steering wheel fingergrips, he wants to press his head against it again, but knows it won't help. He moves the handkerchief from his neck and gingerly touches the skin there. He has stopped bleeding. At the front door, he places his fingers against the heavy oak, feeling the grain. Jan has a doorbell, but he doesn't want to ring it. He knows that Hank is here, that he has to be, but he is afraid to knock. He is also afraid to just drive away.

He does not know how long he stands there, but after a while, the deadbolt clicks and the door opens. "Ray?" Jan says, face in the crack there. Her eyes are slit with sleep. She is nearly absorbed by the dark: black hair, dark eyes. He nods, feels that if he were to speak, the words would come out weeping. "What are you doing, huh? Are you okay, honey?" And with this last word, a name Jan cannot have spoken to him in years, the tears come. She turns on the outside light and pushes the door open. "Is it your dad?"

"What?"

"Did he die?" She steps forward, puts her hand on his arm.

"What?" he asks again. She nods, opens her mouth to speak, but he says, "My band played tonight."

Now Jan is the one to say, "What?"

"At Calhoun's. You know…Hank, he…"

"At Calhoun's?"

"Yeah, I was just checking…"

"Wait," Jan puts her hand up. "Your band played tonight."

"Yeah, I just wanted to know…"

"Wait," Jan says again. "Your band played tonight?"

"Yeah, you see…"

"Lily said your dad had a heart attack."

"What? Wait, now…"

"No, no, no," Jan says, shaking her head. "You…you left Hank with Lily cause you had a gig…" She is chewing on her thumbnail now, looking at the pavement.

"You see…" he tries to explain.

"No!" Jan yells suddenly, slicing her hand through the air. Ray waits, gaping mouth. Then she hits him, open-handed against his chest. The sound is like wet cardboard and hurts, but vaguely, as if the pain is only something someone describes. She hits him again. "Fucker," she says, and Ray feels glad for the first

72

time in a while, thinks, *Yes, hit me. I can do that.* He goes into a crouch as she pounds him—shoulders, back (he can actually hear it in his back and wishes the pain hurt more). He falls to the pavement, curling into the fetal position, and she is still hitting him, the thuds of her fists and palms audible, whispering "fucker" as if this is private despite the fact that they are outside and the neighbors could look out their windows and watch if they were not all asleep.

When she is finished, she goes back inside and closes the door quietly. Ray lies there a long time, listening to the birds singing and his breath coming and going, watching the vapor of his exhale, feeling the tickle of dewy grass on his cheek and chin and the brunt of Jan's fists fading so quickly it breaks his heart.

5

Ray borrows the super's big plastic rake to make neat piles of glass shards in each of his rooms. Then, after brushing off the cushions, he lies on the couch. He is hung over, could barely drag himself from bed.

Jan won't answer the phone. Or, actually, she answers, hears his voice, hangs up. Lily reacts differently, almost seeming to relish his phone calls. She curses at him like a truck driver. Or tells him about the stranger she fucked in the bathroom of The Purple Minny the night before. Or just laughs. He has stopped calling her, but something will not let him stop trying Jan, or driving past her house. It is dangerous to be at home alone. The apartment is depressing and trashed. And Nate, the landlord, keeps leaving messages on his answering machine. Apparently, the downstairs neighbors came home and found a bunch of their stuff—"Very valuable stuff" Nate insists—water damaged. He says, after the third or fourth message, that if Ray doesn't call back, he will have to let himself in. "It says right there in the lease," Nate says, if Ray wants to check: *Lessee agrees leaser may enter premises with 24-hour notice.* Ray figures that gives him at least 48 hours, if not 72 or 96 before the vandalized tub is discovered, along with the rest of the trashed apartment.

The phone rings. Pulling it slowly by the cord, he manages to lift the receiver—after dropping it once—without moving from his reclining position. The day is ending. Sun shines across the ceiling and he knows that if he were to look out the sliding glass doors on his balcony, that the city of Gainesville would look sleepy and depressing. "Hello?"

"What's going, kid?"

"Hi, Dad." He chews on a match, sits and carefully puts his bare feet on the carpet, reaches for his bong, but, of course, the bowl is empty.

"So?" his father asks after a second.

Ray waits. "So…what?"

"Why don't you ask what's going on?"

"What's going on, Dad?"

"I bought Basement Balls. God, I hate that name. Sounds like a fag hangout."

Ray reaches for a pack of Lily's cigarettes from the side table. "Congrats, Dad."

"Yeah, I guess old Carnie couldn't hang on anymore. Finally sold out."

Ray's father owns Gallant Sporting Goods in Myrtle Beach, South Carolina. His only real competition, besides for a corporate big box store outside a mall, was Joe Carnie's Basement Balls.

"I've been busting my nuts, kid. Running back and forth between the two stores, making sure Carnie's employees know who they got to answer to, weeding out the crap he was selling. Soon as I get the operation running, I'm thinking about doing some remodeling. That place *seems* like a basement, know what I mean? Even smells like one."

"Well, you'll get it going."

"It sure would be easier if I had some help."

"What's Tim doing?"

"Ah, Tim's a good guy, just sort of dim."

"Hasn't he worked for you for like fifty years?"

"Ten, smart guy. I don't know I can trust Tim."

"You think he'd rip you off?"

"Hell no. I'd rip his balls off." Ray's dad sighs. "It's just not family, you know?"

Ray knows where this is going, and moves to shift it away. "Why don't you ask Carrie to come in on it with you?"

"Aw, I don't know. Your sister's awfully busy…" Carrie is an accountant at a phone monopoly in Atlanta.

"Make it worth her while."

"Women aren't good with figures and, hell, kid, what are you doing in Gainesville? Didn't you go to college to get a job?"

"I've got a job, Dad."

"A *real* job. You know what I mean."

Ray stares at the smooth, eggshell-white ceiling. "What about my band, Dad?"

"You'd be famous by now if you were going to be. I've been seeing this woman, she's got a boy—real obnoxious, zit-faced, skinny, always got a scowl on his face, god, sometimes I'd love to smack him. Anyway, when I'm waiting on Claudie, sometimes I watch the MTV with the boy cause we've got nothing to say to each other, so I know what I'm talking about. Rock stars are young." Ray twists the phone cord around his finger, scratches his balls, yawns, waits for more. "You're not a spring chicken, you know? And you got a son. You need to start thinking about his future."

"Are you thinking of *my* future, Dad?"

"That's right."

Ray is the one to sigh this time. "Dad, speaking of Hank, I need to go. I'm supposed to pick him up…soccer practice."

"Ah, the kid plays soccer. All the kids play soccer. Claudie's brat plays it too. I'm not sure I understand a sport that won't let you use your hands. Why not? Doesn't make sense."

"Probably not, Dad. He seems to like it."

"Okay, you're not telling me what I want to hear. You'll cave, I can wait."

"I wouldn't recommend it—waiting—I won't."

"I'm not listening to you, kid. Call your grandma sometime. She's old and lonely."

"I will."

Ray hangs up, looks at his watch, but the crystal is still broken.

By the time he gets to the practice space—a storage unit with a metal roll-top door out on Archer Road—Ray has had a couple bourbons and three beers. It's Monday night, Combustion's usual practice time. They're playing an especially sloppy version of the Velvet Underground's "White Light/White Heat." Two other bands are playing nearby. The hardcore one—Snail Pace—sounds typically awful. That synth band with the overdramatic singer is practicing too. The guys in Combustion are smiling at each other like they are having fun despite the sloppiness, and Ray stands in the doorway, listening, can hear the play in the music and realizes it has been months, if not years, since he enjoyed making music. It makes him sad. Then he feels just irritated and awkward.

Jon briefly loses tempo when he notices Ray; Randy stares at the scavenged carpet on the concrete floor; Reese just smiles, or sneers. Ray lugs his Marshall to the back of the Jeep and, as he comes back for his guitar, the song comes to its clumsy end. "Listen," Reese says patiently, "The chorus is two measures of C-G-C, *then* F-C-G, then D-sharp-C-G."

Randy is leaning forward, hair hanging in front of his eyes.

"Actually," Ray says as he picks up his guitar case, "the chorus starts at F-C-G."

"Who asked you?" Reese wants to know.

"No one," Ray admits.

Jon alters the height on a crash cymbal stand, swiping his oily hair from his eyes with the back of a hand.

"Why'd you call Lily?" Ray asks Reese. "You got me in a load of shit. She trashed the apartment." He spits. "I should make you pay my security deposit."

"Why'd you disappear?" Reese asks.

"I asked you first."

"I asked you second."

"Are you quitting the band?" Jon speaks, looking at the brown, beer-stained carpet.

"Yeah, he's quitting," Reese says. "Let's take a break." He puts his Strat on its stand, and takes two canned beers from the Styrofoam cooler at his feet, flicks a few shards of ice off their tops and moves through the door.

The swamp which rims the warehouses is red with dusk light. A huge, blue heron wades in the distance at the water's edge, head moving forward on an elastic neck as it drives its beak into the water, tipping its head back with whatever it has found there. It suddenly alights, moving between the drooping branches of cypresses. Reese and Ray watch it disappear.

Ray sticks his guitar in the back of the Jeep, slams the door, and takes the beer that Reese hands him, popping the lid and drinking. Belching, he leans against the jeep. "I understand the whole band thing," Ray says, gesturing toward the practice space where Randy and Jon are sitting in plastic chairs, leaning back against the cinder block walls, smoking and laughing. "You're right, my mind's not in it. But that was so senseless for you to call Lily. You wanted revenge."

Reese shakes his head, drinks from his own red and black can of beer. He takes a pack of cigarettes from his shirt pocket, gingerly pulls one out and puts it in his mouth, lights up, all with one hand. Unsticking a sweaty strand of hair from his cheek, he finally speaks: "My dad's a career Marine, a major. He thinks I'm a fuck-up, doesn't understand what the hell I'm doing here in Florida when my parents and family are in Colorado. He thinks I fucked up when I dropped out of school, thinks I'm wasting my time playing music, thinks I need to enlist in the military—says even the Navy would be better than what I'm doing now." He laughs softly, stares toward the setting sun over the swamp. A bird—perhaps that heron—is a silhouette skating across the surface of the orange sun. "But he'd know the importance of commitment. He'd know that when you have a deal with people, you don't let them down. He'd understand that."

Ray guns his Sportster up the steep hill, loving the way the seat and handlebars vibrate and the engine whines. He eases off the accelerator at the top and the sudden silencing of the engine is like the opposite of an exclamation point—a void, an explosion in reverse. From here, he can see Lake Walters, its surface glistening like a gasoline puddle in front of his tire. It is finally winter in Florida though the day is only in the sixties. There are two cars and a truck in the parking lot. An old-fashioned box kite struggles in the slate-blue sky. A sailboat tilts on the lake surface, a "V" of bird silhouettes snipping the firmament. The sun is a high, dull gleam.

Pulling up near the picnic tables, he unstraps his helmet and takes the 12-pack of canned beer from the compartment beneath the seat. Hank runs across the grass toward Ray, yelling "Dad, Dad!" Patrick Henry jogs after, also smiling, a chicken leg in his mouth and an orange foam-rubber pointy finger on his hand.

"Hey," Ray says, leaning to kiss his son on the cheek. They hold hands, and Ray tries not to look at Jan's scowl as he gets closer. Rain and Art turn on their bench at the picnic table to watch him walk. Art, wearing long shorts and sandals, despite the chill, comes to meet him.

"Ray, my man. What's up, baby?" He slaps Ray's hand and gives him a one-armed hug. The sun glints off Art's brown, shaven head, a rough palm gripping Ray's shoulder. "You're in time; we're eating lunch."

"Ray, hi," Rain says.

"You guys didn't tell me *he* was coming," Jan says, glowering at Rain, then Art.

Hank climbs up on the bench next to her. "Sit next to me, Dad," he says, patting the side opposite.

"Yeah, sit next to him, *Dad,*" she says.

"I'm kind of surprised to see you too, Ray," Rain says. "*Pleasantly* surprised," she adds, this later at Art.

"Yeah," Art says, looking out at the lake and grinning, "I mentioned it to my man the other day. You know, boys need their daddies."

"Dad, we were throwing the football," Hank says, a mouthful of chewed chicken, "and we're going to some more if you want to play too."

"The boy's got a good spiral," says Art.

"Yeah, and you should have seen this catch I made," Patrick Henry adds, and his father runs his fingers through the boy's curly hair.

"Help yourself, Ray," Rain says, "we've got fried chicken and potato salad and baked beans." She is wearing a white, floppy hat; unlike her husband, she is fair and freckles easily.

Ray pulls open the twelve-pack, pops a can and asks, "Anybody want one?"

"I made sangria, baby," Art says.

"Ah, man, that sounds good. Let me get a cup of that."

"Yeah, drink up," Jan says.

Art glances at her, then pours the punch into one of the plastic blue cups the adults are drinking from. "What my man wants, my man gets," he says, passing the cup to Ray.

"Pass the chicken to your dad," Jan says quietly to Hank.

Everything comes down the table to Ray eventually. They also have coleslaw and some sliced fruit—apples, oranges—and cheese. They have brought some of Rain's hand-thrown plates—glazed sunburst pieces that glint even under the dull sun—and Ray fills his completely, ravenous and suddenly realizing that he has eaten almost nothing but takeout and pre-packaged food since the night of Combustion's gig two weeks earlier. They talk about the weather and Art mentions some homeless guy he is defending for a knifing and suspects that the guy is guilty. Rain talks about one of her students at the children's museum, a disturbed boy from a foster home, a nearly comatose child who makes beautiful cups with handles and round mouths, cups so perfect colleagues of hers in grad school would have been jealous. Hank and Patrick Henry jabber about something that Ray cannot follow, but it makes the two boys laugh, mouths full of chewed food. "Hey, hey," Rain says, "chew your food, *then* speak."

"Yeah," Jan adds, bumping Hank with her shoulder, "say it, don't spray it."

The boys find this particularly hilarious and everyone laughs and Ray and Jan smile at each other briefly, but then she looks away.

At some point, Hank says, "Dad, let's throw the ball."

"Aw, I'm too full, man," he says, patting his stomach.

"Come on, Dad."

"Give me a little rest. Go practice your throw."

"Come on, come on, Hank," Art says, getting up and jogging for a long one. Hank throws and, sure enough, it is a beautiful, perfect spiral. The boys run after Art who sprints toward the swings.

"Come on, throw it back, no fair," they yell.

Rain smiles, wipes her mouth with a cloth napkin, then drops the hat she's wearing on the bench, puts her auburn hair into a ponytail, and kisses Ray on the cheek. "You know, it *is* good to see you," she says. And then to both of them, "Be nice to each other." She takes off, running after Art and the boys. "Hey, can girls play?"

Jan watches them go, then, sighing, twists on the bench to face Ray. He feels awkward like that, so he switches to the other side. It is a long table—really three, end to end—and seems to take an absurdly long time to get where he is going so that he jokes, "I guess you're wondering why I've called you here today."

She picks a bit of fluff off her purple sweater and crunches some ice between her teeth.

"You want some more?" Ray asks, lifting the plastic pitcher of sangria.

"No." She forks the last of her mashed potatoes into her mouth.

"You're talkative."

"So are you."

"You know, it's my week."

Watching the boys play, she laughs and it is unclear if the sound is sarcastic or really meant to express humor. Rain throws the football, Ray notices, *like a girl*. It wobbles and lands near no one. "Baby, you throw like a girl," Art calls and she smiles, flipping her husband off. They kiss.

"We probably need to rethink this whole custody thing," Jan says.

"Oh, *do* we?" He watches Jan wince and it makes him feel kind of sick—the potatoes are a lump in his belly. He finishes the pitcher of sangria, pops a beer.

She picks at the unraveling wrist of her sweater, breathes in. "I don't know what's going on with you."

"Really?"

She watches the sailboat struggling on the lake. "I wonder if my car is still out there? Do they fish up sunken cars, or just let them sit down there and rust?"

Ray watches her look at the water, can see its surface reflected in her eyes. Strange, he sees how beautiful she is even as he finds something repellent about her. He hates her at this moment, and yet, can imagine reaching across the table and touching her cheek, would love to put his finger against her lips and see if she were willing to take it into her mouth the way she used to. He suspects she might bite it off or, more likely, yell at him to get his fucking hand out of her face.

He follows her gaze to the lake. The sailboat is coming in. A man jumps overboard and struggles it onto land. It is a family—dark-haired guy, blond wife and two tow-headed boys. As they walk toward their truck with its trailer and winch, the smallest of the boys clutching either parent's hand, they hum a big top circus sound, lifting the child in the air while he squeals. "Me too, me too," the other calls, hopping in place.

"I'm within my rights to say, 'Come on, Hank, we're going to my place.'"

Jan smiles sweetly. "And I'm within my rights to knee you in the balls."

"Were you always such a bitch?"

"Oh, boo-hoo." She wipes pretend tears. "Is that the best you can do? You don't want to go with me, baby. I'll kick your fucking ass. You're about three sheets to the wind, anyway."

"I am not." His voice rises slightly and he winces at how wimpy he sounds.

"Oh really? How many beers have you drunk?" She nods at the twelve-pack. "Go ahead, count them."

Ray can feel his head turning slightly, but does not look in the box. "Since when do you count the beers I drink, grandma?"

"Since you left my son with your high school cheerleader girlfriend."

"Lily and I are through."

"And that's the point." She rolls her eyes, stands and pulls her sweater over her head. She is wearing a faded orange Gator shirt, long underwear beneath that. "Why don't you come play football with us. You could probably use the exercise if you think you can stand."

"I've got a better idea," he says, suddenly paranoid, listening to hear if he is slurring. "Why don't you go play football and I'll sit here for a bit. Maybe in a little while you'll decide if you can stand to be around me."

She stares at him, a serious expression and, after a moment, smiles. "Maybe. I think I'd like that." She reaches toward him, but short of touching, turns and runs toward the football. "Hey, let me play too. Girls against boys."

He watches them: hiking, rushing, throwing and running. It is the kind of scene he might see on a television commercial: a multi-ethnic bunch enjoying a sunny day, playing "football" although they have too few players for even one team. And yet, their faces do look happy. Hank appears to have forgotten he wanted Ray to play.

Ray reaches into the box, counts with his fingers. The cans

are cool and rattle beneath his palm. Six? No, they are unsteady, moving too easily in their thin cardboard. Five. He tries to remember if anyone else had beer. He can almost picture Art lifting a blue and gold can to his lips, wiping his black goatee with the back of a hand roughened from landscape work while in law school. But that did not happen. Ray pulls a can from the box, pops the lid, walks unsteadily toward the edge of the water, away from the football. He drinks, listens for voices calling: *Ray? Dad? Honey, come and play with us. Our pleasure is sincere. All that keeps it from being complete is your presence.* But there is nothing except laughter, a squeal, a "Hey, good catch," an "Over here!"

The sailboat is long gone: winched onto its trailer and pulled up the hill toward the horizon, disappearing down 441 to Gainesville or Alachua or Micanopy or somewhere else. At the cold and soggy edge of lake, he finds an old wooden rowboat with a hole in its bottom. Flipping it over, he climbs in, intending to sit. Instead, he lies on his back, staring up at the sky which looks leached of blue. Soon, people will say, *It's getting late, we've got to go. Where's Ray? Where's Dad?* And Ray will say, *Here I am, I was just lying in that boat. I'm ready to leave too.* The sky is almost clear, just a trace of cirrus traveling left to right then gone. The sun glints low until it is beneath the boat rim. He places his face against the rough rotting wood and closes his eyes.

When he awakes, it is dark and his teeth are chattering, and his motorcycle is the only vehicle in the lot. Crickets chirp and there is just a sickle of moon, sharp enough to put out an eye.

Ray slows in front of Jan's place. There is light coming from behind the living room blinds that looks homey and makes Ray feel pissed off. He accelerates to the end of the street and turns left. On University, he heads toward Summertree Condominiums.

It is just after nine when he pulls up in front of Art and Rain's place. Patrick Henry and Art are dark shadows outside in the street, faces barely illuminated by burning bottle rocket fuses. Just as Ray cuts the engine, sparks fly from the rocket's tube, spitting fire into the cola bottle on the pavement and whistling into the sky. There is a pause like an inhaled breath and then a pop. Patrick Henry and Art cheer with the enthusiasm of a couple of guys who have watched this more times than they can count. The boy pulls another bottle rocket from the shoebox, sticks it into the bottle, and lights the fuse. His dad has changed from the shorts he wore to the lake into dark slacks, a white shirt and a dark-red vest. He is leaning on that cane he brought back from Zaire last year, his "walkin' cane," he calls it. It is made of dark mahogany with an elaborate lion's head carved out of the hand rest.

"Ray, you're in time for some old-fashioned fireworks. What's up?" Art asks.

"You guys left me at the lake."

Patrick Henry's smile fades at something in Ray's voice.

"We called you," Art says, trading glances with Patrick Henry. "Right?"

"Yeah. We did, Ray. A bunch of times."

"I was sleeping in the boat." Ray's anger slips away, replaced by something else, self-pity perhaps. His head pounds and he suddenly wants to sit, even if on the pavement. He feels dirtier and thirstier than a shower or ice water can fix.

"Are you still drunk, man?" Art asks, still smiling.

"I wasn't...*drunk.*"

Art, smile unchanging, says, without looking at his son, "P.H., I can't find the Wolf Pack crackers. Go inside and look in my sock drawer. If they're not there, check in Mom and Dad's closet—in the back, on the shelf over the shoes."

"They're there, Dad. Right here..." Patrick Henry reaches for the box, but his dad raises it, letting the walking cane go—the lion's head clicks against the pavement.

Art smiles, but looks at Ray while he speaks, and a little of the humor has slipped from his eyes. "Just go look for me, man, Okay?"

"Okay, Dad." The boy runs inside.

"I suppose we're going to have a talk?" Ray asks.

"If you want."

"Not really."

"Then why'd you come over?" Art's smile gets wider. "I talk for a living, man. Listen too. I'm good at it."

Rain comes outside. "Honey?" She's wearing a white skirt and a pastel tank top. One of the straps has slipped and her dark bra shows at her shoulder. "Oh, hi Ray. What happened to you earlier?" Barefooted, she hugs her arms in the chill, stepping from foot to foot. She looks angelically beautiful in the pale light. Ray can imagine how it would sound to hear her sing, wants to ask her to do so, but doesn't know how without sounding completely insane.

"Ray and I are going to get some wings."

She looks at her watch. "Haven't you had enough chicken today?"

He slaps his belly, only a slight paunch as he approaches middle age. "You can never have enough chicken, baby."

Still shifting from foot to foot, she looks at her watch again. "All right, but don't stay out too late. You've got work tomorrow. Bye, Ray." She steps inside. "And don't wake me," she yells before closing the door.

"Okay, honey," Art says quietly, smiling at his friend of nearly ten years.

Ray shakes his head. "I don't want chicken. I'm sick of chicken."

"Then you'll watch me eat."

Ray and Art sit on stools at the bar and Art orders 24 buffalo wings with Super Hot Sauce. Although he didn't want them, Ray eats a few, dipping them in blue cheese dressing to cool the spiciness. Art pronounces them not "super" hot, but appears to enjoy them nonetheless. On the nearest TV there is a football game—Ray recognizes the green jerseys of the Philadelphia Eagles, but is not sure who the other team is: navy jerseys, the logo on the helmets a blur. One of the Eagles catches a ball in the end zone and, after spiking it, flaps his arms like a bird. "I hate that," Ray says.

"What?" Art asks, gnawing a chicken bone, then wiping his fingers on a wad of tissue-like napkins. "These napkins ain't cutting it."

"This." Ray flaps his arms like the player on the screen, a moronic grin on his face.

Art picks up another wing. "They're just celebrating, baby. What's so bad about that?"

"Nothing's bad about celebrating. Do they have to show off like that? It's childish."

Art nods. "That's true. It's childish to play a sport for a living. Sometimes, I wonder if professional athletes ask themselves *Am I really getting paid so much for doing this?"* He shrugs, dips his wing in the white sauce. His hands are huge on his skinny wrists. "But they do. Might as well act childish—it's their job." He chuckles and shakes his head.

"Hey, counselor," says the bartender, reaching over the counter to shake Art's hand.

"Hey, man. How's your mom?"

"Mom is good, *real* good. She's gonna be happy I saw you."

"You tell her I said hi."

"Sure thing, man. What can I get y'all?" He lays cocktail napkins on the bar. There's a gold tooth at the center of his mouth.

Art orders a light beer and when the bartender glances at Ray, he says he will have the same. The guy goes to draw the drinks and Ray stares at the white paper square in front of him, the restaurant's name in black curlicue on its surface. He says in a quiet voice, "I was sure you were going to order us club sodas." He smiles sheepishly at Art who watches the game.

Art shrugs, says without looking at Ray, "I wanted a beer. And you're a big boy. You make your own decisions." He reaches a salt shaker off the back of the bar, sprinkles it over the two napkins to keep them from sticking to the frosty mugs.

The bartender sets the beers down in front of Ray and Art and, when both men reach for their wallets, says, "Naw, man, it's on me." He slaps his barrel chest with emphasis. "You're real people, man." He gives Art the peace sign and then moves down the bar.

Art goes back to eating, gaze moving from chicken wing to TV. The other team, it turns out, is the San Diego Chargers, the blur a lightning bolt. At another table, a group of college students with perfect teeth and tans sing along to the jukebox: "I'm a joker, I'm a smoker, I'm a mid…night toker! I sure don't wanna hurt no one!"

"I got his brother off a drug rap," Art says, nodding at the bartender talking to a couple UF linebackers at the far end of the bar.

Ray nods. "Did he do it?"

"Do what?" Art asks, then "Damn!" when an Eagles wide receiver misses a catch.

"Sell drugs?"

Art looks at him, drinks his beer down to the halfway point in two gulps, puts it back carefully on its napkin. "Dunno. But my man's little bro is taking college classes now, got a part-time job. I guess I didn't ask."

Ray massages his temples. He feels that he has settled into his hangover, that maybe, he has had a constant low-level hangover for weeks. Even though he doesn't want it, he sips a little of his beer—it tastes like sour water. An ice fragment slides down the side of the mug and he flicks it off the bar. "I got kicked out of Combustion."

Art nods at the TV, chews on the last of the wings. "How'd that happen?"

Ray shrugs, turns his mug, takes another sip. It tastes awful. Art looks at him then, and so Ray shrugs again for his benefit.

"Baby, you *know*."

Ray shakes his head, says, "I'm a fuck-up."

Art laughs, pushes aside the little paper boat of chicken bones, finishes his beer and nods at the bartender. "I'm paying for this one," he yells.

"Naw, man, you're my people," the bartender smiles, slapping his chest, already drawing Art's beer. "You all right?" he asks Ray who still has half his. Ray nods.

"I insist," Art says, pushing a bill across the bar top. The bartender replaces Art's empty mug with a new one, puts his hands in the air like he's being robbed. They both laugh and ignore the bill. "You ain't a fuck-up, baby," Art says, sipping on the beer and looking at the TV. A toy bunny in sunglasses hits a drum. Art gestures at the screen, shaking his head: "Look at that, I've seen this commercial a million times and I'm sitting next to my best friend in a bar and can't look away. It's the nature of the machine." He looks at Ray, says, "Maybe you're just finished with that band. Could be it's time for something new."

Ray pushes his beer toward Art, who is already finishing his. "You can have this one too. My dad wants me to move to South Carolina and help him run his sporting goods store."

"You want that?"

"Not really."

"Then why mention it?"

"I'm not sure what else to do."

"You got a job. This is a college town, you'll get in another band. Your boy's here. I know that woman still loves you."

"Jan and I aren't getting back together. You need to let that pipe dream go."

"All right." Art starts drinking Ray's beer. "I just hate to see two people in love who ain't got the sense to be together when they could."

"Too much shit has happened. Neither of us have any financial future. You've got a real career so you don't understand."

A news announcer appears on the screen: "The commissioner today announced that Gainesville police have apprehended the serial killer responsible for the Gainesville murders. Victor Mansley was arrested in Tampa, FL in a robbery and, after matching fingerprints, police say they have their man." The shot cuts to a familiar image: large man in thick glasses, red, messy hair, hands cuffed behind his back. The announcer says in voiceover, "Find out at eleven why this man, Edward Skein, has been wrongly held for the last three months."

"I knew that guy was innocent," Art says, shaking his head, a sour look on his face.

"You did?" Ray assumed the police had the right guy all along.

"Yeah. That's a sad story. The cops wanted to search his place after they arrested him so they read the search warrant to the empty house. His grandmomma had a heart attack when she came home and saw the cops ripping it apart. Dead." Art sips his beer, watches the football game which has come back on. "That bastard was crazy, but not a killer. Now he's got no one to take care of him."

"Why didn't you do something?"

Art turns to him. "And what should that have been, pray tell?"

"You're a lawyer." Ray stares at the bar in front of him, suddenly feeling a little dumb. He mumbles, "Get him off."

Art touches Ray's arm gently. "My friend, I am smart. I am very, very smart. But I can't get everyone off. I hate to disabuse you of your naivetés."

Ray shrugs, wants his beer back, feels absurd here in this bar without anything to drink. He opens his mouth to say *drink up*, but instead, Art yells, "*Yes!*" jumping off his barstool. On the TV that big Eagles halfback flaps his arms like wings. "That's *right!*" Art yells, pointing at the bartender who nods back. For Ray's benefit, he flaps his arms like a bird. "You know you like it, baby."

It is early afternoon when Ray gets to Wooly Bear Records. There are seven or eight customers in varying stages of cool boredom flipping through records and CDs. Billy immediately shouts, "Hey, there's my favorite hipster, Gainesville's most eligible guitarist."

The other two employees working are Jamie, a kid with perpetually greasy hair who plays in a bubblegum rock band and always looks like he is about to cut his wrists, and Sally, a sexily chubby post-teen with a boy's haircut. She wears baggy jeans, a too-tight blue T-shirt and sneakers. Billy slaps his big belly and says, "Come over here and give me a hug, man. Come give me a hug!" He has got a few days' whiskers, red eyes, and is wearing a voluminous T-shirt with the word "Baby" on the chest and an arrow pointing toward his belly. Ray passively walks into his arms and lets his boisterous boss hug him and kiss his forehead, a thing he does so often that no one but Billy seems to find it amusing anymore.

Ray pushes up on the back counter and sits, already tired although he has six and a half hours ahead of him. Wooly Bear sells new and used CDs, but most of their product is used vinyl. The owner, Max Strane—an old, embittered hippie alcoholic— constantly grumbles, "I hate those shiny, little circles," and is famous for chasing a teenager out of the store who, in all innocence, held up a 45 record and asked, "How does this fit into a CD player?" Billy always chuckles and musses Max's hair, says, "Honey, you know CDs are our bread and butter."

Today, Billy is cheerful despite what looks, and smells, like a raging hangover. His hair sticks up in various places and the sour tang of stale beer sweats through his pores. "I'm glad to see you, man. Look at my hand." He raises it slowly to demonstrate the shakes.

The "Incoming" shelves behind the counter are packed with recently bought CDs. "I see you left me all the CDs to price. Way to make our purchases work for us."

"Have you seen my hand?" Billy's frenzied smile shifts.

"Uh, can I buy this record?" a waif in paisley dress and trench coat asks quietly. The cover has Andy Warhol's famous banana print on it.

"Dirtbag," Billy says to Jamie, the least senior employee working, "a customer awaits your skillful assistance."

Ray stares at the stack of CDs, an uneasiness rising from his gut for a reason he cannot quite place. It is not the impending work— he can price CDs while he reads, a tedious task, yes, but not dread-worthy. One of the CD spines draws his eye as he glances up and down the stacks on the shelf, the print on their labels blurred at this distance. The spine is lime green with blue print, unlike the others which are mostly white with black letters. Hopping to the floor, he steps across the aisle to the shelf, comprehension dawning as he works the disc out from the middle of the stack, already well aware of the title, *Pushing Too Hard* by the sixties garage band, The Seeds. He doesn't even need to turn it over—although he does—to prove to himself that his initials, "RG," have been written in the right lower-hand corner above the barcode. And then he is quickly pick-ing out ten, then twenty, thirty, and he is sure there is more, all with his initials on the back. "Fuck, fucking-A!" he yells, over and over.

"Hey, man, what's up?" Billy asks.

Finally, Ray whirls toward him, hands full of CDs, two, then three more falling to the floor, cases cracking. "These are my fuck-ing CDs!" he yells. "Who bought these?" He stares at Billy who glances at Jamie, then Sally, his eyebrows up.

"Uh, I didn't do it," Jamie says, hands up in surrender, hair falling into his eyes. He bats the hair away, raises his palms again.

Sally leans against the counter, eyes down. "Not me." She seems unconcerned though her pale cheeks flush a pretty red. Ray glances around the store as if he will discover the guilty culprit, but there are just three customers and they all stare at him like he is a crazy person.

"I'll find out," he says, slamming the stack of CDs on the counter and taking the purchase clipboard off its hook. He scans down the list and gets all the way to the bottom without finding what he is looking for. He has to flip it over and go to the day previous to see the name: Lily Rongo. He jabs her name with his finger, shouts, "Ah-ha!" and runs his pointer to the spot for employee initials. "JJ"? he asks.

"Oh," Billy says, scratching his head. "The new kid."

"The new kid?" Ray says. "The new fucking kid? Why's the new kid buying CDs? Hasn't the new kid only been here two days?"

Billy nods, raising his palms, "It's been longer than two days. But yeah, it's soon for him to be purchasing. It's not his fault—I shouldn't have had him working alone last night."

"What is he, a moron?" Ray flips to the back of the clipboard to where the new kid has photocopied Lily's ID, standard practice for purchases over 20 bucks. "I've got signs posted all over. I even taped a picture of her right here next to the register." He points at the snapshot: Lily looking young and cute and blond, one hand raised at the camera, at a Ray she liked then. There is a stridency, a near-hysterical note creeping into his voice. "Anyone can read it: *If this girl tries to sell CDs with the initials RG on them DO NOT BUY THEM! They're stolen. Take them from her and call Ray Gallant immediately.* I've got my phone number listed and even some of the more obscure disc titles in case that's not enough. Look: The Seeds!" he says, holding up the disc. "Who else would have the Seeds?"

"Keep your voice down, Ray," Billy says, and his smile leaves for a second, but then is right back. "You're harshing my mellow."

Ray stares at him, then says, "Well, I'm taking these," and moves to pick them up.

"Come on, man?" Billy says, putting his hand on Ray's wrist.

"What? They're mine."

"You know the routine: No one gets his stolen merchandise without a police report. It's the only way Max has of getting his money back. Press charges. What do you care if Lily goes to jail? Do the paperwork and you'll get your shit back. Don't and you won't. That's the way it is. I've heard you say the same thing to poor mothers of crackheads." He pulls Ray by the shirtsleeve. "Come on, leave those there. I want to show you something in the back. Can you guys hold the fort?" Jamie is flipping through a magazine and Sally stares into a tiny compact mirror, appearing to dig something out of a back tooth.

"Yeah," she says around her fingers.

"Hey dirtbag," Billy says, "make yourself useful and price some of these goddamn CDs. *Not* Ray's. Find all the stolen ones and leave them on the back counter for me."

"You know, I've got a name, Billy," Jamie whines as Billy steers Ray toward the back of the store. Inside his tiny office, Billy locks the door and pulls open the bottom drawer of his old, scarred oak desk, uncaps a bottle of cheap whiskey. He lifts a paper cup off its side and sniffs the interior, shrugs, pours a few fingers of whiskey and passes it to Ray. Billy swallows the coffee in a brown coffee mug with the inscription WORLD'S GREATEST DAD, makes a grimace, then pours some whiskey and throws it back, slapping his chest and emitting a weird groan.

Billy used to play bass in Man-Sized Firepower, one of the greatest post-punk bands in Gainesville music history. They even had a record on college radio stations in the eighties. But then their singer caught AIDS from sharing needles and the band fell apart. If he turns his head just right, Ray can still see the frumpy, boyish beauty Billy had then: the kind of untucked-shirt look that probably made him a nerdy outsider in high school, but a Romeo in his twenties. Whereas he looked nonchalantly unkempt then, now he just looks unhealthy. He pours another few fingers and then raises the mug toward Ray, nods and waits until Ray raises his own untouched cup.

"I don't really feel like whiskey, Billy."

"Shut up and drink," Billy says, not unkindly. "To old guys selling records." He kicks back this whiskey, too, in a swallow. "Ah, 'That,' as the kids say, 'is the ticket.'"

"The kids don't say that." Ray swallows his whiskey to be done with it, a shiver working through his chest to his toes. For a second, he wants to ask Billy for another.

"They should." Billy raises the bottle, nodding toward Ray.

"I've got to work."

Billy pours another cup for himself. "I've got to baby-sit. It's Brenda's monthly night with the gals. They wear panties and bras and hit each other with pillows."

"Sounds delightful."

Billy belches.

"Why did you give that chick, Kristina, comp tickets?"

"What?" Billy runs his fingers through his tangled hair, rubs his face with both hands.

"That girl, Kristina. The other night, you know. I was outside."

Billy stares, blankly. "Kristina Quean? That *kid?* What of it?"

92

He scratches the stubble on his fat neck. "I've always given the ladies comp tickets. Why do you care?"

"I thought employees had first dibs."

Billy squints at Ray as if he's emitting light. He scratches his head and a dust of dandruff flakes onto his shoulders. "You want to see Fine? I thought you hated them." Billy scratches his head some more, then tips his chair back so he's leaning against the dirty drywall. "If I'm not mistaken, you always say, 'Turn off that cowpunk shit' whenever I put on the new record."

"It's not the point, I just…"

"Didn't I give you Led Zep reunion tickets?"

"Yeah, but…"

"Maybe you should masturbate."

Ray just stares. "What?"

"You know, your chick left. You seem tense. It might help." Billy pours himself another couple fingers, swallows. When he speaks again, his voice is hoarse: "People think that us married guys have it made. 'Aw, you guys are lucky. You can fuck every night.' That's what that dirtbag said to me at the Minny a few weeks ago. Can you believe that? I said, 'There's nothing like jerking off, kid. Even us married guys do it.' Besides, when you've been with the same chick for ten years and she's getting old, she doesn't care about getting as clean, her tits sag…"

"All right, I get the picture. Pour me some whiskey, you old fuck."

"Now you're talking." Billy grins and pours, probably too much for a guy who is about to work a six-hour shift.

"I'm quitting." Ray takes a small swig.

"Yeah, right. You'll never quit."

Ray winces. "I am." He nods once for emphasis.

"Why are you acting like this?" Billy's voice is loud with a high-pitched squeal to it. "Did that bitch run off with your stash?"

Ray laughs. "Actually, yes. That's beside the point."

"No, it's not. Exactly the point." Billy slaps the desk. "I'm gonna have to…" He pauses, touches his chest, then gestures like an opera tenor and belches so loudly it is surely heard out in the store. His expression never changing, he says, "I'm gonna have to bring Chance out to get a video or he's bound to drive me crazy. I'll be biting the bullet. Plus, fuck, what am I gonna do for dinner but pizza?"

"Chips and soda?"

"Exactly." Billy points at Ray. "When we come out, I'll swing by and smoke a joint with you. It'll loosen you up."

Ray sighs, but nods. "Sure. I'm still quitting. This is my two weeks' notice." He pushes a crumpled white paper bag to the floor, brushes aside a bagel fragment, and picks up a gnawed-on disposable pen with a clump of blue ink on its tip, scribbles on the desk blotter until he gets ink, then circles a day. Billy watches this performance, eyes ludicrously wide as if in horror. "This," Ray says, tapping the day with the pen, "is my last day."

"No," Billy says, shaking his head slowly, "it's not."

"Yes," Ray says, face grim, "it is."

Jamie and Ray work the night shift and it is slow. Tipp, a regular, comes in wearing a shrunken T-shirt, pudgy belly peeking. A part-time security guard at a warehouse on the east side, he wears his hair oiled, slicked across his white dome in a comb-over too sad to even fool himself. He asks Ray to play a couple of songs off a Carpenters' record and listens with his eyes closed like a connoisseur sniffing wine, a quick exhale when the needle pops over a scratch. After a song or two, Ray says, "Yes or no?"

Tipp puts an index finger to his bottom lip. "Hm," he says. "I want to look around."

He does this every Tuesday: asks Ray to play a song or two off an album. Then asks him to play another, and then another. He always asks for three sample listens—Ray's limit—and always buys just one record, invariably one he has not even asked to hear, always one of the cheapest in the store.

Tipp browses for two hours, asks Ray to play a Sinatra hits disc and an album by a band called Corpse Eater. When he brings up a fourth album—something he occasionally does, pretending to have lost count—Ray, too bored to care, puts on the record, a one-hit-wonder eighties band unironically called Kathy and the Hugs (their hit is not on this record).

Other customers drift in and out, ask where the latest Public Enemy CD is, flip zombie-like through vinyl and fanzines. The only moment that dents the pall is when a hippie smelling of wet cardboard comes in and asks in a loud voice if Wooly Bear sells whippets.

Jamie yawns frequently, stretches and, at some point, pulls a shiny American History textbook from his backpack and opens it on the counter. There is something childlike about the way the tip of Jamie's tongue moves into the corner of his mouth, how a greasy lock of hair curls in front of his eyes like a Spanish question mark. Even his movements are childlike: the way he clenches a fat yellow marker in his hand too near the tip, running it carefully along a line of text, brings to mind Hank drawing. The cloying smell of marker evokes both Ray's childhood and his fatherhood and makes him sad and a little annoyed.

Flipping through the latest issue of *Consummation,* some obscure Brit mag of experimental music, Ray asks, without looking up, "What are you studying?"

Jamie swipes that question mark away. "The Revolutionary War."

There is something so intense and serious about the kid that Ray would not be surprised if he quoted a line of poetry. He smiles, sings, "Louie, Louie, woah, woah, me gotta go now...", but the kid just stares, until Ray's smile wavers, and he adds, "You know, Paul Revere and the Raiders?" The kid stares until Ray says, "You know, Paul Revere, the patriot...Revolutionary War?" He shrugs and says "Forget it," stares at the glossy magazine and then closes it, tosses it on a shelf beneath the counter. "What do you want to be when you grow up, Jamie?"

"I don't know," the kid says, staring down at the book, and then running the highlighter over a line of text, and then another. He recaps the pen, taps it on the counter, looks at Ray as if he is waiting for some other question, refuses to see the condescending expression on his face.

"What's your major?" Ray asks. He feels embarrassed, wishes that Tipp would return, takes off the current choice, a poppy selection of cloying Miami pseudo-salsa. "That's enough, Tipp. Want it?" Tipp shakes his head without looking up from the bluegrass albums he is flipping through.

"Business," Jamie answers.

"Really?" Ray resleeves the record.

"Why's that surprising?"

"Usually the people who work here major in things like Art or Philosophy or English. Or don't go to school at all."

"I want to get a real job when I get out." Jamie plays with the chain connecting his wallet to his belt loop.

"What about your band?"

Jamie smiles for the first time and Ray can see what girls probably see at his shows: a shy, clean-faced kid who might write songs about them if they are lucky, who seems standoffish, but probably wants a girl to take care of him. "You know as much as me how few people make it." Tipp brings up another record, this time one of those eighties metal bands, Shifty, the kind where all the musicians wore makeup and had bare hairy chests and sneered or pouted at the camera. Ray shakes his head. "No, Tipp, you've gone over tonight. If you want to hear more, you need to bring me something that's not complete and utter shit."

"Oh, sorry, Ray." Tipp goes off in search of something acceptable, lumbering toward the far corner of the store where the soundtracks and spoken word albums are.

Ray shakes his head and Jamie says, "Of course, if the band made it, I'd be as happy as anyone. I'm not counting on it though. Frankly, I don't much care what I do as long as it's not retail. My god, how can you stand to deal with retards like that daily?"

Ray feels that he is blushing, wants to say something nasty to the kid, actually has an urge to slap him. "It's better than working in an office," he says, speaking to the poster image of the latest sexy, folkie ingénue.

"How do you know that? Have you ever worked in an office?"

"No."

"Neither have I. But I've worked jobs like this. I sold socks and ties at some mall store before this, and more than once I thought it'd be great to sit in a cubicle. I'm not going to say that's hell just because everyone else does. Look at that fuck." Jamie gestures at Tipp, who, at the moment, is flipping albums with one hand and digging in his ass with the other. "People get days off at places like that, with pay. Not just Christmas and Thanksgiving. I wanted Easter and Memorial Day off in the spring and Billy said no, I could have one or the other. What the fuck's up with that?"

"You're willing to work some dehumanizing job just so you can get a few days off?"

"That's simple. Is it lazy or selling out just because I want to go surfing with my friends? Is it lame that I want to go to my folks' barbecue because it's on a Sunday and most normal people don't have to work?" The kid does not wait for an answer. He is already highlighting a line of text. Ray wants to ask if he even knows what he is marking, but he senses the kid would have an answer. He stares at the cash register, would like some reason to jab numbers into its face, even wants to poke the "No Sale" button just to hear the drawer pop open and the dings of the register tape jerking up.

Tipp appears with a beat-up record with a fat man's face on the cover, the shot in close-up so his pores are tiny craters. There is a zany expression on the man's face, a frayed hat pulled low on his head, and a cartoon bubble flowing from his mouth: "LET'S GET WACKY!!!" he suggests. Tipp stares blankly at Ray as if there is no question that this is a step up from the heavy metal stylings of Shifty. Ray doesn't bother sighing. He unsleeves the record and places it on the turntable, lifts the needle over the wax and gently sets it in its groove.

It is past close in Wooly Bear's and Ray is alone. He let Jamie go as soon as the last customer left which is against the rules. Both closers are supposed to take the day's earnings to Florida Federal ever since an employee got hit in the face with a lock in a sock a few years ago. Ray imagines there might even be some pleasure in that—not in the teeth, maybe against his cheek or temple. He would wake in the street, look up into the worried faces of strangers, a drizzle sprinkling his face. He would touch his forehead and there would be some satisfaction in the way streetlight gleamed off the blood on his fingertips. He knows that this will not happen though, and wonders why that is disappointing.

Wooly Bear seems run-down and lonely now in the murk. Sporadic cars drift by on University, a car horn, squeal of brakes. There is just one string of lights on along the back wall casting a dim glow by which Ray will add up the day's purchases and sales. But first he wanders over to the Rock/Pop section, the Ps, flips slowly through the records until he sees it, Tom Petty's first album. Bringing it behind the counter, he takes the record from its sleeve, sights along the vinyl—just a slight warping, a few hairline scratches, fine. He places it on the turntable, turns it on and sets the needle in the groove of the last song. There is that jangly guitar, the syncopated snare-bass beat that almost upsets Ray's heartbeat, and then Petty's voice, a snarl like Dylan's but with more complexity. Ray closes his eyes, can feel the dimness against his lids, listens: "Well, she was an American girl, raised on promises. She couldn't help thinking that there was a little more to life…somewhere else." *What happened?* This is the song, the album that made him want to play music. His earliest musical fumblings were some approximation of this trebly playing. His first band in high school, Refuge (the name makes him cringe now), played two Petty covers, and Petty forebears—a few Byrds numbers and Dylan's "Like a Rolling Stone."

In Combustion, he didn't want to just copy his biggest influence. Combustion had never played a Petty cover, nor a Dylan for that matter, and the only Byrds song they did was their cover of Jimi Hendrix's "Hey Joe." There had been a constant tug-of-war between Reese and Ray about the band's aesthetics. While Ray's sense of composition favored the lyrical, the bright, Reese embraced the jagged and dissonant: the heroin-induced deadpans of the Velvet Underground, the scary chaos of the Stooges. Ray liked that music too; it was fine, even good that he and Reese loved different music.

But that tension never created anything that Ray felt good about. Reese and Ray had not been able to make their different tastes combine into a fresh, compelling sound in the way of their influences: Reed and Cale, Strummer and Jones, Jagger and Richards, Lennon and McCartney. Combustion had never brought that many to the bars, and few people had ever asked him—or few except flirting girls (and as he got older, there were fewer and fewer of those)—"When are you guys putting out a CD?" They *could* have put one out. Everyone did nowadays. Ray knew half a dozen guys in Gainesville alone who owned 4-tracks or digital recorders, guys who would have recorded Combustion for beer or dope.

At the end of the song, he lifts the stylus and places the needle at the beginning of the record. He counts the ones in the register, loses count on the number twelve, recounts and loses his concentration at fourteen, then nine. He slaps his palm against the pile of money, suddenly feels a surge of anger at

Jamie, wonders why the fuck he let the kid go. And then he wonders why Billy didn't return to get him high like he promised, and wonders why he even wonders because Billy constantly says he will do things he doesn't. Without thinking, Ray picks up the phone and dials.

"Dad? Am I calling too late?"

"Ray? What's going, kid? Where you calling from? You sound funny. You talking on one of them walking-around phones?"

"No. Dad: listen to me."

"Yeah, sure kid, what's wrong? You in trouble? Be straight."

"Dad, okay. I want to know…if I were to work at the store…"

"I'm listening, kid," his father says when Ray pauses too long.

"Could I have Memorial Day off?"

"What?" Ray's dad chuckles. "You kidding?"

"No, Dad. I want Memorial Day weekend off. I want responsibility too. I don't want to just run the register. I want to matter, you know? Or I can't imagine doing this."

"Kid," Ray's father says, his voice deep and careful, "what you're saying is real responsible and very doable. You're making your old man happy, really happy."

"Thanks, Dad. I'm going to look into moving. I need to figure some stuff out, so it'll be a few days before I can tell you when I'm coming. Okay?"

"Great, kid, take your time. Let me know what I can do. I'm looking forward to it."

Ray hangs up, puts his palms against the wooden desk. The record has played through and the broken phonograph arm has failed to lift and travel back to its perch. The needle glides out across the smooth gap at the end and skips against the paper circle, a repetitious hiss like the sound of waves on a beach. When Ray moves back to Myrtle he is going to surf like he did in high school. At least three times a week, no matter the weather.

Ray knocks at Jan's door, waits. The blinds are drawn, but there is a light in the living room so he knows she is up. He is about to knock a second time when the door opens. Jan scowls at him in sock feet, pajama bottoms, a faded punk band shirt which looks too big for her.

"What do you want?" she asks.

"I need to talk."

"It'll have to be another time."

Music drifts from inside, the Pretenders. *Wasn't that my disc?* he thinks. "Who's here?"

"None of your business." He tries to peer over her head. The person there is cut off by the edge of the living room wall, but Ray can see a giant black Converse high top perched on a blue jeans knee, toe-tapping double-time to the music.

"Is that your boss?"

"You've got to go." She tries to push the door, but Ray's palm is pressed against it.

"William," he calls. The foot immediately freezes.

"Shhhh," she whispers, "Hank's asleep. Are you drunk?" Her voice is a shiv.

"*No.*" He lets his hand drop from the door. "I'm leaving."

"Good." But some of the anger has left her voice. She catches the door before it swings closed. "I'll call you in the morning."

"I'm leaving town."

"When are you coming back?"

"I'm not."

She puts one foot on top of the other, toes curled. "What are you talking about?"

"Dad's asked me to help run his stores. I'm going to. I'm moving to Myrtle."

"What about your son?" He leans against the jamb. Their faces are close and he can smell the lotion she still rubs on her cheeks and hands and legs each night. Her breath is shallow and her eyes gleam in the dim light coming from the living room. He peels an inch-long splinter off the jamb, holds it up to her and she takes it from his hand, tosses it away. "Answer me."

"I need something." His voice breaks. The music ends and, after a pause, some zither music Ray's not familiar with comes on.

Jan opens her mouth, but then just nods, stands on her toes, leaning toward him as if she will kiss him. But she pauses, the breath catches in her throat. He leans suddenly toward her, but she leans back, takes a step away. "Bye," he says, turning, but she grabs the front of his jacket. Before she can pull away, he snatches her wrist and pulls her close, kisses her on the mouth. They are leaning into each other, clutching, tongues touching, and even though it only lasts a few seconds it will stretch far into the future, into realities that will never exist.

6

Someone whacks weeds outside William's apartment although it is 7:30 in the morning, sidewalk complaining when the blade gets too close. The groundskeeper is an early riser, *the bastard.* William rolls over, but Jan is already out of bed, hunched, an arm in front of her bare breasts, padding silent as a cat to the bathroom. He runs his fingers through his beard. His cat Flann is perched in the window, watching sparrows dart after each other.

In boxers and T-shirt, William grinds coffee, dumps it in the filter and places it in the drip basket. He pours the water and flips on the switch which glows a reddish orange. The shower cuts on in the back of the apartment, pipes groaning with hot water. Drinking a tall glass of orange juice, he stares out the window. The sun seems high for so early, the pine's shadow a stumpy shrub. Renaldo, the groundskeeper, a Cuban immigrant, yanks crabgrass away from the sidewalk, throws it over his shoulder. Two sparrows fight in the tree branches, wings a whir, chirps slicing through the glass. William realizes that one is perched over the other's back. *Fucking, not fighting.*

Jan and William sit on either side of his tiny kitchen table and crunch on day-old garlic bagels with cream cheese, sip bitter coffee and read the paper. "What's the weather like?" she asks without looking up from the front section.

William flips to the back of the sports section, snaps the paper. "No rain. High 90."

Jan stares at him, an ambiguous expression, and he looks back. She walks across his living room, brand new flip-flops flopping and opens the door, leans her hands upon the iron railing, head looking right, then left into the parking lot.

Things have been weird. It has been over half a year since Victor Mansley's killing spree, since Eddie Skein was scapegoated, since Jan and William slept together for the first time. They stopped sleeping together for a few months, but have started again, occasionally, when Jan is in a good mood. Sometimes, she throws her arms around him, leans into him and kisses him playfully on the neck. Sometimes, she looks through him like he might be glass. She never says more than "Hi" at work, says, "How much are we pricing the John Grisham book?" or "You think I can go on break?" She barely smiles, lets her eyes linger on his, but still Jessica asks, "What's with you two?" and Erik asks, "Is Jan coming in today?" William snaps without thinking: "What do you mean?" "How should I know?" "I'm busy."

Today he is not sure what to expect. Perhaps soon, she will climb into his lap, and say, "Kiss me, goddamnit." Then again, she might order, "Take me home. I've changed my mind."

They are supposed to go to the beach for the weekend. Ray lives in South Carolina now so Jan has Hank all the time. But Rain has taken him for the weekend so Jan can have fun. She has been working full time since she decided not to return to school this semester, and has been taking extra shifts from her fellow workers whenever they want to go to a concert or are too hung over to work, or would rather go to the beach instead of slap the cobwebs off a *Hardy Boys* collection.

William's brother, Tad, owns a lawn service and, with the money he has put aside, managed to buy a cabin at Crescent Beach. It is a little run-down: unfinished wood floors, scraps of dead lawn, an intermittently running A/C unit perched on two-by-fours in a sand-filled flowerbed. Tad's wife worries they can't afford payments on the house plus their home in Gainesville. But William's older brother is an obsessive surfer and also a charmer of his wife and it has been an easy sell.

At a 7-11, without a word Jan jumps out of William's truck and pumps the gas. She taps her foot and watches the digital numbers speeding toward full, a fingernail-bitten hand on a hip, a tuneless sound coming from between her teeth. "What do you want?" William asks.

"What?" She turns, visibly annoyed, eyes flickering toward the traffic.

William grins although he can feel an uneasiness like sour stomach, the rumblings before sickness. He pantomimes drinking and eating, nods toward the store.

She shrugs, lowers the sunglasses on her head so that he can no longer see her eyes.

Inside the chilly store, he grabs a twelve-pack of beer, a bag of chips, one of pretzels, a can of nuts. He wants to take Jan to his favorite seafood restaurant for dinner, but this will hold them over. He drops the armload of snacks and beer on the counter, says to the cashier, a teen girl with bony hips and braces, "Also a bag of ice and whatever's on…" He gestures outside. "Whichever pump the rusty truck is on." Jan stares into the store. William waves, but maybe she cannot see him because of the glare, because she offers no reaction, leaning against the truck, fingers in her pockets. She spits on the pavement and yawns. The cashier has said something in a quiet Southern drawl. "I'm sorry?" William responds. She taps the readout on the cash register, blows a big pink bubble, lets it soundlessly deflate.

He drops the bag of snacks in the back of the truck, puts the twelve-pack on the concrete and trots back to the outside cooler. "How much was it?" Jan calls.

"Don't worry about it." He pulls open the glass door and retrieves a bag of ice. It is bracing in the humid morning—once again, Florida has skipped spring in favor of summer.

"No, really, how much?"

He shrugs and it looks for a moment as if her lips will break into a grin. But she shakes her head and looks away. He pulls the Styrofoam cooler from the truck and smacks the bag of ice against the black pavement to break it up. The cool damp contour of ice feels good against his palm and the smack of pavement against plastic, he realizes, is the first real pleasure he has had this morning. The sour stomach dissipates a bit. Jan toes the twelve-pack and that silver ring on her second toe glints against the sun. He took her toes into his mouth last night and tasted its metal along with the warm skin which was slightly gritty. She giggled and pulled away, said, "No, don't, I'm ticklish."

Now, she says, "I hate Nate's," toeing the box again. "It's bitter."

William stops smacking ice, hears himself sigh, or groan. He pushes his glasses up on the bridge of his nose, leaves his palm on the cool bag, places the other against the pavement which is nearly too hot to touch. "You drank it last week. At Linda's."

"That's all she had."

"You were smiling." William smiles as to offer a sample, and yet the feel of his lips seems wrong somehow. "That usually means pleasure."

"I was faking," she says with no attempt at levity. Her eyes are invisible behind those cheap, dime store shades. "I like to fake. I do it often."

William has to look away from those brown lenses. A guy in a Greek T-shirt gassing up a Trans Am, a scrub of beard on his chin, watches. "Do you mind?" William asks.

"Naw, man, go ahead," the guy says, hawking and spitting.

"This is fun," Jan says, clapping, "Fucking fun. Really!" She gets back in the truck, slams the door.

William slowly finishes loading the cooler, rearranging cans so that they all fit with the ice. Putting it in the truck, he watches Jan sitting rigidly in the passenger seat, staring out the front window. He slams the tailgate, runs his fingers along the rough metal, counts to himself, *10, 9, 8, 7...*

In the truck, he fingers the keys in the ignition, staring out the front window with Jan at nothing—cars passing on 13th, a dumpster with its lid thrown back, plastic bag struggling in the wind, anchored by something inside. "I'm sorry," William says to the windshield, waits. "I'm not even sure what we're fighting about. *Are* we fighting?" Then he says, "I could get some other kind of beer. Or Cokes." He looks at Jan then, his Adam's apple working convulsively. "Water?" he manages to croak.

"Don't," she says, turning to him, "bother."

He nods and, without thinking, turns the key, revs the engine more than it needs. Squealing tires, he pulls onto 13th and takes a right. "Slow down, Bo Duke," she says, putting a palm on the dash, but he takes the light on University, speedometer vibrating toward 60. "You're going the wrong way," she shouts over the engine. "What's going on?" she asks when he pulls into a space in his apartment complex and shuts the engine off.

"What do you think?" His voice has risen and Jan leans back as if he might be violent. "I'd rather do something else this weekend. Maybe wash my bathtub. Or rearrange my books. I've been thinking about organizing them by color. Won't that be pretty?"

She laughs at this, finally, and he frowns, thinks that maybe they will go to the beach after all. But she says, "Fuck it," still laughing, opening her door and getting out.

"Yep," he says quietly to himself, "fuck it." He grabs his overnight bag and then pauses halfway across the parking lot. Jan stands at the staircase, hands on hips. "What?" he asks.

"My bike's in your apartment. Let me get it and I'll be out of your hair."

"Fine." He brushes past, bag bouncing against his thigh.

"Yeah, fine," she says, following him up the concrete stairway and flip-flopping angrily after him down the walkway.

He stops at his door so suddenly she runs into him. "What?" she hisses into his shirt.

Holding a finger to his lips, he nods at the glass sprinkling the pavement beneath the living room window. The door is slightly ajar. He puts his hand against the door and feels Jan's fingers digging into his arm. She mouths *no*, shakes her head, gestures over her shoulder, taking a step back. He gently peels her fingers away, mouths, *It's okay*, puts his palm up and whispers, "Stay."

The refrigerator door is open and William can see a back curved above it, a voice coming from inside. "Want something?" a man says, words wet as they work around the food in his mouth. "There's lots to eat." Jan pulls William's arm again and he shrugs it away, lifting a Phillips head screwdriver off the window ledge. That is when the dog rushes into the room. He is fast and nearly silent, like a low-flying bird of prey. But then he is barking that high-pitched, rapid small-dog bark. He is a strange mutt: terrier's head; body like a dachshund; dirty, peppered coat like there might be a little Dalmatian.

Jan screams, pointing to the kitchen, one hand over her mouth. Blood oozes from the knuckle on the guy's left hand, leaving painterly splotches on the white linoleum. In his other, he clutches a dill pickle, bitten in half. He is soft, fleshy, and pale, bright red hair sticking up in sweaty corkscrews, thick glasses askew. His filthy blue flannel shirt is open, revealing a T-shirt with the words, *Gainesville Blood Drive 1990: Give Till It Hurts!* beneath a cartoon drop of blood. He is short enough that William can see down onto his white bald spot as perfect as a tonsured monk. He seemed larger on TV.

"What are you guys doing here?" he asks in an avuncular tone.

"This is my apartment," William says. "What are *you* doing here?"

"I sublet it. Remember? I'm staying here while you're out of town."

"But we're not out of town," William says, gesturing to Jan and himself.

"Will…" Jan says.

"No, really, I did," the guy says, rummaging through a black garbage bag which seems quite a few months from new. "See?" He pulls out a scrap of newspaper and lunges toward them. Jan lets out a little scream and William puts his hand on her shoulder. He glances at the paper as if it actually might be a contract. It is a bra ad for a department store, skinny women with suburban haircuts directing pointy breasts at the camera, demure smiles on blank faces.

"William," Jan hisses, and he holds up a hand as if he is trying to read. The dog still barks, the guy's breath a rasp, William's temple pounding in rhythm to both sounds.

"Yep," William says finally, handing back the fragment of paper, "looks like everything's in order."

"Will…" Jan says.

"Come on, let's go," he says, pulling her through the door, screwdriver in his palm slick with sweat.

"Maybe you guys could stay here with me?" the guy calls from the doorway as they hurry down the sidewalk.

"No, it's okay," William calls over his shoulder, pulling Jan by the hand. The dog wags its tail as they move away, tongue happily hanging. "We're going to the beach."

"Really. There's room for all of us. You could sleep on the couch." The dog yips once as if he agrees.

At the foot of the stairs, William knocks at the door of Mrs. Freidrick, the landlady. "Was that…?" Jan asks, but then a tiny gray-haired woman in sneakers, housedress, and glasses opens the door. "Mr. Mannix," she says with a pleased smile. (William is always prompt with the rent.) "Is this your girlfriend?"

"Mrs. Freidrick, I need to use your phone to call the police."

"Oh my." She clutches her housecoat. "Is someone hurt?"

"Someone broke into my apartment."

"How awful. Yes, please, come in." She leads them to a white rotary phone next to an ancient wooden television. Cowboys shoot at shrieking Indians in black and white. Mrs. Friedrick turns down the volume as William dials 911. The room's unscarred antique furniture is speckled with doilies. Over the off-white couch, there is a kitschy oil painting of a 19th century hunt with frothy dogs and horses and mustachioed men. Mrs. Friedrick asks Jan to sit and she perches on the edge of the couch, knees together, saying "No, thank you" when her hostess tries to force a plate of wafer cookies on her.

The operator asks, "Your emergency, please?"

"Eddie Skein has broken into my apartment."

"Who?"

"He's the guy…Never mind, just some guy broke into my apartment. He's still here."

"Give me your address, please."

A box fan whirs in the kitchen doorway, clicking the Venetian blinds against the window in a steady rhythm. Identical blinds are in each of the units, although the slats of William's are broken where Flann has repeatedly pushed through to sit in the window.

"The police are on the way," the operator says. "Stay on the line until they arrive, please. How do you know this person?"

"I don't know him."

"You called him by name."

"He's the guy that got blamed for the serial killings. Look, I hear the sirens. I'm going outside to meet them." He hangs up without waiting for an answer. Realizing the screwdriver is still in his hand, he shoves it into his back pocket.

Three cruisers pull into the parking lot, one after the other, lights dull flashes in the bright day, sirens whining to a stop. "Where is he?" one of the cops says, unstrapping his gun. William, Jan, and Mrs. Friedrick are warped cartoon characters in his mirrored shades.

"I don't think you'll need that," William says.

"Sir," the second cop says, "the apartment?" He's short and stocky, has an identical buzz cut to the first.

"25," Jan says, and the cops run up the stairs.

The third cop, a couple decades older than the others, and quite a bit chubbier, ambles over from his car, trying to work a little notebook out of his back pocket. "All right," he says, scribbling on the lined paper to get some ink, "tell me all about it."

William does, voice breaking off when they hear the shrieks of Eddie Skein and a struggle, the dog barking. Mrs. Friedrick says, "Oh my," again, and Jan leans against William. He can imagine the struggle upstairs: one of the cops on Skein, knee in the back, the other forcing his arms into handcuffs, a bloody string of drool hanging onto the brown carpet.

When the cops lead Skein downstairs, sure enough, blood is running freely over his bottom lip. Both cops are wearing surgical gloves and sweat glistens on their forearms, dampens their armpits. The dog trots behind, barking the entire time. "I said we could share!" Skein screams at William and he feels ashamed and looks away. The chubby cop picks the dog up and it immediately stops barking, tail curled between its skinny legs.

"You're a big boy," he says to the dog who licks his nose, making him laugh. "Let me put this puppy in my cruiser and we'll talk some more."

"Where are you taking him?" William asks.

"Aw, man, I'm telling you," the cop says, shaking his head, looking from William to Jan to Mrs. Friedrick. "We've had so much trouble with that boy since his grandmama died. This is about the fifth time we've picked him up for something or other. We'll take him back to County. They'll feed him some pills, shoot him full of electricity and drop him on the street again. He'll definitely kill somebody someday," he adds, affable smile never faltering. The cop with the mirrored shades is pressing down on Skein's head to direct him into the back seat of the cruiser, but he hits his head anyway, shouts, "Ow!" The chubby cop shakes his head and grins as if to say, *That guy.*

"Not him," William says. "Where are you taking the dog?"

"Oh," the cop says, looking down at the dog as if to verify that, yes, that is what just licked his nose. "Skein must have picked him up somewhere. Probably some kid's." The cop shrugs. "No tags. Got to take him to the pound. Dogs aren't allowed at County."

As the cop turns toward the cruiser again, William says, "Wait. Let me take him."

"What?" the cops says.

"William…" Jan says.

"Mr. Mannix," Mrs. Friedrick says, her sentences clipped and business-like, "I'll have to ask for another pet deposit if you take that dog. One hundred dollars. Non-refundable."

As the cruiser with Skein pulls out of the lot, the cop in mirrored shades strolls over. He takes his glasses off revealing the fading yellow of a shiner, folding the shades into his shirt pocket and taking a can of Skoal from his pants, lower lip already thrust forward.

"The kid wants to take the dog," the chubby cop says, even though William must be at least a decade older than his colleague with the black eye.

Jan squeezes William's elbow. "He's right. The dog probably belongs to some child. You can't just take him."

William leans away so she is no longer touching, says, "What if he doesn't? He'll get gassed at the pound."

"Nah," the younger cop says, a wad of tobacco pinched between his thumb and pointer, "we can't just give him to you." He shakes his head slowly as if even the suggestion might be dangerous. "That would go against procedure."

William paces his living room, dissonant German music on the stereo. He sips a can of Nate's, picks up the phone, listens to the dial tone, puts it down again, stares at the numbers scrawled on the pad next to it. Then, picking up the phone again, he dials quickly, listens to the ring tone. Mrs. Friedrick's oafish son, Hugh, has patched the broken window with a duct-taped slab of cardboard, the upside-down message, "THIS SIDE UP" with downward-pointing arrow. Supposedly, Hugh can't get a pane until Monday.

Someone picks up, says, "Animal control."

"Yeah, I'm calling about a dog…"

"Please hold."

Some muzak plays and William waits, chewing a nail. As he

comes to the realization that the song he's listening to is "You're Having My Baby," someone says. "Kennel." There is the rhythm of barking behind the voice.

"I'm calling about a dog. I think the cops took him there yesterday afternoon?"

"What kind of dog?" It sounds like she is chewing something as she speaks, gum or maybe a sandwich.

"I'm not really sure. It's a weird mix. He's short, brownish, spotted, short-haired…Pointy ears?" he adds when the woman says nothing.

She sighs, says, "I'll ask. Hold on." This time he is not put on hold. The phone bangs hollowly against something, and the sound of barking seems to increase. After several minutes, the woman returns, "Yep, cops brought him in. I seen him. Funny looking fellow, ain't he?" The smacking again, definitely gum.

"He hasn't been claimed?"

"Aren't you?"

"No, he's not mine. I was just here when the cops picked him up."

"Oh, well, no one's called. I thought he was yourn."

"No. What's going to happen to him?"

"He's got no tags, and if no one claims him…You hear that?" The sound of barking is louder. "If no one claims our friend, well, I hate to say it, but he's not long for this world."

"Can you call me before he's put down?"

"Aw, naw, I'm sorry, hon. We're understaffed here. We can't—"

"Fine, how long does he have before you kill him?"

"Hey, it's not like we take him outside and shoot him. It's very humane. He gets a little shot, then goes to sleep."

"Okay, how long before you put him to sleep?"

"It's tricky, hon. We can't turn any strays away—even if some crazy lady dies and leaves a house full of cats, we gotta take em. We try to keep all animals for a week, but you heard how crowded it is."

"Thank you for your time." He hangs up before she can answer.

Although William adopts the dog on Sunday, he cannot pick him up until Monday. The pound requires a 24-hour waiting period while they neuter the dog and call the landlady to see if it is true that she allows dogs. And she does, as long as William is willing to pay the hundred bucks—he is.

On the way home from the pound that afternoon, the dog sits in the middle of the truck's vibrating seat, uninterested in the open window next to him, tiny tail curled between his legs. Impulsively, William drives by the bookstore.

"Oh my god! What a weird dog," Jessica shouts when William brings him inside. Something about her voice seems to calm the dog and he makes a funny little sideways dance toward the desk to meet her.

"I can't believe you got that thing," Jan says. "Your landlady is going to shit."

"She doesn't care," William says without looking at her. "She's got her deposit."

"What's his name?" Jessica asks, rubbing the dog's belly.

"Harry."

"That's a great name," Jessica says.

"Why Harry?" Jan wants to know. She seems annoyed, but William ignores this.

"I just read *Kermis Contortionist*. The dog makes me think of Leath. Scrappy, hangs out with the wrong crowd...Oh shit," William whispers, looking around. "Harry's not here, is he?" Author Harold Leath is a store regular.

"You're cool, babe," Jessica says, standing and bending to crack her back. Harry looks at her as if he is in love.

"What do you think Flann will think of him?" Jan asks from behind the counter where she prices a stack of romances.

"We'll see," William answers.

Flann doesn't like Harry. She hisses at him, the hair on her back standing on end. Harry tries to be passive, realizes that she is the alpha pet, keeps his face turned away. However, his new love for William is so intense he cannot be dissuaded from following him, even if he has to tiptoe around the cat he instinctively seems to know could shred him. Flann pretends indifference to William, as if this introduction to their household is an unforgivable affront, even goes to the trouble of taking a dump in the bathtub. Harry sits on the floor, watching William pace the apartment talking to himself. Within days, he learns William's reaction to stimuli: When the kettle boils, William goes to it, and so does Harry. When someone knocks at the door, William answers, and so does Harry (he also barks at whomever is out there). When the phone rings, he beats William to it, waits for him to pick up the receiver and seems to eavesdrop.

"Billy Boy."

"Tad," William says into the phone. "How you doing?"

"Good, buddy, good. How was the beach last weekend?"

"We didn't go."

"Really? Why not?"

"It's a long story." Harry looks up at William, tongue out, tail thumping the carpet.

"You want to go this weekend?"

"I don't know, Tad." Harry's tail beats faster and he yips once.

"What's that?"

"That's Harry. My dog."

"No shit. I thought you hated dogs."

"I sort of do." William scratches behind Harry's ear, under his chin.

"Bring him to the beach. Dogs love the beach. Besides, you need sun. You look like a fucking vampire."

"None of your surfing buddies can make it?"

"Is it weird that I want to spend some quality time with my little brother?"

"Yes."

"Fuck you. And yes, none of my surfing buddies can make it. Come out Friday; I'm taking off work early, letting the grunts handle it." The "grunts" are a pair of bearded twins who work for Tad at his lawn service.

"I've got to work Friday. But I'll come out Saturday with the dog."

"Good. Don't bring Karl Marx or Heidegger. You read too fucking much."

On the road, William flips through radio stations until he hears James Brown sing "I Feel Good." He slaps the dashboard and the wind—cool enough that he is wearing long sleeves—rushes in the open windows. Harry perches on the passenger side, front paws pressed against the door. Every time they pass a car with a dog in it, Harry barks and follows the other dog with his eyes.

At Tad's, the key is under a big rock on the porch, the word "KEY" painted in white on its side. William opens the door and Harry immediately runs off, sniffing, tail wagging. "Harry," William calls several times and finally the dog returns. Harry is mostly house-trained, but William has learned the dog sometimes finds the difference between inside and out ambiguous. William kicks off his shoes and changes into T-shirt and shorts. In the hammock strung between two palms, he reads a science fiction paperback and drinks one of Tad's cheap beers. When Harry gets too close to the road, William yells, and eventually the dog learns to stay in the yard chasing horseflies that look like bright blue miniature helicopters, lapping the bowl of water William has set out for him on the porch, or fetching a soggy tennis ball until William tires of the game. Pale and easily burned, this is as close as he wants to get to the beach. He can see strips of blue water between dunes, daubs of cumulus between palm branches, gulls and sea oat struggling in the wind. He can hear cars blasting classic rock and rap, the whir of jet skis and beneath that the white noise of waves hitting sand.

Tad appears after William has drunk a couple of his beers. Like William, he is tall, but muscular with straight hair which is wet and hangs to his shoulders. His crooked teeth are very white in his tan face and the incisors are prominent and pointed, giving him a predatory look. He carries a surfboard under one arm and, in his wetsuit and sandals, he might pass for a Roman god or perhaps a comic book superhero. William has hidden his sci-fi novel and pretends to read a thick paperback edition of *Das Kapital*.

"Dickwad," Tad says and, with typical accuracy, hits the center of the book with a shell. "What did I tell you about Marx?" Tad leans his board against a palm tree to dry, backhands wet hair from his face, says, "So this is the dog." Kneeling, he scratches Harry under the chin. "Kind of funny looking, isn't he?" William watches Tad rub the dog's neck, then chest. "You leave me a beer, baby boy?"

"Sure, there's some left." William tosses the empty bottle and, just like he knew he would, Tad catches it in one hand, without blinking or even seeming to move. "Get me one too."

"Don't be a bitch, bitch."

Tad makes bologna sandwiches for the two of them and feeds Harry the remainder of the luncheon meat. "Feed any animal if you want a friend," he says. Sitting on the uncovered slab of concrete which serves as a porch for the cabin, they munch on Cheetos out of a bag perched on an upside-down plastic red crate with the words "PROPERTY OF FINE LADY DAIRY" stamped in white on its side. When William tosses one to a gull that has hopped up on the porch, Tad says, "Don't feed the birds. I hate those fucking things."

"I want it to be my friend." William finishes his fourth beer of the day.

"Don't change the subject."

"What was the subject?"

Tad thumbs over his shoulder at the board. "You're going out with me after lunch."

"No, I'm not."

"Yes, you are."

"I'm sorry, but my doctor told me never to swim after eating. Ever."

As they both know will be the case, Tad goes surfing by himself, but just for a couple more hours "The best surfing is always early in the morning or after a storm," he says behind his hand as if he is keeping a secret from his enemies. After a quick shower and change into jeans and Gators sweatshirt, Tad wraps potatoes in foil and shoves them into the coals in his squat, battered grill. Slicing the fat off for Harry, Tad grills thick steaks and they listen to the same Johnny Cash tape over and over, until both are singing, "I shot a man in Reno just to watch him die." Harry falls asleep on his back, front and back legs spread like he is tanning himself beneath the full moon. Tad rolls a joint and William smokes with him, although pot usually makes him paranoid.

Tonight is no different. In the middle of a rambling overly-detailed summary of a movie Tad saw the previous weekend, William suddenly interrupts: "Are they watching?"

Tad turns his head to follow William's pointing finger across the street to a neighbor's house. The blinds in a window are pushed to the side, but then they fall back into place. After a moment, they move again, then fall back into place. Harry snores and William stares at Tad, looks at the window, and then back at his brother. He opens his mouth to speak, but it is too dry, so he takes a swallow of beer and, finally, Tad says, "I think it's their fan?" He looks at William. "You know? Tapping the blinds?" Then he immediately launches back into the movie narrative. William cannot remember anything about the film: its title, who was in it, whether it was a comedy or drama or action movie. Heat lightning flickers over the ocean and the waves say, *Shhhh, shhhh*. Tad's words are a gentle murmur at William's left. His brain feels like it is wrapped in an athletic sock.

He is still uneasy. Something is wrong, something nagging. His fingers go to the tender spot on his right outer thigh, a spot which has been irritating him for days. "...and then the guy realizes his partner is really working for the other side..." Tad drones on. William presses the spot which seems to throb and is large and hard like a ball bearing. As he stares at his brother's lips, William wonders how he could have walked around in shorts all afternoon without a comment from Tad. Surely, he has noticed this tumor on his leg.

"I need to take a leak," William says suddenly, and Tad stops mid-monologue.

They stare at each other and, finally, Tad nods at the house. "You know where it is."

In the dim light from the overhead bulb, William squeezes the throbbing zit, or whatever it is. It feels as if he has got a jagged foreign object under the skin, like a rock, or a burr. Electrical tendrils thread off from the zit, snaking through his thigh. He squeezes again; the pain is enough to bring tears but nothing comes out except a little milky water.

Tad raps at the door and opens it without waiting for an answer, two beers clutched in a hand, eyes squinted, red and sleepy. Harry is at his feet, and cocks his head at William as if to say *Where did you go?* "Whatcha doing, taking a dump?" Tad asks and then, "What?" when William only stares at him.

"Look at this," William whispers.

He expects Tad to say, *Oh, my god,* to express shock. But his face is blank.

"Isn't it huge?" William whispers.

Tad seems to recognize where this is going—he knows his brother. "It's a *zit.*"

"Are you sure?"

"God," Tad says loudly, rolling his eyes, "don't be a pussy. It's a zit. Now drink your beer," and he thrusts the wet bottle into his hand and goes back outside.

The brothers' aunt died of skin cancer. William has her pale skin. He remembers vividly the last time he saw Aunt Candace. William was only five or six and didn't understand the reason for their trip to Virginia. He assumed they were on vacation. So it was a surprise to be taken to a hospital, to see this white, skeletal woman with dark splotches under her eyes who he did not recognize as Aunt Candace at first. She gestured in her shadowy hospital room, hand a claw. "Billy," she said, voice like ripped construction paper, "come see me." He pressed his face into his mother's thigh, hot tears in his eyes, not wanting to see this wraith, this woman who looked just enough like the vibrant, healthy aunt William had seen not more than a year earlier. He never saw her again. William's not afraid of serial killers, or planes falling out of the sky—those disasters happen and you barely have the time to say, "What—?" But illness, the wasting kind, makes you deal with your dying, makes you face it and think about it, makes you measure it against the minute hand and that ray of sunlight moving across the floor.

William finds his insurance file in a drawer in the spare room at home, flips through the papers he has never closely examined before and scans the list of GPs. He snaps his fingers to the Charlie Parker in the next room and Harry licks his foot. Flann sleeps curled in her cat bed, oblivious to the two of them, already adapted to, or at least tolerant of, this hyper addition to their household. "How do I decide?" he asks the pets. Running his finger down the list of doctor names and then back up, William pauses on one: Dr. Singh. How could a doctor with that name bring bad news? William imagines a handsome charmer pirouetting into the room, flinging out his arms and singing:

"You've got nothing to fear, my man.

Nothing to fear.

Don't you hear?

Nothing to fear!"

His blond nurses would take synchronized steps behind him,

belting through impossibly red lips, "Listen to him, boy, you've got nothing to fear!"

Dr. Singh, naturally, does not sing. His one nurse is a dowdy woman with a pallor to her skin. The doctor is small with jet sideburns and a brown bald head with wisps of hair which float in the drafts coming from the overhead vents. He nods, tapping a fingertip against a front tooth while William—on the papered examination table in boxers and T-shirt—tells him about his aunt in halting tones and the nurse pencils some notes on a pad.

At the end of William's monologue, Dr. Singh stretches some latex gloves over his fingers, and removes a long, thin needle. He grips William's thigh with surprising strength, says in a clipped, English accent, "Please hold still." Lancing the growth, he squeezes some of its milky interior onto a slide, as William hisses a breath and grips the metal table. "It's probably nothing," Singh says, eyes invisible behind spectacle gleam. He hands the slide to the nurse and she affixes a round yellow sticker to it, writes a number, a letter on it. Singh peels off the gloves, drops them into a wastebasket, rubs his palms together, wipes them on his slacks and tightens his tie which does not need it. "Good to see you again," he says to William although they have never met, and shakes his hand. The doctor leaves the room and, after the nurse fills out a form and sticks it in a folder, she says, "Just bring this up to the desk when you're ready, hon. We'll make another appointment. These things usually take about a week. Maybe less." She pushes through the door after the doctor and William stares at his jeans in a clump at his feet, the metal table chilling his thighs.

"Hello?" Jan says when she picks up, and William can hear that frayed sound in the word which means she is stressed or tired or preoccupied or maybe all three.

"Hey, it's me."

"Hey," she says. There is a popping noise behind her voice which immediately brings to mind BBs against aluminum cans as an adolescent. "Are you sick?"

"No, do I sound funny?"

"Erik said you had a doctor's appointment."

"Oh, yeah, that…"

"Honey, could you turn that off? Yeah, that's it. Thanks, buddy. We're making popcorn," she says, to William.

"Oh, that's nice. Is it movie night?"

"We're watching *Old Yeller.*"

"That's one of my favorites."

"Mine too. I just cry at the end. I suppose everyone does though, so big deal, right? Are you working tomorrow?"

"Yeah, I'm—"

"Good. I've got to go. I'll see you. Bye."

The phone is cool and solid in his hand and William watches Harry watching him, waiting for dinner or just a pat on the head. Flann sleeps in the large blue arm chair on the other side of the room. If William were not listening to the dial tone, he might be able to hear the cat snoring.

"Negative," William hears even as he drives down the street, the memory of Dr. Singh's cool, dry handshake still lingering in his palm. "Sometimes pimples become infected. Our bodies usually have no problem fighting off low-level infections like this, but sometimes these subcutaneous battles leave little bundles of scar tissue behind. We'll just watch it for now, but I predict it will go away by itself within a year or so."

Why do they call it "negative" when it's good? William wonders. There is a second when that three-syllable word comes through a doctor's lips that a patient does the mental translation: "negative" = "well." But before that, there is a leap of fear, claws at the heart.

He wants to call someone and share the good news, but no one knows he was afraid he had cancer. Tad will laugh at him if he tells him he even went to get the "zit" checked out. Without deciding to, he drives up Main Street to Air, the tattoo parlor where his friend Jimbo works. Air is meticulously clean, looks more like a hair salon than a place where people get tattoos and holes punched into their skin. William sits on a white vinyl couch in the front where there are notebooks and magazines full of "modern primitive" photos: skinny pale boys and girls with tattoos, piercings, scarification. Most of the customers who enter Air will get a tiny stud in their nose or a chain or vaguely tribal image circling an ankle or wrist or even a corporate image like a pack of cigarettes or a Nike swoosh permanently inked into their skin.

On a pad, William carefully draws a circle, then dissects that circle with a line and then again with two others. It is a Buddhist wheel of life. Buddhists believe in reincarnation; the wheel symbolizes rebirth. He knows that if he works at it, he will be able to explain to himself *Why this tattoo? Why now?* But he does not want to, will not let his mind touch that thought. He just wants to do it and that has to be enough.

"This is the one I want," he says to Jimbo who flips through a hotrod magazine at his workstation, chewing on a toothpick. The tattoo artist lingers over a 50-something red Chevy with gigantic silver exhaust pipes, a grinning and bikinied blonde on its hood, and then delicately closes the magazine. Although Jimbo is obsessed with hotrods, William has only seen him going anywhere in Gainesville on foot or a gigantic skateboard. When William commented on the size of the board, Jimbo said, "I'm old, man. Tricks are for kids."

He studies the sketch pad in William's hand, shakes his head and burps. "Whatever." Jimbo's tanned, hirsute skin is covered with laughing skulls and purple spiders and anatomically impossible axe-wielding fantasy chicks. He reties the bandana on his shaved skull and drops a couple of eye drops into each eye. "Sit down," he says, slapping his chair. "Where?" he asks, then, when William stretches out on his back, rolls up the left leg of his baggy army surplus shorts.

William taps his left outer thigh, the spot directly opposite his zit which already hurts less now that he knows it will not kill him. "Here." This will be his ninth tattoo.

"Black?" Jimbo asks, and William nods. Jimbo runs a straight razor across the hair on William's thigh, sprays the spot with disinfectant. Then, sitting on the floor, he holds the pad up to the light and, moving his head left to right, from symbol to leg and back again, he carefully reproduces it in blue ink on William's leg. "Well," he says, finally.

William cranes his neck and stares at his leg and, after a second, nods, says, "Yep."

Jimbo stands, cracks his knuckles, then pours black ink into a heavy plastic cup. He pops open the autoclave on the counter and steam escapes from its mouth. The boxy machine, with its large glass dials, looks like a contraption from a 1950s sci-fi movie. Jimbo removes a needle, fits it into a hand grip, steps on a floor pedal, and there is a buzz like a sewing machine. When William feels the needle on his skin, the first shock is like a wasp sting, but subtler, and then it is just a slight pain, a pressure reminding him that he is alive.

The only other person in the shop is Holly, a black-haired Goth with silver studs protruding from her lips and eyebrows and nose and that space between her chin and bottom lip. She is sucking on a red lollipop and when her tongue emerges from between dark red lips, William can see the glint of another stud. She sits dangerously on the back of her chair, feet on the seat, a magazine open between her clunky shoes.

The tiny bell on the front door tinkles and two blond women come in giggling, their tans so dark that their teeth and eyes appear to glow. The younger says, "I called before. We want our navels pierced."

"Sure," Holly says. "Step into my office." She gestures toward a curtained alcove and, after a pause, the two women shove and pull each other into the small space. Holly raises one drawn-on eyebrow at William and sticks her studded tongue out, then steps in after the two women, pulling the curtain closed behind them. There is silence, then the murmuring of voices. Holly has a deep voice and, although the two blondes have higher, somewhat squawky tones, all the words travel across the shop as fragmented vowels and consonants until one of the blondes, quite clearly, says, "Come *on*, Mom, it doesn't even hurt that much."

Jimbo is concentrating on his work, tongue pinched between lips, gripping William's leg firmly, wiping away excess ink and blood with a paper towel. Staring up at the ceiling, dropped Styrofoam like you might find in a doctor's office, William allows his mind to go blank, eyes to close, the needle buzzing as it projects ink just beneath the skin.

In his office at the bookstore, William runs his finger down the time sheet, stabbing numbers into an adding machine. When he gets a total, he inputs that number into the computer, the program calculates another total and he fills out a check, ripping it from the checkbook and sticking it into an envelope with a slip of Book Purgatory trade credit—an employee perk. He seals the two documents in an envelope, scrawls Erik's name on the front. There is a knock.

"Yeah," he says and Jan opens, sticks her head in.

"Hey."

"Hey. I got a late start. I'll do your check next if you want to wait."

"Sure, no prob." She pulls the door shut behind her. "What's his name again?"

Harry is standing on his blanket in a crouch, tail wagging.

"Uh-uh," William says sharply to the dog who freezes, leaning forward, eyes flickering toward his master. William waits a second longer, then says. "Okay." The dog moves quickly to Jan, tail wagging again, licking her calf. "Harry," he adds, flipping through the clipboard to find Jan's time sheet.

"Pretty impressive." She scratches the dog's chin, then his hindquarters.

William punches some numbers into the adding machine. "I grew up around dogs."

"New tattoo?" She nods toward the gauze bandage on his thigh.

"Yeah." He smiles. "Want to see it?"

She shrugs. "Do you think you'll ever outgrow it?"

His shoulders tense, but he speaks some numbers to himself, adds them into the machine, enters the total into the computer.

She speaks into his ear. "I've got salmon and a bottle of merlot."

"That's nice." He fills out a check. "Payday."

Jan rubs his shoulders. "You seem relaxed. What happened?"

He rips the check out, fills in a trade slip, swivels to face her. "Need an envelope?"

"No, man," she smiles, taking it from him, leaning close like she might kiss him, but not. "Want to come over for dinner? Hank's got a soccer game this afternoon. He'll probably be tuckered out and hit the hay early."

William stares, something that might be a smile on his lips. "No, thanks."

She stares back, smile faltering, then turning into a frown. "Got plans?"

"I don't..." He gestures between them. "...I don't think we should do this anymore?"

"Eat dinner?"

"Yeah, eat dinner."

She turns her head as if trying to hear better. "You don't want to be my friend?"

He chews on his lip, ponders. "I don't know. Let's try to just be co-workers for a while. What do you think?"

She nods, looking at the floor, head tilted as if she is listening for something. Giving him a brittle smile, she says, "I changed my mind. I do want an envelope."

7

It is late morning when William pulls into Jan's driveway. He closes the truck door quietly as if he does not want her to know that he is there. That old, green Mercedes her parents bought her sits in the carport covered with a pale-yellow film of pollen. At the curb, he yanks out the envelopes jammed into the mailbox. It is mostly junk with cellophane windows promising 0% APRs and sweepstakes winnings, but its heft feels like the days and hours since he has heard from her and there is a slight tickle of fear in his chest. He knocks on the front door and waits, feeling absurd with the mail under his arm like he is a child playing postman. After a few seconds, the fear is in his breathing and he tries to keep it slow and shallow. The street is quiet—no cars, lawnmowers, no dogs barking. It is like one of those *Twilight Zones* where a guy realizes that he is the last person in the world. William rings the doorbell, listens through the wood—hears it ringing inside, barely, but nothing else. It is completely silent. Well, no, there is wind, birds chirping.

Several weeks ago, when Hank went to his father's in South Carolina for the month, Jan showed up at work the following day with an intense smile, in a manic good mood, seemed eager to make jokes. She tapped William on the shoulder, said, "What's up, man?" the first light phrase she had offered in months. She made small talk, asked if his band—an experimental noise trio called Hatchment, a band she has admitted before she cannot stand—would be playing soon, seemed eager to bring back sandwiches for everyone from the deli across the street at lunch. She asked Erik if he had read *Desire in Language,* wanted to know what he thought of it, and seemed amused when he stammered out a few half-sentences and disappeared to his romance novels section at the back of the store. Near the end of that shift she said to her coworkers, "I'm feeling like a youngster. You guys need to go out drinking with me tonight." Erik cleaned his glasses on his "Question Authority" T-shirt and mumbled something about needing to write. But Jessica and William traded amused looks: *Sure, what the hell.* At the Purple Minny, Jan programmed R&B standards into the jukebox and after two beers stood up, said, "You guys, let's dance." They wouldn't—it was not that type of bar. But it turned William on to think of Jan dancing by herself. He missed sex with her, Gainesville seemed empty of anyone he wanted, and many nights he masturbated, imagined her tanned skin, the touch of her hair which had grown into short boyish curls. "Go ahead, we'll watch," he said, winking. She immediately lost her bravado, and slumped into her chair, sipping beer in a sulk. William and Jessica smiled and shrugged at each other, talked about some noisy band they thought was "interesting." Younger girls with belly shirts and navel rings stood at the bar ordering drinks, the occasional red-faced frat boy yelling fun-time nonsense. Jan said after a while, "You guys are so boring." When William said he was tired and wanted to go, Jessica stayed to catch a ride with someone else. He dropped Jan at her house and she said "Bye" without looking at him.

It has gone downhill from there. The next day at work, her manic good mood had disappeared. Whereas the day before she had seemed to be trying to look like a hipster in vintage sundress and sandals, that day she looked like the tired single mother that she was. Wearing a handkerchief on her head, jeans cut off at the knee, a too-large Sonic Youth T-shirt, and black high-tops with holes in the soles, she looked like she had dressed to clean house—she even smelled musty. She yawned constantly and William had to say everything to her twice. Late in the afternoon he asked, "Didn't you get enough sleep last night?" She just shook her head and walked away, scratching her jaw.

This behavior intensified over the next couple weeks. She would forget to shelve the children's books and they would build up in the ancient Dr. Pepper crates they were stored in, spilling onto the carpet. William would sarcastically say, "Maybe we should hire a high school kid to shelve these books. What do you think, Jan?" She would look right through him. Once, he found a half-cooked frozen dinner in the microwave and walked around the store asking the employees who it belonged to, realizing as soon as he saw Jan pricing children's books with comic book price stickers that she had simply wandered off and forgotten. It was like although her body was here in the store, her mind had traveled up the coast with Hank.

She started calling in sick. A lot. Thursday, she had worked, but looked tired and distracted if not a little ill. When she went to shelve the Horror novels in her bare feet, William asked her, only half-joking, "Are you on drugs?"

"Yeah, William, I'm on drugs."

He waited, then stammered, "You shouldn't do that. It's against the rules."

"Really? Show me where it says that in the employee manual."

His nose twitched like he had to sneeze. "There is no employee manual."

"Great," she said walking away. "Just great."

Then she left work fifteen minutes early without telling anyone and called in sick the next day. "What's going on?" William wanted to know, but she hung up without answering. Then on Saturday, she did not bother calling. William talked to her answering machine four times over the course of the day. The first time he was angry, used the phrase, "If you don't want your job…" The second time he sighed and asked her to call. The third he offered her a series of questions, and the fourth he told her to "Pick up, pick up, pick up, damnit." That night was the first time he had gone by. Her car was out front, but there were no lights on and no one answered when he rang the bell. Sunday, he called Rain. She was no help, said she had not heard from Jan in days in a distant tone which suggested she did not care. Monday, he pounded on the door with more force, tried to peer around the edges of the blinds which were all drawn, yelled, "Jan, open up." Later in the day, when he came back, he faintly heard her yell, "Leave me alone. Go away." He was relieved to hear her voice, but also upset and *did* go away. "Fuck this," he said, even though he was not exactly sure what "this" was.

After a nearly sleepless night, he has come back. He does not know what he is worried about. If she is yelling *go away*, at least she is alive. But worry gnaws at his belly which growls back because he has had nothing today except coffee and a piece of dry bread.

He clears his throat and pounds on the door again, leaning close to hear through the wood. He wonders if he hears footsteps. The frustration surges through him and he pounds again, no longer concerned about disturbing the neighbors. He had promised himself that he would break in today if she does not voluntarily open the door, but he dreads the thought. It seems crazy, and probably unnecessary. "Jan, open the damn door," he yells, knocking again.

It sounds like someone yells, "Leave me alone." Then someone definitely yells, "Go away."

William drops the mail and it scatters at his feet even as he turns to go. But he pauses, stares at the white dot of doorbell, and instead of going, jabs it as if it were an eye or some other object he could put his finger through, something he could destroy. He jams his finger and the pain travels to his elbow. Pounding the doorbell with the flat of his palm two or three times, he yells, "Open up," and then pauses, takes a breath, counts, *10, 9,8, 7*...Smiling, he rings the doorbell. Again. Again. He pushes the button with what must be maddening regularity inside. He can barely hear the dull *ding-dong*, the click of the button outside louder as he presses it with the regularity of a metronome. Perhaps Jan yells *stop* or *go away*, but he is not sure. He feels like a child again, locked out of the house by his older brother—annoying, tireless, brattish behavior the only recourse. He smiles.

The door opens quickly, doorbell intruding on the quiet morning, and he forgets to stop smiling. The smile drifts off his face slowly, though, as he forgets what was so funny.

She is in bare feet, wearing a ratty green T-shirt with a large rip at the neck and jeans with a smudge of dirt or chocolate near a pocket, fraying around the ankles. Her hair is a mess—frizzed out on the sides and flat on top. It might be comical if she did not have such a desperate look in her eyes, sleepless and swollen, creases in her face like she has been lying on it for a long time. She might be a bag lady, someone who would scream gibberish or mutter racial slurs on the bus. She says, "Could you please fuck-ing stop?" By that point, though, William is no longer ringing.

"Jan," he says, mouth open for several seconds in silence, "you look…" His lips work silently like a child searching for a state capital, and then, "…tired."

She smiles and her cheeks dimple, there is an echo of humor in her eyes. Then it is gone and, as if embarrassed, she looks at her feet, puts one over the other. "Why don't you say what you really mean?" she says quietly. "Why don't you say I look like some-thing the cat dragged in? Or death warmed over? I look like shit, right?" There is the beginning of tears in her eyes. "William…" She steps forward on tiptoes to reach around his neck. "I feel so alone." He picks her up and can feel her legs encircling his waist, slept-on hair bristling against his cheek. He can feel her hand on the back of his head and it gives him the strength to kick the door closed behind him and walk her through the living room toward her bed.

"The couch," she says, just barely, voice phlegmy with tears.

He stops. "You want to lie on the couch?"

He can feel her nodding, something like a "uh-huh" barely next to his ear. Walking her to that ugly beige couch already dented with her body, its stuffing bleeding onto the scarred wooden floor in two places, he helps her to lie down, cradling her head onto a pillow. She cries freely now, chest lurching silently as she turns her face to the back of the couch, holds his hand to her eyes. Her breath is warm on his fingers and he sits on the coffee table, leaning close to feel her tears, putting his other hand on her shoulder as if to hold her down, or hold himself back, keep him from kissing her eyes. A dress is on the floor in a clump at the foot of the couch. One black high heel is on the off-white chair on the other side of the room, the other on the coffee table. There is an ashtray crammed with butts and ashes even though Jan quit several years ago. The air is full of the dirty scent of stale cigarettes. The television is on with the sound off, on one of those channels she barely gets—a catamaran surges over a wave partly obscured by TV snow.

She stares at him, the tears suddenly gone. Smiling, she inhales a deep and shaky breath. "Jan, what's wrong with you?" He doesn't mean for the words to come out so hard, this brittle anger appearing as suddenly as his sense of play had at the door-bell. He opens his mouth to explain, but cannot think of words.

She rearranges the pillow beneath her head, says, "Why did you dump me?"

"Come on, surely this," he gestures helplessly, "whatever it is you're doing, isn't about that. It happened months ago and you didn't bat an eye."

She closes her eyes then, says "Mmmmm," as if she has just enjoyed something—eating chocolate or having sex. She still holds his hand to her face, shows no signs of giving it up. "Did you come by to fire me?"

He smiles despite himself. They are playing a game. "You're not going to answer my question." There is a pause. She wipes away the tears on her cheeks, in the process smearing her dark makeup clownishly. He leans forward, speaking in a whisper. "You know, there's something very poetic about your suffering." He pauses, but she does not answer. "You're smelling a little ripe, by the way." Her breathing deepens as if she were sleeping.

She slowly opens her eyes as if coming out of a dream. "Don't mock me." Sniffling, she says quietly, as an afterthought, "Asshole."

He leans closer, runs his hand over her hair, smoothing it against her face. Then he licks his fingers, wipes them against her cheeks, rubbing the mascara on his cut-offs, licking his fingers again and repeating this until her face shines. He leans even closer, can hear her breath, the quiet parting of her lips, an artificial smell like rubber on her teeth. "What's going on?" They sit frozen in the almost-silence of their bodies living, the house ticking with the whims of physicality—vicissitudes of temperature, invisible crumbling that comes with the passage of years, a myriad of outside sounds not worth noticing. Time stretches and they remain still, tableau-like. If they were to move, they would stretch into the future, possibly be torn apart. They are afraid of breathing, momentum.

William can wait all day, all week, all year if he has to; he can see his resolve in the reflection in a dark eye, his face half-hidden in the shadows thrown from the blinds. And he can see her see this in the way she curls her lip slowly as if she is afraid of sudden moves, afraid to disrupt some intuitive equilibrium. "William," and her face crumbles in on itself as if she will weep, but her eyes remain dry. "William, this isn't me."

"Who is it, then?"

"Don't be facetious."

"I'm not. What do you mean?" He cups her cheek and then waits in the stillness.

"God, William, I want to be me."

"What does that mean?" He feels a surge of that irritation again. He wants not to care.

"I knew I'd miss Hank, but I had no idea it would be like this."

"Like what?"

She closes her eyes, squeezes his hand and bangs it softly against her forehead. "William. Billy." She smiles. "You know, I thought I was really going to enjoy being by myself for a month. Like maybe I could just sort of take care of me for a change. Find out who *I* was." He wants to say something, but keeps his mouth shut. She sees this hesitation and smiles at his silence, caresses his hand. "That first night when you and Jessica and I went to the bar, it really hit me in the face. I'm not a kid anymore." He breathes in to speak, but there are no words, just a sigh. She notes this, nods once. "Good." Taking a breath, she says, "I talked to myself. The house was so empty, so big. At first, I was talking to myself, but then I imagined talking to Rain or you. And Hank, too." She crinkles her nose. "You guys would answer me back and then I'd say something else. We'd have a complete conversation." She nods, eyes wide. "You think I'm nuts?"

He squeezes her shoulder. "You know you're not crazy."

"No. I suppose not. Craziness would be something I could understand. I'm talking to myself because there's no one. No one here, no one in my life with my son gone."

"You've chosen that. You could call Rain, you could call... anyone."

She puts her fingers against his lips. "Listen: I've not figured this out, so don't ask me what I'm talking about. I'm thinking, just thinking out loud. If you don't want to hear it, I understand. But then we have to be quiet."

His brain is screaming: *Just be quiet, be quiet.* He knows they should just sit here, that he should make sure she is okay, ask her when she is planning on coming to work, and then escape. But he is strangely, intensely happy and cannot think of anything but the words she is about to speak. He is eager, ravenous to hear them. He cannot speak, can barely nod.

"All right. I don't know who I am, even what I *like*." She turns away and reaches for the blinds behind the couch, puts her index and middle fingers through a slit and spreads them. That tiny slit lets in a brightness too intense to stare at in this perpetual dusk, so he just watches the light on her cheek, the dust motes drift, until she lets go, looks back at him. "I know I've not really talked about my childhood much. Mainly, cause it's kind of boring." She runs her hand through her hair. "God, I must look like shit." She glances at him shyly and then at the ceiling. "I know, I'll stick to the topic. I'm kind of tired." She closes her eyes and speaks: "I wanted to be a poet when I was a girl, a teenager. I loved Anne Sexton. A lot of poets, but especially her. She was so beautiful. I love that photo where she's resting her neck against her hand. If I were to define 'perfection,' it would be Anne Sexton's eyes. I probably liked that she was so depressed, that she killed herself—somehow, that seemed romantic." There is a long pause. Finally, she turns her head slightly and opens one eye. Smiling, she blows a brief raspberry and then closes the eye, turns her face back to the ceiling. She licks her dry lips.

William is afraid to move, even though that happiness is still panting in his chest like an injured bird. He will not even breathe until she speaks. Her eyes still closed, she says, "I used to stay up all night writing. Poems, I guess. Horrible things, I can't even read them now without cringing." She opens her eyes and smiles at him, nose crinkling in that way he loves. "Well, sometimes I wrote. I had insomnia a lot. I would usually tell myself I was writing, but mostly I watched TV. I felt isolated and worthless. William," she pulls his hand to her chin, pauses, whispering: "I had an abortion in high school." She takes a deep breath. "You know, I don't buy that Catholic bullshit I was brought up on. I don't think I ever have. When I got pregnant I knew I was too young—forget the father, he was just a kid from the school play, a skinny, quiet boy named Michael who smelled like lotion. He had beautiful eyes. Eyes that looked like he'd been beaten every day of his life. God, they were amazing. Everything else is the cliché: it hurt like hell, was over in, like, five seconds, he acted like I was a leper from the moment it was over until I never saw him again. Blah, blah, blah." She sighs again and this sigh is so deep, so protracted William worries that she is finished. He knows he has been given something precious, but wants more. He has known her for over a year, slept with her for part of that time, but feels like he barely knows her.

Her smile is bitter. "Mother also knew I was too young. God, I was terrified about telling her. I couldn't even imagine what it would be like. I knew she'd be disappointed, but what would she *do?* She just shook her head, said, 'Well, I suppose we better get an abortion.' I could barely speak. 'What about Daddy?' I asked. She said, 'Don't worry about your father.' I assumed that meant it would be our secret." Jan squeezes William's fingers, almost to pain, but then relaxes again. "She must have told him though. He seemed different from that day on. Don't ask me how. Just different." She shrugs, eyes closed again. "Who knows? Maybe Mother didn't tell him. Maybe he still doesn't know. Maybe it's my imagination. I could ask him. But I can barely speak to him." She turns on her side and opens her eyes, holds William's hand in both hers. "Ray wanted me to have an abortion when I got pregnant with Hank. I told him he could leave if he wanted, but I was having the baby." She frowns at William's hand which looks gigantic in her two small ones and they both smile as if this is funny, mouths open to laugh. "William?" He doesn't say anything until her eyebrows raise and he realizes that she wants him to answer.

His mouth is dry and he swallows first. "Yes?"

"William," and then her lip shakes and she cries, faltering, fat tears on her chin where they pause and fall to her shirt. "William, I know we're not together anymore. But please, William. Will you just stay until I fall asleep, will you just sit here and hold my hand?"

He smiles, moved beyond words, that happiness like a danger in his ribcage. "Of course, I'll stay." He leans closer whispering, his hand on her cheek, fingers in her hair. "I'll stay as long as you want."

"I'm sorry, I'm so sorry." Her eyes close while she moves onto her back, clutching his hand to her chest. "You're good, you're so good."

William is not sure how much time has passed since Jan stopped speaking, since her breath became the slow, sleeping timbre he has not heard in months. The light seems to have changed, but it is difficult to know with all the blinds drawn. Thirty minutes? Three hours? He might believe either answer, but suspects the truth is somewhere in-between. A brief time after closing her eyes, Jan's hands slipped away. When William sat upright his back sounded like a walnut cracking, but her eyelids did not even flutter. He moved from the coffee table to the rocking chair, has been sitting and staring at nothing for what seems like a long time. After a while, he turns his head, lets his eyes focus and stray, allows himself to notice things he hadn't since he has been here: a spray bottle half-empty on the end table. Drinking glass resting on its side next to a wall. There is what looks like a toy army man on the short stone wall rimming the fireplace. And then he realizes it is an empty candy bar wrapper. On the coffee table, next to where he was sitting a while ago, is an open book, its spine in the air. There is a capped ballpoint pen next to it, flush with its edge. The cover is plain, glossy black, a diary. William focuses on the journal until it takes up his vision, until it seems to pulse. He is not breathing, and does not move his head as he shifts his eyes to Jan, counts slowly: *One, two, three, four, five, six, seven, eight, nine, ten, eleven, twelve, thirteen, fourteen, fifteen, sixteen, seventeen, eighteen.* Without even deciding to, he picks up the journal, eyes never moving from Jan's face. She is so still, like a corpse at wake, so still he stares at her chest, throat, until he sees slight movement, then allows himself to breathe too. The glossy, black spine of the diary is facing him, pages against his knee. It is not the type of journal he would expect a girl, a woman, to have. Something pastel maybe. But Jan is unlike many women he has known, although he has not known many well. He turns the book over and glances at the page, reads the last sentence she has written:

Hank is coming home in a week. Im very excited and for some reason scared.

He looks up quickly, but she has not moved at all in many minutes. He allows himself to breathe deeply for a few seconds and then flips to the front of the journal. On the inside cover Jan has written "June 6th, 1991" and a dash with a blank space. The handwriting on the facing page is familiar and not; it is Jan's, but charged, a crazed energy that frightens him, the script pushed sideways as if reaching for the lines it stands upon. He can feel the text's indentation on the page through his fingertips, cannot believe the person who has written it can sleep so peacefully.

He feels he is about to dive into a pool where he knows the water is freezing. The entries are written without paragraph breaks, words crammed together in their narrowly lined pages. As he flips through the journal, he reads in the way he imagines the words were written: with intensity, ingesting whole blocks of prose in a single thought, flipping the page even as his eye traces the last few lines, not really reading individual words and sentences as much as ideas, dropping the occasional word or letter in his mind, as if imitating Jan's own quick carelessness. He hears her quiet voice speaking to him from her dreams on the couch:

6/06

Hank on the road now, somewhere on I-75, Georgia probably. Maybe at a hotel, but knowing Ray, theyll drive as long as he can stay awake. Hank strapped in the back seat, wind on his face, head bobbing, road winding, road lines dot dot dot. Drooling in his sleep. I cant stop staring at the map we decorated his wall w/ so he could see where dad lived. Ray looked good. Hair shorter than Id seen, blonde from the sun, arms thick, more muscular. Hitting golf balls, for godsake. All he could do was smile & blush; god, his teeth are white, must be bleached. It seemed like he was giving up when he quit his band & moved back to Myrtle to work for dad. Maybe it was good. Girlfriend seemed nice. Wanted to hate her (like the chick-what's-her-name he shacked up w/ when here). Alright I guess. Toothy smile, firm handshake. Cute if you like that sort of thing. Girl next door—not exactly Rays type. But I liked how she knelt and looked Hank in the eye. Shook his hand & didnt do that little child voice I hate. Seemed sincere. I miss my son so goddamn much. I can feel it in my chest, in my breathing. Can I last a month. Damnit I'm going to have fun.

6/08

Talked to Hank—it helped. Hung over though only had two beers. Slept two or three hours; thought about calling

in. Went for a walk in the woods to clear head. Quiet creek soothing. Saw a flock of sparrows, about a dozen, perched in a rotting pine. They were so still, like splashed gray & white paint on black bark, like in The Birds when they go outside. Necks swiveled when I passed, watching. Leafless tree rotting wet needles & leaves beneath it, overcast day. Felt like winter, though hot as hell. Strange sensation they were waiting for me to talk. Put a lump in my throat. For no reason they flew off.

6/10

Worked ten-hour shift—mostly uneventful very tired. At lunch, Jessica asked if Id like to go w/ her & Sandy to Universal Studios. Going to do acid & look at special effects. Said it was a shame she hadnt tripped last time cause it was: "like, totally psychedelic, like, you know, like, we ate lunch in a booth like that car from Back to the Future." Told her I couldn't afford ticket or LSD & she shrugged: dismissed. Truthfully, I couldnt afford it. Anyway taking drugs & going to an amusement park is the height of silliness. Scary too. Shes young—maybe ten years younger than me but that seems like forever. Stylish in her tight jeans, black pageboy, ring through the nose, thick schoolmarm glasses. Flipping through some rock & roll magazine, pulling a string of gum from her mouth, sipping diet coke. Shes very sexy, can even imagine kissing her, how itd feel. God, I feel so old sometimes. Been feeling that way since I dropped out again. Working around these college kids doesnt seem so hip anymore. William was reading Nietzsche and it was good to tease him about it. We had beer after work. Also good. Made me miss him.

6/15

Scrambled too many eggs, toasted too much toast—been doing that. Nothing else happened.

6/18

Cant sleep. Called in sick. Am I a stereotype? Depressive thirty-something failed poet, failed college student, failed mom, failed girlfriend. Cant get out of bed. Want to drink but know itll be worse. Keep putting my index finger to my head. BANG. All that blood in my pillow & mattress. So much the fabric would get hard like plaster of paris. Cant get out of bed to eat, let alone get a real gun. William thinks I should see his shrink. Something appealing about sitting in office w/ a stranger sharing my whiny life. She would be kind & smile & nod. Offer advice tell me I was a good person. She might want to talk about my father or dreams or sexlife. Id have to choke up $90. Can see myself chewing on a hangnail while she wrote out a prescription for Prozac. Then in the grocery store in a checkered dress, comparing ingredients in jars of peanut butter. My face cracks w/ smiling.

6/20

Sick today. Called last night, but Hank wasnt there—at some kids house, neighbor boy. I was a little nasty to Ray, & he told me to relax which pissed me off worse—I hate when he tells me to relax. He was angry too and said he & Julie are engaged & going to get married next year. He wanted to hurt me. He did—it was like a punch in the stomach. Couldnt take it, told him I had to go and drank my last three beers. I called Rain. She left Patrick Henry w/ Art and picked me up, took me to Sandys, where I got drunker. And uglier. I think I insulted Rain which makes me just ill. I smoked a pack of cigarettes, drank beers, knocked over Rains drink, ridiculed the white-boy blues band: What does that slick goateed idiot know about the blues? I dont think Rain was even looking at me by then. All he cares about is getting laid I said. Hes only got the blues cause he cant get his dick sucked. Rain told me to keep it down & ordered two soda waters. The thing: I knew I was being awful. It was like I was sitting at another table & watching myself, horrified by this drunken bitch, trying to ignore her, hoping shed go away. She didnt.

The cat rubs against William's leg then, cries, and Jan sucks in a breath and he freezes, unable to do more than glance up from the diary. He feels how guilty he must look. But Jan just opens and closes her mouth, and then rolls over on her side, face to the back of the couch. William's heart beats in a frenzy and he cannot seem to breathe nor move. Jan lies still, arm flung over the back of the couch, hand hanging down, face up against the beige fabric. William turns the book back to the last page. Moving slowly— very aware of the cracking sounds from his bones, cautious not to let the rocking chair tip—he sets the book back where he found it, moves the pen flush with its edge. The cat cries and William scratches its back so it shuts up. He stares at the diary, leans and readjusts it again. Picking the cat up, he carries it to the kitchen, finds food and refills the dish, refreshes the water. He fills a glass for himself, drinks a few gulps, pours it out, stares out the window at nothing, runs the faucet some more and stares at the beads of moisture on the glass. The clock on the wall says it is almost five; he has been here five hours. He was supposed to go to work to pay bills today and he touches the white receiver on the wall. Taking a few steps back toward Jan, he stands in the dining room, staring at the table there.

Across the blemished oak there is a pile of diaries, ten, twelve, some open in positions similar to the one on the coffee table. They are all different: ringed binders, checkered faux watercolors, glossy brass tints, pseudo-American Indian designs. There is a squat, antique trunk on the floor which William has seen before, but never open. It is usually positioned next to the wall with a quilt draped over it, antique lantern on top. It is full of diaries, maybe forty or fifty. Suddenly exhausted, William sits in the chair next to the trunk, puts his elbows on the table, rests his head in his hands. There is too much here to read. What would he be looking for anyway?

"William?" Jan calls suddenly and that one name knifes the silence. Jan groans in the next room, and William knows she is sitting, arching her back, stretching arms above her head. "William?" she calls again. He stands blinking at the pile of books and the cat rubs up against his leg again. "William?" she calls again, "Are you still here?"

"Yeah, just a sec." He makes himself turn from the pile of diaries and walks into the living room, feels he must look guilty as hell and even opens his mouth to confess.

"What have you been doing?" She smiles shyly, takes her head in both hands and twists until her neck cracks. "I slept."

He sits back on the coffee table, takes the hand she offers. "I'm glad. Are you hungry?" She nods. "Do you want to go somewhere?"

She closes her eyes and lays her head against his arm. "Thank you for staying while I slept. It was sweet." He can smell the bitter unwashed scent coming off her and touches her head, his fingers in her curls, feels the contours of her skull.

She leans further into him, says something muffled into his shirt. "What?" he asks.

Turning so the back of her head is resting on his leg, she smiles up at him. "Egg drop soup. That would be nice. Would you take me someplace to eat egg drop soup?"

He cups her face. "Yes. I'll buy you a bowl as big as a child's swimming pool."

Jan and William sit in her car in front of the dollar movie theater. After a cheap and good meal of egg drop soup, egg rolls, chicken fried rice, and Chinese tea at Happy Family, they decided to drive up University to see a movie. They have just watched a stupid comedy about two guys who want to be rock stars. It felt good to laugh. In the car, they take turns pointing out the idiocies of the movie as the parking lot empties, as a clerk in the theater runs a vacuum cleaner back and forth over the same spot of floor. William touches her cheek. "You seem calm."

She puts her hand over his and smiles.

And then three guys in a pickup pull into the space next to the car. They fall out of the truck and the way their boots hit the pavement, the way their voices jar against each other, makes it quickly apparent that they are drunk, aware of William and Jan, and are going to get off on fucking with them. They circle the car, faces leering close, laughing, saying, "You guys making out? Don't stop, we're curious. She's awful pretty."

Without speaking, Jan and William lock their doors. William doesn't look at Jan when he says, "Start the car and go."

She does as he says, but as soon as the engine catches, the largest of the three—a fattish oaf with a few days' growth of beard and a rebel flag hat with the bill so bent the outside edges are nearly touching—steps in front of the car. Jan inches forward, jabbing the horn, yelling, "Get out of the way!"

He guffaws, hands on his wide waist. "Don't run me down, missy. I'll get outta the way. Just gimme a minute."

"Go on," William says, voice rising just past control, "run the son of a bitch down. Go." Out of the corner of his eye, he can see her staring at him, but he is looking out the window—eyes narrowed, jaw rigid and grinding. Popping the clutch, Jan slams on the brakes and the car stalls. Rebel flag skips back a step, a glimpse of fear appearing on his flushed face; but that is quickly replaced with anger and then the same stupid, happy meanness. He sprawls on the hood, face inches from Jan's, and she screams. "Goddamn," William says, hands on the dashboard.

Then the guys are turning their heads and looking away. It takes a second for William to realize some woman is yelling. She is in her sixties probably, gray hair and wide hips, jabs a finger at the men while speaking: "Get out of here! Leave them alone. Go on! Don't you have anything better to do?" Her husband, a thin and worried balding man, is tugging her arm. To William's surprise, the three men exchange glances, look at the pavement, remove hats and scratch scalps. They climb in their truck muttering "bitch" and unintelligible words, the engine roars, and they squeal their tires out of the parking lot. The old couple continues toward their car, holding hands as if nothing has happened.

Jan laughs. She laughs until the tears run from the corners of her eyes. William feels he should laugh too, but there is something abrasive about her laughter, he can hear it in his skin.

A coiling snake of rage squeezes his chest and he wants to punch the window shield. He stares at Jan until she stops laughing, suddenly, pleasure gone from her eyes. "*What*," she says, the word more curse than question.

"I'm going to call the cops."

"Why?" She groans. "They're gone."

"They're obviously drunk. You think they're going to be happy with that little scene? The next couple may not be lucky enough to have a little old lady to scare them off."

Rolling her eyes, she says, "Oh William, just leave it. Let's go."

But he is already opening the door. "No. I've got to throw

139

away my cup anyway." He raises the paper cup, the Coke logo blood-red under the parking lot lights.

"Fine, whatever, hurry up." She falls against the seat, chewing a nail.

As if they can sense he is out of the safety of the car, the truck pulls off University Avenue and speeds across the parking lot. Over his shoulder, William sees them coming, but something will not let him quicken his pace. His back stiffens, shoulders tight, waiting for what is surely about to happen. They speed past, guttural laughter emerging from a window. There is a sudden silence, a displacement of space, and even before William hears anything, he knows an object has been thrown. He keeps walking, a robot man now, the glowing lights of the theater his only goal, and the bottle shatters feet away. He thinks he hears Jan's scream coming from behind rolled-up windows. Without pausing, he turns, raises an arm and flips them off. "Fuck you!" he yells in case they are too stupid to realize what he means. The rage simmers now, now that it is out of the car and has room to breathe. Rage moves his body forward through space and time. There is the squeal of brakes and the truck does a U-turn and pulls to the curb.

Inside the theater, William squints at the light bulbs running along every straight line. *Right, throw the cup away.* He pushes it slowly through the metal flap in the garbage can, metal mouth opening to receive its soggy morsel. Turning to the wide-eyed clerk behind the counter, a calmness descends upon him and he even smiles. "You better call 9-1-1." The clerk seems to be reaching for something, a phone hopefully. His mouth is open and he is staring at the doors which William can hear being pushed open, laughter following him in from the pavement. He turns to meet the fist blotting out everything. Even as his head is snapped back, he swings and feels his fist go into something soft, hears a grunt. Someone says "faggot" and a boot, or knee or fist, connects with his groin and he goes into a crouch, feels something against the back of his head and he is on his knees, a wet pain in his gut, sucking air. He looks out at the world through fish-eyes as things happen to him. It will only be later that he can reconstruct the final events: door opening, wiry thing coming through it with the speed of a spider. She screams, "Bastards!" and is lifted from her feet and flies through the air. As she lands on her ass, the impact travels through the red carpeting toward William's ear, sticky with blood. That coil of rage comes back momentarily and he lifts his face, mouth open to speak, wet running over his bottom lip. But something rushes toward his skull. He turns slightly to follow it: A worn boot, stitching coming undone. At one time it must have gleamed with promise, smelling of cured leather, the scent of stemmed animal rot and the sweat of human hands shaping skin for purpose. Something shines just beneath the toe of the boot: a tooth in a puddle of blood, stark as a sugar cube in a bowl of cranberries. William can feel his brow wrinkling to wonder *Is that mine?* But the thought never has a chance to form.

8

When William opens his eyes, the world is all slow-motion strobe. He is lying on a gurney moving down a brightly lit hallway, watching the square lights passing overhead, tiny pinholes in the white ceiling blurring like that bit of road near the window that always hypnotized him on long car trips as a child. He feels so light he imagines he is looking down at the ceiling and lights, at the faces staring up at him, tossing questions in rapid succession: "William, do you know what day it is? Do you know where you are? How many fingers am I holding up?" Jan's face is at his side and she holds his hand. William realizes that he is gripping the gurney's handrail, so he lets it go and puts his hand over Jan's, feels her fingernails. He lifts his hand to touch her face, but the movement dislodges something in his chest and he lurches to breathe, regain some strand of breath as if he has been kicked in the stomach. Someone pulls her away, says, "You'll have to wait outside, Miss," and her fingers coming from his hand feels like heartbreak. But William's eyes are already closed, everything is gone.

When he opens them again, he is in a hospital room, hooked to a heart monitor which glows and beeps in the shadows. Jan is with him, in a large brown chair next to the bed. She leans forward, smile tentative and eager. The only light other than the tiny red dots and dashes on the heart machine comes from two lamps on a table on the other side of the room. As Jan takes his hand, he wonders why someone would put two identical lamps next to each other, and then realizes that it is just one, its reflection in the window, a night black and thick as mud on the other side of the glass. "Hey," Jan says in a whisper, and William tries to lift his hand, but it is weighed down with a cast, and he closes his eyes and sinks again.

Morning light inches along the windowsill and flings a rainbow fragment against the mottled ceiling. Jan and his mother, a slight, stoop-shouldered woman with still-dark hair, stand next to the bed, speaking in low tones. William has that disorientation that comes from not knowing how long one has been unconscious—he would believe weeks as much as hours. His mother is the first to notice his eyes are open and she smiles, says, "Honey," touches Jan's shoulder. Jan turns and the way she smiles and pulls in a slow breath makes William glad to be alive, so glad the feeling becomes physical, in his shaking lips, aching chest, and he is crying. Then coughing. A wheezing comes from his mouth and below his chin somewhere and he gasps for breath, claws at his lips to help. His mother jabs the call button and Jan disappears—he hears her sandals slapping the hallway, voice loud and panicked: "Could someone come, please! Please help us!" And then she is back and leaning over him, almost lying against him, her hand against his forehead, mouth so close he can taste the scent of the coffee she has drunk that morning. "Please, calm down, William," she says. "Breathe. You're all right, but breathe." And he does. A nurse comes then, there is a pinprick of something cool in his arm and he sleeps.

The next time his eyes come open, Jan and his mother are still there. Jan has changed into a skirt and the light has changed also. He looks out the window, but there is too much sky. The earth undulates in the distance, speckled with cars and buildings and the ant-like bodies of people. Movement comes to his brain blurry and his eyes ache with the light.

"Hey, buddy," comes a deep voice to William's right. It is his brother who reaches down and squeezes his shoulder. His wife, Laura, is there too, blond and small next to her husband. "Oh, Billy," she says, and William opens his mouth, but no words come when he speaks. Jan caresses his head and reaches over him slowly to press the call button.

A skinny, efficient nurse with ruddy cheeks appears and tells everyone to leave. "One person can stay," she says.

Jan heads toward the door, but William's mother plucks the sleeve of her white blouse, says, "Jan, why don't you stay?"

"Oh…" she says, neck tensed as if she is going to refuse. But something invisible runs out of her, and she says, "Okay."

William has a tube in his chest, next to his right armpit. The nurse tells him his lung collapsed and had been leaking air and blood into his chest. "It would have killed you if we hadn't operated," she says, nodding somberly. "The tube allows that air in your chest to escape. You'll most likely be coughing for weeks. It's very important for the next few days to *make* yourself cough. Every fifteen minutes or so." She puts her hand over her mouth and coughs. "Like that. Now you do it." Nodding, he coughs into his hand, and a wet pain flashes through his chest. He winces, but the nurse does not seem to notice, beaming like he is the brightest child in the class. She pats him on the shoulder, says, "Good work," then consults a clipboard hanging at the end of his bed. "I'll tell Dr. Hanson you're awake. Also, Dr. Shelley, the dental surgeon will probably be by to talk to you later this afternoon. Are you in any pain?" She peers at him over the clipboard, eyes bright, demeanor as perky as if she had just asked him if he would like either cherry or grape Jell-O.

"Yes. Much," he manages, voice wet with his missing teeth, words dull as if the consonants have been worn off, bits of letter lodged in his chest. He takes a deep breath and his hose whistles and he coughs, eyes watering. "I hurt." He feels broken everywhere—in his jaw, his back aching wherever the bed touches it, arm throbbing in its cast, his neck, even the skin is irritated by the hospital gown as if he were sunburnt. The word *body* suggests *pain*.

"You poor thing," she says, a perfunctory pat on the hand. "I'll bring you some Tylenol. Don't worry, it's the good kind." As she goes to the door, she says to Jan, wagging a finger, "Now, don't wear him out."

Jan gasps and sputters, "Well, okay, sure, all right," then looks at William and laughs. She puts her hand on his cast, kisses his forehead and he closes his eyes, just smelling her—the soap she has washed with, the detergent she has used to clean her clothes, the toothpaste on her breath. They are quiet and still for a long time.

William never sleeps well in the hospital even though he is on pain pills. The room is so clinical, clean. He is not a messy person, but there is something comforting in a dog-eared book on the floor or an empty glass forgotten on an end table, a hand smudge on the wall next to a light switch. Also, that smell in the hospital: recycled air, antiseptic, the plastic scent of killed germs—a constant reminder that beneath that odor is the stink of human waste and illness and death.

It is quiet in the room, everyone very sensitive. He hears them coming and going on tiptoe, his mother and Jan taking turns sitting with him, sleeping on the small cot brought in by the orderly—a huge guy with a shaved head, a guy who always says "What up, Chief?" Jan and his family speak to him cheerily whenever he is awake, seemingly unconcerned that he often doesn't answer. When he reemerges from drugged sleep—never for more than an hour or so—he often finds them whispering. Once, Jan, leaning forward, has a palm to her eyes, shoulders shaking, and he wants to reach out, touch her shoulder, pull her down to him. William's mother has her back to him, words unintelligible and sibilant. Then Jan takes her hand away and he sees that she is laughing, not crying, and struggling to keep quiet. Something like pure happiness is nestled down in the center of him at this moment, in the middle of his fear and pain, and he reaches for it, stretching to touch it even as he slips back under.

And then one morning, William is going to have his bridges put in and he awakens slowly as if coming up from deep water, straining for consciousness like he might for air. He opens his eyes, inhaling as if he could take light and consciousness into his lungs. His hose, which they are supposed to take out today, whistles in his chest, and he coughs up air which feels solid. His eyes water and chest aches in a way it did not even when he smoked, even on mornings-after when his ashtray was overflowing with butts. Jan dozes in the chair next to the bed and, amazingly, does not wake. Her face is slack, mouth open, eyelids fluttering. He can see the exhaustion in the suck of her lips as her chest rises and falls, in the bruised skin beneath her eyelashes. The love he feels for her at that moment is so intense he suspects he might break. Strangely, though, there is no fear in that fragility, it is delicious and has nothing to do with his battered body: he *wants* to break.

He also wants to touch her. He can see his fingers against her cheek, or on her wrist. He would love to see her eyes open slowly, see her smile. To hear her ask how he felt, to see her stretch and knuckle her eyes, to see her lips spread and throat throb as she yawned. He does not touch her though. Somehow, he knows that he will be sad if he breaks this moment. He looks out the window at the blue sky. They are cutting back on the painkillers in preparation for his leaving and his vision is clear. He notices this, notices the thoughts which allow him to notice, the words and sentences in his brain explaining things to himself. Clarity is a novelty and simple thoughts give him pleasure—*window, sunny, sky, blue*—as if he is thinking thoughts for the first time in the history of the world. It is interesting outside his window: He now knows what street they are on, University, which hospital he is in, First General. He knows the cars disappearing over the hill are heading toward the mall, that what had been a throbbing haze before is really I-75, tiny cars speeding back and forth across its overpass. A thin, white line cuts slowly across the blue expanse of sky, jet exhaust turning into clouds of tiny icicles which gasify and disperse. All that movement out there, that going to and fro, makes William tired and a little anxious, and he brings his gaze back inside.

He runs his fingertip around the lip of the hose in his chest, its plastic smooth, only slightly rougher than the shaft sinking down into this hole in his body. He presses his finger against its side slightly and feels it move inside his chest; the sensation gives him a shiver and he removes his hand. He has become sentimental about his body even while he is horrified at its stitching, its yellow and purple bruises, new gaps in his mouth, the shards of teeth and dried-black blood. He touches himself constantly. Not in a sexual way, but in simple amazement that his body has held together, that now he can walk to the bathroom unaided or to the chair by the window. The previous night he had walked the length of hallway outside his room and back with Jan's help and had been so moved he almost wept. Even thinking of it now makes his eyes water, he can feel that lump rising in his chest. It is a physical exertion of will to keep the sobs back even though he knows there would be a relief in the crying, the grief so sweet he would not want it to end. Jan might open her eyes then, lean forward to cup his chin, and ask, "What's wrong?"

The ten floors of hospital above press down like deep-sea pressure as he waits.

9

Ray presses a finger against Hank's arm. When he pulls it away there is a spot, fading after a couple seconds. "Pal, I think you need to put a shirt on. You're getting burned."

"Okay," Hank says, clutching the fishing rod, staring out at nothing, a horizon blanched with sunshine. Ray takes the rod, which is really too big for his son, and with one hand, manages to slip a T-shirt over his head.

"Help me out, pal." Hank shoves arms through the holes, pulling the neck over his wild, sun-bleached hair. Ray speaks into his ear, "Are you still having fun?" Hank smiles and nods, open mouth revealing a gap where his baby tooth was. "Not ready to go back?"

"No way."

"All right." Ray smiles and kisses his son's tanned cheek, but inside he groans. *Ray* wants to go back. He is sick of being on a boat, the constant sun, fishy smell of salt water, sticky feel of wet on skin, his neighbor Mike Rayvor's constant loud jocularity. ("We're both Rays!" he bellowed the first time they met.) The boat is twenty-eight feet long, and there is a pure, clean feeling Ray gets in his fingertips when he touches the new fiberglass, when the sun reflects off the sparkled blue hull, when his bare feet touch that hard plastic stair leading to the shadowy berth where the toilet and cabin are. But they have been out for two days and, despite nothing but water, occasional gulls, and air in every direction, Ray feels hemmed in. All that keeps him from suggesting they head back is that he has not been able to deny Hank a thing he has asked for this summer, which truthfully has not been much: the occasional ice cream cone, a ride on the Ferris wheel at the beach, to stay up a half-hour later. Also, Mike's son, Jimmy ("Boy," Mike calls him), gets along well with Hank. The two kids have spent as much time chasing each other around the boat, engaged in some sort of pretend world of superheroes or cops and robbers, as they have fishing. Mike seems not to approve as, after a while, he will boom out, "Boy, come over here and let me show you how to bait a hook," or "Boy, get me a beer." But Ray has been touched by the boys' friendship. Even though Jimmy is two years older, and a good foot taller, he treats Hank like an equal. Or maybe like a little brother. On their first morning, Ray saw Jimmy put his arm around Hank's shoulders and whisper something in his ear. The boys slouched in giggles, and Hank said something back causing more laughter. It was like they had a secret language; there was an ache in Ray's chest and he looked out at the sun throwing yellow over all that dark blue ocean, shadows of waves turning into black triangles and foam.

It was only because Mike had a son about the same age as Hank that Ray became friends with the older man anyway, who he regards as a blowhard, a Nebraskan who cannot stop reminiscing about his youth. Last night, after a dinner of marlin and cole-slaw, Mike said, "Out in the country you drive early—thirteen, fourteen. Even before I had my first taste of beer, I bottomed out my mother's Dodge on a country road, jammed a stump so far up under the drive shaft it took my daddy and uncle leaning on a crowbar to get it out again." He playfully punched his son's shoulder and sipped beer, said, "Fun times." Ray, not knowing what to say, drank from his own beer—he was a little drunk as there was not much else to do—and wondered why people thought the South had a monopoly on rednecks.

Ray mistrusts this sport, feels it is luck more than skill, although fishing poles are one of the best-selling items at his father's store. He has learned to lie though, counting on the ignorance of prospective buyers, and throwing out vague adjectives—"flexible," "light-weight," "durable"—in an authoritative voice as if he could not wait to get back out on the water. In fact, he wonders if Mike is pulling his own scam. They have moved the boat several times for no apparent reason and in no consistent direction, and Mike has thrown back a few medium-sized fish which he calls bonitos, with only the statement, "Not good eating." Still, Mike did catch a marlin larger than Hank. As soon as he hooked the fish it ran the line, spinning the reel super fast, and bending the pole nearly in half. Mike never panicked. He told Ray to strap the belt lying at his feet around his waist. Ray did as he was told, reaching around Mike's wide belly, positioning the round, leather circle at his navel so Mike could pull the end of the pole against his stomach without pain. After a struggle of close to an hour, Ray was worried for Mike's health. Although a former University of Nebraska linebacker, Mike is in his mid-forties and his bulk has turned mostly to fat. His arms shook with the intensity of struggle, face a bright red, and his breath wheezed through gritted teeth.

When they finally hauled the fish into the boat, Mike could not stop yelling and laughing. "What do you think of that, boys?" he asked the two boys who jumped up and down, squealing in excitement, eyes wide. "Yeehaw! Isn't that what you Southerners say? Yee haw!" His voice carried across the water toward the strip of land in the distance. Mike slapped Ray on the shoulder, saying, "Now *that's* good eating." And for a while Ray liked the big man, stopped thinking of him as a reminder of the suburban life he has chosen, stopped wondering what the hell he was doing out here in the ocean with the owner of a used car lot.

But Ray is tired now. And bored. And a little drunk. His head aches. Nothing has happened in over an hour, and he looks forward to dinner. And then sleep. Mike yells from the other end of the boat, "How you fellows doing over there?"

"Fine," Ray yells back. "You?"

Before Mike can answer, Hank says, "Dad," eyes wide, pole bending in his hands, arms jerking. He steps into the side of the boat, leaning forward as if he will follow the fishing pole rather than relinquish it. This seems to happen in slow motion and Ray gasps, jumping forward and grabbing his son's shoulder with one hand, the pole with the other. They huddle at the edge of the boat—a bead of sweat forms on Ray's nose and drops to his son's arm—and then Mike is behind them.

"You boys catch something?"

"Yeah, I think so," Ray answers. "I better take care of this, pal."

He takes the pole from Hank, but it is only when he is upright that he realizes how feeble the pull is. There is barely a tug, and when the fish breaks surface—black tail, thin and shining in the late afternoon light—Mike says, "You got yourself a bitty baby."

At night, Ray and Hank lie on an inflatable mattress on the deck beneath a quilt. Despite the day's heat, there is a cool, salty breeze. Hank, breathing quietly in his sleep, leans into Ray, head nestled into his father's armpit. Ray stares at the sky: the night is cloudless and the stars seem to float just yards above as if he were looking down at specks of gold beneath black water. The boat's beacon throws soft light on their legs and then dips them into shadow while the waves lap lazily against the side of the boat. Although it has been hours since Mike dropped anchor and cut the motor, Ray can still feel the throb of engine in his stomach. He thinks about that fish he and Hank caught earlier in the day. Except, in Ray's mind, instead of reaching forward and grabbing his son and pole, Hank's slick, sun-screened arms slide through his hands. The boy snakes into the water, plopping like a rock.

Ray is surprised, and perhaps a bit disturbed, that his son is not afraid of water. For Ray, ever since the wreck, there are times when the fear wells up from nowhere, a helpless knowledge that he cannot do anything to save his son from danger. These spells intensified when Ray moved from Gainesville at the beginning of the year. He felt as if he were abandoning his son.

Finally, he slips off to sleep, but he is immediately in a bad dream, a shadowy nightscape, running from a woman with a knife. He grabs an umbrella which sends him flying through the air like Mary Poppins, and then he is falling. "Dad, wake up," Hank says, nudging Ray in the side, "you're having a bad dream."

He opens his eyes, breathing the salty air, the world rocking beneath him, sky a tinge of orange on the horizon, details of the dream slipping away, and wonders where he is.

The two men sip coffee while their sons eat soggy sweetened cereal out of the miniature boxes they came in. Besides the slurp of coffee and milk, an occasional cough, Mike's frequent hawking and spitting over the side, they are silent, somnolent, staring at the nothing of ocean. The morning is gray and hazy, only two blobs of cumulus in the sky. Ray is not fooled; he knows by noon the sun will have burned away all cloud covering. His back is as tight and fragile as the skin of a balloon.

Mike is the first to break the silence. "Fellows, my boy and I were talking this morning and we're thinking we might like to head back around dinner. How about it?"

Ray fights the urge to grin; instead, he turns to his son. "What do you think, pal?"

Hank shrugs, tilting his head to the side. "You want to go back?" he asks his friend.

Jimmy also shrugs, says, "Yeah, I guess so. I miss my dog."

Hank nods.

"Well, it's settled then, fellows," Mike says, voice booming again. "I want you two to fish like you never fished. Who knows when we'll get out here again?"

Ray's spirits suddenly lift, coffee buzzing, a light breeze on his sunburned arms. He whistles and smiles as he shoves his hook through the neck of one of the tiny fish they've been using as bait. "Kiss it for luck?" he asks Hank, and the boy grimaces. "All right." Ray shrugs, "have it your way." He plants a loud kiss on the dead fish and casts. The ache in his muscles and the tightness of his sunburned skin suddenly feel good; it seems as if he could cast the line over the horizon. The reel spins like the chain on a bicycle, and there is a light plunk as the weight hits its wave. "You want to hold the rod, pal?"

"Not yet, Dad." Hank reaches an arm around his dad's thigh, leaning his head against his leg, and Ray feels an intense surge of love, almost a pain, and his eyes sting. They stand without speaking for a while, the murmur of Mike and Jimmy's voices coming from the other side of the boat. Ray stares at the diamonds of light on the calm ocean. He feels happy thinking about getting the salt and layers of sunscreen off his skin. He thinks about his fiancée, Julie. He is going to put Hank in front of the TV, or in bed, and take a shower with her. She will scrub his back with the loofa, run her palms down his sides, put her hand on his dick. He will make her lie on the floor and bend over her, putting his mouth on her pussy, tasting her musk, his fingers between the floor tiles and her ass, feeling her mouth on his cock, a hand on his back, her wet hair against his thighs...

He is giving himself a hard-on. Turning slightly from his son, he forces himself to think of the fish they will clean this afternoon, fish he will insist on keeping regardless of whether they are "good eating" or not. He will chop their heads off, scrape a blade across their scales, slice along their bellies and pull the black guts out.

His thoughts are interrupted by the yells of Mike and Jimmy. Reeling in, he and Hank reach the other side of the boat just as a fin emerges from the ocean and dives again, tugging the line, spinning the reel's crank. "We've got us a shark here, boys," Mike yells. "Ray, you better strap me in; it's gonna be a haul."

It is. The boys chatter at each other, running the length of the boat and back, racing to be the first to shout, "Thar she blows!" Mike becomes quiet, squints, huffs, face red and round like a ripe tomato. Ray holds Mike's beer to his lips, now and then wipes the other man's sweating face, urges him on. He feels inconsequential, slightly absurd, like at Hank's birth. Ray had murmured encouraging words then too, put his hand on Jan's forehead, speaking into her ear, kissed her lobe. Jan and her sheets were wet with sweat and she screamed for hours, panting like she was getting ready to split in half. As Hank's skull emerged slick and dark-headed between her thighs she screamed, "Fucker, fucker, fucker..." and it was unclear if she were cursing Ray or their new son. But when the doctor lifted Hank, cut the umbilical cord, and Hank's tiny, squinting face contracted, mouth opened, and he inhaled to scream his first sound, Ray felt a dizzying surge of pride.

As Mike reels the shark toward them, it drifts, tail offering the side of the boat a wet and hollow slap. The boys giggle and Jimmy says "Woaaa!" Mike, propping the end of the pole in the leather belt with one hand, wipes the sweat from his brow and motions for the beer. He takes a long pull, belches, and says, "All right, Ray, you got to help me here."

"Tell me what to do."

"See that gaff? Yeah, that's the one. When I get the shark up to the boat, you're going to have to hook him in the side. Don't be squeamish. Sink it in good and deep cause you're gonna have to help me pull him in the boat."

Ray does as he's told, jamming the hook deeply into the shark's side. Mike says, "On three," and the two haul the shark up and let it drop with a thud to the floor, shuddering the boat. Pale blood oozes from the side where the gaff was and the shark's gills gasp. Other than that, it is strangely still, black eyes unblinking, mouth open and packed with rows of tiny, sharp teeth. Ray puts his hand on Hank to know where he is.

"Easy, boy, stay back," Mike says, putting his hand on his own son's shoulder. "That fellow still has some bite in him."

"He's smaller than I thought he would be," Ray comments.

"Yeah, he's just a youngster."

Ray kneels next to the shark which is almost as long as Hank is tall. He cannot resist touching its side despite a subtle anxiety that it will somehow twist around and sink its teeth into his arm, pull him between its jaws. The shark's skin is slightly damp, smooth, thick like rubber. The alcohol, sun, and excitement spin Ray's head and he has to place a hand on the deck to steady himself. Mike unstraps the belt and Ray says, "I suppose he's not good eating?" but his tone means, *Now what?*

Mike does not look up. "Some people eat shark; I've never had a taste for it." He drops the belt to the deck with a thump and then snaps a long oar off the side of the boat.

"So, then…why did we bother pulling him in?"

Mike smiles and shakes his head as if he cannot believe how naïve Ray is. "You can't throw a shark back, buddy. This fellow is going to grow up big enough to eat my boy and toss little Hank back for dessert. It'll just take a second."

He raises the oar and brings it down with a thud on the shark's snout—a sound like wet cardboard. A couple teeth snap and click against the deck. But other than more rapid movement of the gills, it is as if Mike has not yet begun to kill the shark. He brings the oar down again and Jimmy blinks as if something has flown into his eye, but his smile remains, if a bit thinner. Ray can feel Hank pressing his face into his thigh and he puts his hand in his son's hair which is spiked with salt spray. The oar descends.

Ray pulls into the driveway and, hooking the six-pack with his middle finger, scoops Hank from the seat. At the front door, he barely manages to press the bell. Julie opens and her face breaks into a smile. "I didn't expect you for another day."

"Yeah, we're tuckered out." He kisses her. "Could you take these?" He carries Hank upstairs to his room and, as he puts him on the bed, Hank murmurs. "In just a second you can go to sleep," Ray whispers, pulling off his son's sandals, T-shirt, shorts. As he pulls Hank's pajama top over his head, the boy looks at him through slit eyes, hair sticking up in wild curlicues.

"Are we home?"

"Yeah, buddy, we're home."

"Mom calls me 'buddy.'" He falls back onto the pillow.

"I'm sorry, pal. Are you *her* buddy?"

"Yeah," he says, eyes closed. "I'm yours too."

"Do you miss your mom?"

But he is asleep and, after a second or two, Ray leaves, keeping the door open a crack with the hall light on. In the kitchen, Julie is washing and cutting vegetables. There is something about the buzz of kitchen lights which makes Ray realize how tired he is. Getting a bottle of beer from the refrigerator, he opens it, takes a long swallow.

"Are you going to unload the car?" she asks.

"I'll do it tomorrow. I'm beat."

"I was just going to have a big salad. But I'll heat you up some leftover vegetable soup. Or make some pasta if you'd like?"

"Soup would be great."

She opens the refrigerator and rummages for the Tupperware container. "Hank's mother called while you guys were gone." For Julie, Jan is only *Hank's mother.*

Ray sighs. "About what?"

"She said she might not be able to pick Hank up on Monday."

"Really? Did she say why?"

Julie puts the container in the microwave, presses a few buttons, and returns to the sink. "Something about a friend in the hospital."

"Which friend?"

"She didn't say. I didn't talk to her—it's on the machine." She breaks lettuce into two large bowls. "Sir Stephen called too."

This is what Ray and Julie call Ray's father, a man who insists that even the employees who have worked for him for years call him "Mr. Gallant." Since Ray has come to work, he has made an exception and lets Ray call him "Steve" at the store, but never "Dad." Sir Stephen is suspicious of open affection, especially between men. He has been in a much better mood in the past year since his only son, a "sensitive" songwriter who let his hair grow and was probably involved in drug abuse and other perverse activity in Florida, has quit his rock band "hobby" and come home to work at and eventually take over the family business.

"What did he want?" Ray asks. "He knew I was supposed to be gone until Sunday."

She shrugs and looks up from the tomato she is cutting. "He seemed to have forgotten. Asked me if I needed anything."

Ray shakes his head and drinks the rest of the beer. "Watch out for him, baby."

"You think your dad is going to 'put the moves' on me?"

"I wouldn't put it past him." Ray moves closer, mouth next to her ear. "You're awfully cute." He bites her lobe softly and she pulls back, smiling, wrinkling her nose.

"You stink."

"What did you guys do today?" Julie asks Ray when they meet like this again the next evening. She pours green and white pasta spirals into the strainer, steam billowing to the ceiling, water hissing softly in the sink.

"Hank and I went to the beach for a couple hours. We both took long naps this afternoon." Ray sips from his scotch, ice tinkling quietly. Cartoon *boings* and *clunks* come from the TV in the next room.

Dumping the pasta back into the pan, Julie salts it, cranks the pepper mill over the coiled shapes. "Must be nice." She grates nutmeg over the pasta, pours a little olive oil on it and sets it back on the stove. Without hesitation, she removes jars of spices from a rack hanging over the gleaming stainless-steel stove. All the neatly labeled jars—turmeric, allspice, cayenne—make Ray feel unnerved sometimes. There is a middle-class perfection to their lives here in Ocean View, the gated community Julie was already living in when he met her. The house is just decades old—cream walls, eggshell-white trim, gray carpeting, new leather on wooden furniture, grass which looks incapable of thirst, garden beds with roses, petunias, lilies. The yard is perfect, yet so tiny that if the house were to tip over, it would be on their neighbor's property. It is the kind of home, community, Ray never thought he would live in as an adult, despite the fact that he grew up in one not too dissimilar, not too far from this one. Julie looks up from the food, flicks a strand of hair from her mouth. "I'm surprised Sir Stephen gave you another day off." She is not smiling.

"I didn't tell him I was back." He sucks an ice cube, waiting to see where this is going. She nods, stirs. Ray pulls the bottle of scotch from the cabinet and pours another couple of fingers. "I've been promising all month to show Hank how to surf." He considers leaving it at that, then continues: "Actually, I don't know how excited he was about the idea, but you should see him. He got up several times. He really needs a smaller board. I would have gone by the shop, but I don't want Dad to know I'm back."

She shakes her head. "Kind of late to start teaching him to surf, isn't it? I mean, *if* he's leaving on Monday."

"What's going on?"

"What?" She opens a cabinet looking for something.

"What are you pissed about?"

"Nothing. I'm not upset." She rummages.

There is a pause and Ray takes a step closer so that his face is inches from hers. Her eyes shift toward him, but she keeps her gaze on the pan, sprinkling red pepper flakes over the pasta. He gingerly touches her arm. "I want Hank to stay here and live with us."

She stops stirring, stares into the pan where the noodles hiss. "What about Jan?"

"I called her today. She wasn't there. I left a message that we need to talk."

Julie switches off the heat and turns to face him, drumming perfect red nails against Formica countertop. Ray is feeling that clenching in his stomach that comes every time they fight, in fact, every time he has any sort of confrontation with anyone. But he is also struck by how pretty she is in this light, dusk sun making her hair blond, fair skin glowing, cheeks slightly flushed from the stove and anger. "I'm not sure what I think about this, Ray."

"What's that supposed to mean?"

"I don't know if I'm ready to have a child, you know? Maybe I'll never be. I worked hard in law school so that I could be in a successful practice and have a good life. You *know* I'm trying to make partner. I don't want to be a mom."

"You're not a mom. Jan's his mom."

She steps closer so that he can feel her breath on his chin, voice an angry hiss. "It's not that simple. Look at me." She gestures toward the pasta. "I worked ten hours today and you spent your time sleeping and playing, but who's making dinner?"

"You didn't have to make dinner. I could have made something."

"Oh, *could* you? When did you think this was going to happen?" She jabs her finger at the clock on the stove. "It's almost eight o'clock. You've got a five-year-old in there. Were you just going to give him a bag of chips and a soda?"

Ray drains the rest of his scotch. There is a pause, but he cannot think of anything to say.

"Your mom left your dad because he treated her like a slave, right? Those are the exact words from your mouth, right? You don't see the possibility of a pattern here, do you?"

He stares out the window. It is dark now and he cannot see anything except for their reflection—Julie is standing close enough to bite his ear.

"I don't know why I even bother talking to you," she says, throwing her hands in the air, walking out, "you'll just do what you want to anyway."

On the couch in the basement, Ray plays a blues progression over and over, sometimes pausing for a lazy solo, then returning to the same repetitive, generic riff. The amp is loud, low notes vibrating the tiny windows at ground level which give the room a sleepy feeling on hot afternoons. After sundown though, with the overhead light illuminated, the bare walls have a dull, yellow sheen which reminds Ray of hangovers. In fact, there is something boozy and dull about the blues, too, he thinks. He is not a fan, rarely listens to it, hardly ever goes to see blues bands perform. He finds most contemporary blues derivative, rarely deviating from the freshness it had in the first half of the century. But like many young boys who took guitar lessons in hopes of being a rock star one day, his first experience was playing the blues. His guitar teacher, an old hippie who always carried an earthy smell—which Ray realized years later was marijuana—spent six months teaching him blues scales and riffs despite Ray's insistence that he only wanted "to rock."

When Julie first invited Ray to live with her, he imagined the basement—carpeted in deep, brown shag and now furnished simply with a yellow, second-hand couch—as a practice space for a band he would form. When Julie had first bought the house, she kept intending to do something with the basement, but between her work and beautifying the rest of her home, she had barely been down there except to store boxes of photos, her dead mother's china, anything she thought too delicate for the unventilated attic. She was glad to surrender the space to Ray, blushed and touched the side of his head tenderly whenever he talked about the band he would form, squinted her eyes in mock pain when he warned her about how loud live music could be in a home. Perhaps it was his proximity to the beach, but the band in his mind was a surf rock combo. He would advertise for local talent and his band would somehow reinvent surf rock. They would play in beachfront bars until they built a local following and then they would tour the coast. But he has never advertised for musicians. In fact, he rarely comes down here anymore, has not played his guitar in months. Since he has become manager, he is too tired after work to think about playing music, let alone finding musicians. At first, he was flattered that his father trusted him enough to give him so many responsibilities so soon—banking, ad designs and purchases, and then personnel—although a half dozen of the employees have been there longer than Ray has. Now he wonders if his dad is trying to keep him too busy to play music.

"Dad!" Hank yells over the guitar, standing at the foot of the stairs. Ray stops playing and gestures for Hank to come closer. "Dad, I'm really, really hungry."

Ray looks at his watch; it is almost nine. "Dinner should be ready soon, pal."

Hank looks doubtful. "Who's making it?"

"Julie."

"She left."

"Where did she go?"

"I don't know. She didn't say anything to *me*. Can I have chips?"

"Yeah, sure." He frowns at his son who is leaning against his leg. He would take them to a fast food restaurant, but thinks he is too drunk to drive. "I'll order pizza, so don't get too filled up. You want pepperoni?" Hank nods and takes a step away from the couch, but Ray does not get up. He pulls Hank closer, kissing him on the cheek.

"Why were you fighting?" Hank asks.

"Sometimes people who love each other fight."

"Like you and Mom?"

"You remember us fighting?"

"Yeah."

Knocking back the last of his ice, he cracks it between his back teeth. "Have you had a good time this month?" The words sound sleepy.

"Yeah, really good. I'm going to miss you. And Jimmy and his mom and dad and sister and their animals. And the beach."

"Jimmy and you really get along. Do you wish you had a brother?"

Hank shrugs. "I guess so."

"Do you think you might like to live here?"

Hank's eyes widen. "I don't know. I like it here, but I would really, *really* miss Mom. I wish she lived here too."

"I do too, Son, but that's probably not likely." Ray smiles. "If you lived here you would be able to walk to school. With Jimmy. And he could look after you, introduce you to the other kids. And I could buy you a smaller board and we could go surfing every day. If I got you a wet suit we could surf year-round. Would you like that?"

Hank does not answer, or look in his father's eyes. He traces his finger back and forth over the long, thin scar in Ray's cheek that he got from a bike wreck in high school. Usually invisible, it turns white when he has been out in the sun. "I don't know," he answers after a bit, his voice breaking. "I need to talk to Mom."

After another pause, Ray says, "Okay."

And then the next pause is even longer, so long that the amplifier hum becomes impossible to ignore and Ray clicks it off. Hanks sighs. "Can I have some chips now?"

"Of course, Son," Ray says, not making a move.

Jan's answering machine picks up when Ray calls again so he hangs up without a word. He bites into another slice of pizza, and then tosses it back in the cardboard box which he shoves to one side of the coffee table. Putting his feet up, he glances at his watch. It is midnight and Julie has not come home. Ray puts his arm along the back of the sofa, plays with a lock of his son's hair. Hank is watching a rerun of some sitcom set in a courtroom. The uproarious laugh track bursts from the TV speakers, but Hank is impassive, slowly digging in a nostril. The television is the only light in the room, and it spills deep shadows into Hank's eyes and open mouth.

"Are you tired yet, pal?"

"No," Hank says, in a trance.

When the show ends at midnight, Ray clicks off the TV. "Time for bed."

"I'm not tired," Hank whines.

Ray isn't either. He stopped drinking hours ago and his buzz has turned into a headache. He knows he should make Hank go to bed anyway, but instead says, "Do you want to go to the park?"

Hank looks suspicious. "Why?"

"We've never been there at night. I bet it will look different. It'll be an adventure."

Hank seems to like the sound of this. "Okay."

Sliding the glass door open, they go into the back yard. There is a full moon; Ray notices the difference between the few, dull stars in the city sky compared to the display out on the ocean. He takes Hank's hand and they go through the gate and walk down the bike path which leads to the local public park. They have come over here several times during Hank's stay—to play on the jungle gym and merry-go-round, throw a baseball, *father and son stuff* Julie calls it. There is no one around, no movement of cars on the street, most of the nearby houses dark except for perpetually burning porch lights. Trees stretch long shadows across the grass and the moon is so bright Hank's face is illuminated like a glowing dial. A dog barks somewhere, but then is quiet. From far away, there is the sound of a horn—a car alarm—but then there is a *beep-beep* and it goes silent too.

At the park, Hank stops walking, staring up at the greenhouse on its little hillock. It was built at the same time the city put in the public swimming pool, a planning commissioner's idea of an educational addition. Unfortunately, the horticulturist committed suicide after only a couple weeks' work and was never replaced. The glass has a sheen of algae and the shapes in the greenhouse appear murky under a nearby streetlight. Vandals have broken several of the panes. The building is overgrown with weeds and many of the plants have died. Three dead palm trees—long, thin shafts—branch up from the floor like gigantic, arthritic fingers. Ray wonders why they bothered to plant palms a couple miles from a beach front littered with them. He wants to ask Hank if he likes it here, wants to ask him again about staying in Myrtle Beach. The summer seems short—the sporting goods store, the marriage pushing inward on his life. He wants to sit on a bench and talk to his son. But he is afraid to speak, as if a sound will shatter the building in front of them, as if its gigantic glass shards will fall and rip the world apart.

Ray lies barefooted on the still-made bed, Hank finally asleep in his own room. He is wearing the same clothes he has worn all day: T-shirt, shorts, socks. The sour scent of sweat drifts in the air and makes him sleepy as the television glows on the dresser, a baseball game. A pitcher in gray, dark letters across his chest, stares just right of the camera, shakes his head once, twice, nods, and throws. His arms and legs move in slow motion, sidearm awkward, like he is doing some strange kind of dance. But then the ball rockets across the plate with amazing speed and accuracy. The umpire makes a guttural sound which is probably supposed to mean "Strike!" and jerks his thumb over his shoulder. Ray knows that Tampa Bay and New York are playing, that the score is tied and the game has run into extra innings, but he does not know exactly what inning he is watching, the numbers at the top of the screen a blur without his contacts. The fact that it is almost one, that his five-year-old son has just gone to bed, and that his fiancée has not returned from wherever she has gone makes this night stretch in front of him like a desolate highway, an endless line of dashed white splitting the black.

The inning ends still tied and the front door downstairs opens and closes. After a few minutes, Julie comes in. She is wearing a white summer skirt, a blue tank top. "Hi," she says, voice flat, kicking off her sandals. Zipping down her skirt, she lets it fall. She puts her hands behind her head and when she takes them away, her light-brown hair falls about her shoulders. Ray notices how skinny she looks in this light, even sickly. The image of emaciated bodies stacked in Nazi Germany flits through his head, and he remembers his sex fantasy on the boat, tries to place the last time they made love. A week? Maybe ten days.

She slips under the covers, slides an arm beneath her pillow, face toward the far wall. "Are you going to tell me where you went?" he asks.

"To the movies. With Cindy. We had a few drinks after."

"What's going on, Julie?" There is silence for a long moment and then he says, "Do you still want to get married?"

She groans. "Can we talk about this in the morning?"

Ray imagines jerking her by the shoulder, breaking the silence with his hard and jagged voice. *Hell no*, he would yell, *we can't talk about this in the morning. You're going to talk now!* But the game is on. And from the sound of Julie's breathing, she is already asleep.

Ray sits at the kitchen table, drinking coffee, rubbing his eyes. The phone cuts the silence and, before he can stop him, Hank has answered. Ray knows it will be his father, that he will be expected to show up for work. However, after a second of listening to the laughter from his son, the murmured words, he knows it is not Sir Stephen.

Hank hangs up. "Nellie's babies are hatching," he says, grinning.

"Who the hell is Nellie?"

"Jimmy's *boa constrictor*." Hank draws out the name of the reptile as if his father is too stupid to speak quickly to.

"Oh. Sweet." Over the years, Mike has bought his son and daughter a wide variety of animals: a dog, three cats, a couple of fat and lethargic hamsters, a comatose tarantula, three birds, and the boa. Ray thinks the Rayvors' house smells like shit.

"Can I go?" Hank jigs in place impatiently.

Ray smiles despite his hangover. "Got to pee?"

"Dad, come on."

"All right, but come home for lunch. Mrs. Rayvor is going to think I send you over there for the free food." Hank runs to the door. "But give your old man a kiss before you go." His son rolls his eyes, but grins as he comes back to give his father a wet kiss on the lips. He runs out the door just as the phone rings again. Ray thinks about letting the machine pick up, but then answers after the third ring.

"Hello?"

"Ray, hi. It's me."

"Jan."

"Yeah, sorry I haven't been in touch. I thought you guys were going to stay out longer and then I was gone all night and didn't get your message until this morning." Ray leans across the kitchen sink, close to the window so he can see Hank look both ways before crossing the street. He thinks he should have made him wear shoes as he watches the boy quickly tiptoeing over the black pavement in his bare feet. "I've been in and out of the hospital all week. A friend was beat up pretty badly."

"Yeah, that's what Julie said. Who was it?"

"William."

"Is he going to be all right?" Ray runs water over the dishes, cuts the faucet.

"I think so. They let him go home last night. A few broken bones. They kept him so long because he had a collapsed lung. He'll be okay."

"What happened?"

"It's a long story. I'm still picking Hank up on Monday, right?"

Ray takes a deep breath. "That's what I wanted to talk about."

"What?" suspicion already in her voice.

"What would you think about Hank staying here to live?"

A loud exhalation, a pause, the light crackle of connection. "Ray, what are you pulling? I don't need this shit right now, in case you're wondering. I'm about to explode."

"Calm down. I just thought you could use a break, maybe go back and finish your degree. It could be a trial thing, see how Hank likes it here."

Another pause, then "What does Hank think about this?"

"He seems excited."

"Really?"

"Why is that so hard to believe?"

"I don't know." A longer pause. "Let me speak to him."

Ray can see Hank waiting at the Rayvors' front door. "He's not here." Jimmy jerks the door open and Hank disappears inside.

"This seems fucked up, kind of sudden." Ray can imagine her chewing a nail, staring out her own kitchen window. "I've got primary custody, remember?"

"Relax." He is starting to get mad. "We're talking about what's best for our son."

"I wonder." There is the sound of breathing. "You know, sometimes I think it might be nice if Hank lived with you for a while too. It's hard raising him by myself."

Her voice catches and Ray feels a lump in his throat. "I know."

"Yeah, well, I can't make a decision like this without talking to Hank. I can't decide like this over the phone anyway. I'm coming on Monday like we planned. I'll be there late afternoon, three or four."

"Jan, just listen for a second..." She hangs up though. Ray calls back immediately, but as soon as he says, "Jan," she hangs up again. He slams the phone down, headache worsening.

After dinner, Julie disappears upstairs to a closed-door bath while Ray loads the dishwasher. When the phone rings, Hank runs for it as he always does these days. Ray closes the washer door and, as it clicks on, Hank's face widens with a smile and he yells, "Mom!" Ray just stands there, staring at the phone as if he expects it to do something, then goes to the living room and pulls a random book off the shelf. Sitting in a chair with his back to the kitchen, he stares at the black print, listening to his son's half of the conversation. At first, it is all excitement—the fishing trip, staying up past midnight, baby snakes—but then his son's answers become monosyllabic, hesitant, quiet.

"I guess," he says. A long pause. "Yeah…I know." Another pause. "I don't *know*, Mom." Pause, quieter: "I miss you." A very long pause. "Uh-huh, yeah. I love you too." Hank puts the phone in its cradle on the wall carefully as if it were fragile. Ray focuses on the print, really reads: *For a young person cannot judge what is allegorical and what is literal; anything that he receives into his mind…*

"What are you reading?" Hank leans against the arm of the overstuffed chair, peering at the book in Ray's lap.

The book is part of a large set of leather-bound hardbacks Julie owns. He turns it over and reads the spine. "Plato."

"Hm, Play-doh. Is it good?"

"Yep. How is your mother?"

"Fine."

Waking, Ray looks up into Julie's face, complexion clear of makeup, hair pulled into a tight bun. "I'm leaving," she says.

There is a lurch of fear in his chest, and then he realizes she is in the black tights she wears every Saturday when she goes to dance lessons. She was a ballerina throughout her school years and went to college as a performance major, but quit after going into the hospital with chest pains, the precursor to a heart attack, a result of a long-term eating disorder. She says that dance nearly killed her, but she has not been able to abandon it completely, spending Saturday mornings with an instructor and a room full of women—other professionals and housewives.

Ray touches her hand, the one holding the car keys. With the sun creeping around the blinds, her fine cheekbones dappled with soft light, she is slender and beautiful. Although motionless, she seems graceful, as if she were a rare bird about to take flight. "He's not going to stay," Ray says.

"What?"

"Hank is going home." For some reason, the word "home" makes him pause, catch his breath. "On Monday."

She sits on the edge of the bed, gingerly touches Ray's chest. "He decided?"

"He hasn't told me yet, but I can tell."

She looks at the floor, jiggles her keys lightly. "Ray, I'm sorry…" There is a slight catch in her voice and a wetness at the rims of her eyes. "I feel like I've been a bitch."

He pulls her close so she is lying against his chest, her cool face against his neck, the scent of strawberries coming from her hair. "No, you've been wonderful."

Ray stands just at the edge of the window, spying into the back yard. Hank and Jan are talking, sitting in the two swings of the set Ray put in at the beginning of the summer. Julie comes up behind him, slides her arms around his waist, lips against the side of his neck. "Hi," she says. "How are you doing?"

He leans his head against the wall, the window frame cutting off the view of Jan and most of Hank except for his Keds kicking at the dirt beneath the swing, the thicker grass surrounding him like a green ocean. "A few weeks ago, I was helping an old lady try on some walking shoes at the store. She said I had such 'good manners.' I felt like a child, but also kind of old. I've been running away from being grown up my whole life, and it's finally caught up to me. You know what? It's boring."

Julie kisses his neck again, squeezes him. "Babe, you can't avoid getting older. You don't have to be boring."

He wants to say something, feels that there is a rebuttal to this. But all he can do is sigh.

Ray carries Hank's suitcase to Jan's Mercedes while she lugs his toys in a milk crate. "So, how's the bookstore?"

"It's a job. I've decided to go back to school and finish."

"That's great. What are you majoring in this time?"

"Name it. I figured out I can get a History, English, or Philosophy degree within a year. I guess I'll do whatever is quickest and easiest—I just need to finish."

"That's a good goal."

She leans the crate against the back bumper and rummages in her oversized shorts for the keys. "Yeah, and Rain has been showing me how to throw pots. I figure if I take a ceramics class, I can use the school's wheels and kilns." She pops the trunk and shoves the crate in toward the back.

"What's all this stuff?"

Jan looks up at him, hand raised to block the sun, head tilted sideways. "Some of Hank's stuff—toys, clothes, books." She waits while Ray stares at her blankly. "Remember? I thought Hank wanted to stay here."

Ray swallows, clears his throat. "I thought he did."

She keeps staring for a moment, then puts a hand on his shoulder, squeezes. "I know. He's only five; it's probably hard for him to know what he wants." Ray shoves the suitcase in the trunk and slams it.

"You ready, buddy?"

Hank is speaking quietly with Jimmy. "Yeah," he says then. "Well, see you."

"See you," Jimmy answers, punching Hank's shoulder and going home.

"Give me a hug?" Ray asks, crouching, arms wide.

Hank takes a step and pauses, lip quivering, and then he is crying. "Dad, I'm sorry."

"What's wrong?" Ray asks, pulling Hank into his arms. Hank shakes and quietly sobs. "Son? Why are you sad?"

"I just…" But there is nothing more.

"Pal, this has been such a great vacation for me. I've had so much fun." Ray pushes his face into his son's shoulder, inhales the scent of detergent from his T-shirt. "I'm very proud of you." This makes Hank cry harder. Ray glances at Jan, but she stares off, across the street. He can feel his son's small fingers clutching his arm and shoulder, Hank's open mouth against his neck, the baby teeth pressing his skin. A plane flies overhead, there is the call and response of birds. No one says a thing.

10

Jan and Hank have been on the road for a couple of hours. They have mostly been silent since they left Ray's place. Jan glances at her son who occasionally rubs his eyes still swollen from crying. She feels a surge of guilt for some reason and wants to touch Hank's curls, or his cheek, put her fingers against his collarbone, but knows he wants to be left alone. Turning on the radio, she spins the dial to the first station she can find. Grace Slick's deep mannish voice comes from the tiny speakers in either door, singing "Somebody to Love." Usually, this song makes Jan sing along, but now it just makes her sad. Flipping the blinker up, she turns into a rest stop. She has been a vegetarian for about a week and can already feel it changing her guts. When she gets cramps and goes running to the restroom, she tells herself that it is good for her, that she is getting all that bad stuff out of her system and starting over.

Rain has been nagging her for eight years, ever since she has known her, to stop eating meat. *Yeah, I know,* Jan always said, without really considering. But last week, sitting with William in the hospital, holding his hand, the fingers curling out of the cast on his palm, a nurse had brought a plate of food and set it on the tray attached to the bed. Like most hospital food, it looked bland, nearly colorless: turkey and gravy, volcano of mashed potatoes, over-cooked, dull-green beans and soggy corn. There was something about the turkey though—its oval shape, off-white color— which put a quiver in her stomach. Except for a tiny tear in its side, it could be something man-made, plastic covered in brown gravy. That tiny tear though—echoing the split in William's cheek held together with black stitching, bottom lip swollen and cut near the corner of his mouth, the long gash over his eyebrow swelling his eye shut—was distinctly nauseating, the meat-ness of William's face, his body, of everyone's, suddenly clear. The nurse cut the food on William's plate into tiny pieces because his new bridge had just been put in and his teeth were tender. When he spoke, the words emerged with a sort of delicacy, as if they might be too hard for his fragile mouth: "Could you please bring a plate for my friend?" Jan sensed the gag reflex before she felt it, stood slowly and went to the bathroom, closing the door. Kneeling over the toilet, she stared at the dark reflection of her face, hair hanging down into that unnaturally clean receptacle, and then, without vomiting, lay down, cool tile against her cheek. She was so exhausted she slipped into a brief sleep. When she awoke a few minutes later, she knew that she was going to stop eating meat.

She parks in a space at the rest stop—travelers in sunglasses and pastel shorts move slowly toward the one squat, brick building surrounded by scrub trees as if they are surgery patients learning to walk again. They sweat, leaning into the hot air like it will catch them if they fall. Jan smiles at Hank. "Need to go to the bathroom, buddy?"

Looking at the floorboard, he says, "I don't know. I guess." He takes her hand in the parking lot as they cross the pavement to the sidewalk. She relishes the feel of his small hand in hers. Tired, she feels the weight of the waffles she had for breakfast in her stomach, can taste the syrup still on her chapped lips. She wishes it were not so hot, that she could breathe. They pass through the milling fat people sweating and gazing at vending machines full of overpriced, unhealthy snacks snug behind bars. A stooped old man in a baseball cap reaches a trembling hand through the peeling black bars to retrieve a bright green can of soda. Holding Hank's hand, Jan pushes against the restroom door, but he pulls up short, fingers slipping from her fist. The move is so sudden, Jan gasps and takes a quick step toward him as if someone has snatched him. But he is just standing there, shaking his head. "Mom, I can't go in *there*."

Her forehead wrinkles and she cocks her head at him, confused. "What?" The ache in her stomach is sharper.

"That's the *ladies* bathroom."

She smiles, thinks he is joking, then realizes he is serious. An overweight woman with thin, delicately blue-veined legs pushes past, smiling down at Hank, eyes invisible behind enormous sunglasses. The words *Oh, come on* form in her brain, but something in Hank's fixed expression keeps her quiet. She pulls him aside, squats, knees cracking. Looking into his solemn eyes, she realizes he may have grown in the month since she has seen him. "You don't want to go in with me?" she whispers so the people silently lumbering over the shadowed pavement will not hear.

He whispers back, voice urgent, "I *can't*."

Jan quickly scans the clusters of people: some children, a teen with bad skin, a beer-bellied avuncular man, a stunning brown-skinned couple in designer clothing who seem reluctant to part and enter their respective restrooms. Jan tells herself that no one here looks deviant. She then tells herself that deviants usually do not look deviant—the image of the Gainesville serial killer, Victor Mansley, in his wireframes and rumpled button-down looking like a librarian, flashes through her mind. Her bowels ache with pressure and she chews her lip. "Can you hold it?"

"For a bit."

"Good. Okay, here's the plan: I'm going to go in there." She points toward the women's restroom. "I want you to stand here by the door, okay?" He sighs, rolls his eyes. It is the duplicate of a gesture of Ray's and she feels nostalgic and annoyed at the same time. "Humor me, all right, buddy?"

"All right."

"Don't talk to strangers. And if anyone says anything wrong, mean, creepy, bad to you, yell my name. Okay?"

"*Okay.*"

She runs a hand through his hair. "Good kid." Hurrying into the bathroom, she ducks into the nearest stall. This is not the dirtiest bathroom she has been in, nor the cleanest. The floor is damp like it has been mopped, but there is a dinginess to the tile as if the years of human tread and waste are wearing it down. A toilet runs incessantly somewhere. There is an intense ache in her lower stomach, intestines maybe, and it is good to sit against the cool plastic seat. She rests her chin in her palms, listens to the high-pitched laughter from a few stalls down. "Henry wouldn't let me sleep *at all* last night." "Uh-*huh!*" someone responds and then and more laughter. A sink is running over somewhere, water dripping to the floor. The sudden joyful scream of a child outside the bathroom makes Jan hold her breath. She tries to hear Hank's voice in the mix, but, of course, he should not be talking—anyone he would be speaking to would be a stranger. She bites her thumb and does not call his name.

Even though the sun is down, it is hot in Jan and Hank's house, the air conditioner broken again. The landlord keeps saying he will come over to "look at it," but has not appeared in over a week. Jan has a sinking feeling that she will finally see him right before rent is due. At the kitchen counter, she stretches her back which aches from the drive and carrying in all of Hank's clothes and toys. The crickets are singing outside the window, and moths bat at the screen, a breeze refreshing against her hair still wet from the shower. She chops the tomatoes Rain brought a few days earlier from her garden. She whistles to the tune drifting from the living room stereo, Neil Young's sweetly imperfect voice accompanying. Hank comes in and hooks an arm around her thigh. "What are we having for dinner?"

"I'm making gazpacho." She squeezes the seeds out, turning the red orbs to mush between her fingers.

"What's that?" His voice is suspicious.

"It's like a cold tomato soup."

"Yuck."

"*Yuck,*" she mocks, laughing, lightly pinching his cheek, leaving a wet spot he wipes away. "You like tomato soup."

"Not cold."

"Have you ever tried it?" She raises her eyebrows at him.

"No," he admits.

"Well, see? You'll just have to try it. Do you want a grilled cheese sandwich too?"

"No, baloney."

"I'm sorry, buddy, we don't have baloney. I've sort of stopped eating meat."

He looks at her with such an expression of horror that she laughs. She kisses his head. "Don't worry, we'll go shopping tomorrow and get you some baloney and anything else you want. You can eat as much meat as you ever did."

"Promise?"

"I promise," she says, hand on her heart, realizing, too late, that her palm is wet with tomato slime. Picking a tendril from her recently clean T-shirt, she swipes at the red splotch with a damp towel. "Now see what you made me do?" She pops the towel at him, letting it snap a few inches from his butt.

Giggling, he scoots away. "Missed me, missed me."

"That's right," she says, turning back to the cutting board.

Dishes done, Jan finds Hank lying on the couch in the living room, watching TV. It is an old black-and-white war film, chiaroscuro soldiers shooting each other in a desert setting. The camera cuts to a close-up of a leading man type with tense expression, eyes so light in his face, they are obviously blue, and then cuts to a shot of the ground exploding, a different man flying through the air, pinwheeling arms. Explosions and gunfire vibrate the tiny speaker in the TV. "Is it loud enough?" she yells. Hank's eyes flicker at her, and then back at the screen as he turns down the volume with the remote next to his face. "What are you watching?"

"Dunno."

"I'm going to go lie down; I'm exhausted."

"Lie here." He pats behind himself, moving to the edge of the couch.

"Are you sure there's enough room? You're awfully big these days."

He nods, pats the couch again which makes her smile. Climbing over him, she groans as if it takes a huge effort, and then has her chest to his back, palm on his stomach, a leg hooked over his bare feet. Kissing his ear, she whispers, "I love you very much." There is a pause, terse talk from the leading-man type, and she says, "I missed you."

"I missed you too." He stares at the screen, running men and explosions reflecting in his blue eyes. Putting her fingers into his curls, she is just starting to follow the narrative, suspects she has seen the movie before, long ago, when Hank says, "Why did William fight?"

"Who told you that?" she asks, although she knows.

"Dad."

"Well, he didn't exactly fight. He was beat up."

"Who beat him up?"

"Some guys."

"Why did they do that?"

Jan rests her chin on her palm and looks down at him for so long that he finally looks up. "You know, I don't really know why they did it. I was there and it didn't make much sense."

He stares at Jan for a second and then says, "Oh," turns his face back to the screen.

Feeling her answer has been unsatisfactory, she adds, "Sometimes people are just in the wrong place at the wrong time."

Hank seems to ponder this for a moment, licking his lips and then scratching his nose as there are more explosions. "It's scary."

Jan kisses his head. "You know, I wouldn't let anything like that happen to you."

There is a pause and she thinks the conversation is over, but then he says, "You couldn't stop it from happening to William."

She cannot think of a thing to say as the movie continues, as bombs explode and bullets fly and men scream.

Coming through the door of William's apartment, Jan crouches, lets Harry off his leash. Hank leans against the couch, holding a comic book in one hand, scratching William's cat Flann behind the ear. The tiny dog, panting, constantly hyper, runs across the carpet toward Flann and, as usual, she arches her back, hisses, and takes a swipe. The dog hops back a couple steps and barks twice. "Stop it, Harry," Hank says calmly, not looking up from the comic book, petting the cat until her orange fur lies down, until she rubs against him again.

It is just after ten o'clock in the morning, but Jan's T-shirt is already sticking to her. She falls on the couch which is frayed where Flann has sharpened her claws. William, at the kitchen table, bends over a bowl of gazpacho, a glob of sour cream and bits of scallion floating on its surface. His breathing has that labored rasp it has had since the fight. "What took you so long?" he asks, words coming slow. He is still getting used to the new bridge, moving his lips carefully as if afraid to shatter these fake teeth.

"I took him by the halfway house to see Eddie." William takes Harry to see Eddie Skein, Harry's previous owner and wrongfully accused serial murderer, every two or three weeks, but had not been for over a month.

"Oh, thanks. I was starting to feel guilty."

"Eddie was worried about you. He told me to give you this." She puts a beat-up Superman comic book next to the bowl of gazpacho. "I can see why you do that."

"Do what?"

She kisses him on the forehead. "Take your dog to see Eddie. That guy's been through so much. It was nice to see him playing in the yard with Harry. He was so grateful, he couldn't stop thanking me." Pressing her knuckles against William's old wooden table, her eyes shine. "He's got a part-time job."

"No way."

"Yeah," she says, rubbing William's back. "He runs errands or something down at the courthouse. He showed me his I.D. He wears it on a lanyard. Even at home."

"Not bad," he says, pushing the bowl back. "I've never had gazpacho."

"Me neither. Though I'm not sure it's meant for breakfast." William shrugs, belches.

Hank laughs and Jan says, "You're gross," but smiles. She stares out the window. "It's so damn hot. I wasn't sure what else to do with the tomatoes. Rain's in a gardening co-op. She's always bringing me stuff." Jan picks up his bowl, but he puts his hand on her wrist.

"Leave that." He stretches to kiss her, but she turns her mouth away at the last second and his lips glance off her cheek. Hank is watching.

"You about ready to go, buddy?"

"Yeah," Hank says, getting up and brushing his shorts though there is nothing there.

William still holds her wrist, but his grip is gentle. She looks at his hand and then his face, raises an eyebrow as if to say, *Well?*

"Andrea called today to ask if you were still working for us," he says.

"What did you tell her?"

"I said yes, that you would be in tomorrow. Is that correct?"

"That's correct, boss."

He lets her arm go. "Don't call me that." Smiling at Hank, he says, "You want this?" offering the comic book.

A shocked look appears on the boy's face. "That's a gift, William."

Jan nods at William, a slight grin on her lips.

"You're right, Hank, I'm sorry." He looks down at Superman punching some white-cloaked villain, a bubble full of exclamations coming from his mouth. "Would you like to borrow it when I'm through?"

Hank shakes his head. "I don't like Superman."

"Why not?"

"He's too perfect."

William stares for a long time, then nods and grins. "I'm glad you're back, Hank. I missed you."

Jan feels strangely touched and kisses him next to his ear, says, "I'll call you later."

In Book Purgatory, Jan figures out how much they owe a smiling little old lady, a regular named Sandra who always smells faintly of glass cleaner. It is Sandra's usual biweekly dose of historical romances with their nearly identical illustrations of erotic rape-in-progress on the covers. William pushes through the front door and Jan takes in a breath, can feel something like a lurch in her chest. Since the fight, she is always surprised by the way he looks. The bruise over his left eye has turned yellow, that eye smaller and redder than the other. "My god," says Jessica who has not seen him since before the fight. She is the only employee not to visit him in the hospital due to a childhood fear arising from when her mother died after a long bout with breast cancer. William's cheeks are red, brows together, jaw tight—that look that says he is in a rage.

Jan tries to smile, keep her voice from shaking. "Why are you here? You should be at home; we've got things under control." Then she notices the blood oozing from his arm just above the elbow, the big smudge of dirt on his blue button-down. "What happened?"

He stares at her for a second, hands on hips, jaw working, then says, voice scratchy, "Someone stole my truck." He shakes his head and coughs into his hand. "Tried to." He closes his eyes, inhales deeply. "It was that guy."

Jan stares at William's truck, forehead wrinkling. *What guy?* There's no one there, the truck looks fine. She glances back at him. "What guy?" But he is stalking toward his office. Jessica watches him go, thin, dark eyebrows going up and down dramatically, as she rings up the comic books of some freckled kid with braces. Jan finishes tallying Sandra's trade credit and leans against the counter, watching the closed door of the office, waiting for Jessica to finish talking to the kid who appears to be telling her about one of the characters in a comic book, flirting. It is the first full day Jan has worked in nearly two weeks and she feels wiped out. She rubs her eyes. William's presence is gnawing at her; her eyes twitch behind the lids. When she opens them again, the kid is gone and Jessica is staring at her. Jan meets the stare, waits for her to drop it. When she keeps staring, Jan says, "What?" louder than she means to.

"Are you going back there?"

Jan keeps staring at Jessica. Although she and William have not been involved romantically in months, everyone at the store assumes there is something still going on. Realizing her mouth is still open, she lets it close, breathes through her nose, frowns. "Will you be all right by yourself?"

Jessica pops her gum, nods once. "I'm all over it, babe."

William is sitting behind his desk, doing the breathing exercises for the broken ribs, hands on his hips, face shiny. "Are you all right?" she asks. He shakes his head, breathes out. "Why did you come in? It doesn't make sense. What were you talking about out there?"

Holding in a breath, he stares at a frayed Eric Dolphy poster. "I'm not sure why I came in." He looks at Jan, then the floor. "I'm scared. They know where I live."

"Wait, slow down. Who? What are you talking about? Those guys?"

"I wanted to take Harry for a walk—I'm fucking out of my mind being in that apartment." His voice is hushed as if he is afraid someone will overhear. A child whines nearby and his mother drawls, bored, "Come here or I'll beat you." Jan pushes the door closed. "As soon as I hit the first step to the parking lot, I saw him. The bastard was in my truck—I could see his stupid rebel flag hat bobbing up and down behind the dash."

"The guy from the movie theater? What was he doing in your truck?"

"I don't know. Trying to steal it, I guess. The idiot pulled a bunch of wires from under the dash." William puts his forehead on the desk. Jan considers shoving the books stacked on a metal folding chair to the floor so she can sit. But there seems to be something wrong in keeping the desk between them. Then again, she does not know if she should squeeze between the scarred wall and desk to stand next to him. Would she put her arm around his shoulders, lean close and kiss his head? Would he want her to? The pause electric, she bounces on the balls of her feet in an uneasy stasis.

William rests his good fist on the cast, props his chin on top of his hand and stares at Jan's stomach. She is wearing a short shirt, tanned belly showing, and instantly feels awkward, but there is nowhere to turn. Swallowing, she stares at the top of his shaved head. "I just stood there," he says, speaking like someone in a trance, lips barely moving. His new "teeth" are unnaturally white, perfect, their perfection strangely disturbing in the dingy office and she looks away to a smudge on the wall. "Harry was yanking at the leash. I thought I was seeing things, that there wasn't really anyone in the truck, that it was a trick of the light and my paranoia. And then I thought it wasn't my truck. But it was definitely the same guy. And there was that gap of rust near the back fender, you know?" She nods. "The paint was peeling in the same spots too." His voice breaks: "How *couldn't* it be my truck?" He looks into Jan's face, eyes damp with fear. "I feel like I'm losing my fucking mind. I'm exhausted and anxious. Pretty soon, I'm just going to jump out of my skin." He raises his good hand. "It's not just the redneck. Look at my hand. I've been shaking since I woke up. I can't even shave."

Without thinking, Jan sits on the edge of his desk and takes his hand. "Will, you've been through a lot. For the last week and a half, you haven't done anything but lie in bed and sleep or watch TV. You've been hurt really badly. Anyone would be loopy."

He looks at her hand, gripping it almost to pain. "I don't know when I started walking again, but at some point, I realized I was getting closer. I was just a few yards away when he saw me." William shakes his head. "You'd think he'd be scared. He just smiled."

"You should have called the cops. He might have had a gun."

William puts an index finger against the skin peeking through the hole in the knee of Jan's jeans as if he is not sure what it is. "I know. I wasn't thinking. He got out of the truck and told me I probably wanted to drop the charges, that he and his buddies knew where I lived. I didn't say a thing, but Harry barked. I was too shocked by the whole surreal thing and dropped the leash and Harry was biting the guy on the pants leg before I knew it. The fucker laughed and picked him up by the scruff of the neck and threw him."

Jan puts a hand to her mouth. "Is he all right?"

"I think so. It scared him. He ran under a car." William bites his lower lip, teeth gleaming under the fluorescents, and Jan stares at that tattoo of two arrows pointing in different directions. It fills her with longing and pathos; she fights the urge to touch it. William spaces his words as if they were volatile: "I lost it. I ran at him. It was stupid even though he looked scared for a second. I'm worthless as a fighter. All it took was one punch in the gut."

He stares at Jan for so long she squeezes his hand, leans forward and kisses his forehead right next to that yellow bruise. "What then?"

William takes a breath. "Nothing, really. It knocked the wind out of me and he was saying something, but I don't remember. I just stood there with my hands on my knees and Harry whimpered at my feet and after a while I could straighten up again and he was gone." He rests his cheek on the blotter and Jan strokes his moist hair, pausing occasionally to wipe the sweat on her jeans, and then stroking it again. "He might have killed me if he wanted," William says, face pressed to the blotter. Jan tries to speak, but an unexpected sob rises solid as a rock from her chest. She lightly squeezes the back of his neck. He puts his arm across Jan's lap and she pushes closer on the desk, knocking something off which hits the carpet with a dull thud. "I've upset you." She takes his hand when he reaches to wipe her tears.

"You should see a doctor."

"I know."

"And you need to press charges."

"No."

"Why not? The idiot is obviously counting on that. How arrogant to think he could just attack you in broad daylight and get away with it."

"Is it? He did get away, didn't he?"

"But he's probably left fingerprints all over your truck. All you have to do is go to the station and he'll be back in jail."

William shakes his head, tracing the large shaky letters of Hank's signature on his cast with a finger. "I'm scared. When I woke up in the hospital, all I could think about was you. I felt how much pain I was in. My body was like a sack with all these different bones and muscles and cartilage rattling around. I could feel the needle going in and out when they stitched me, and felt them setting each bone in my hand. It hurt to breathe, felt like breathing fiberglass. All I could think was *What have those guys done to Jan?*" His voice breaks. "I know we're not together and I accept it. But I couldn't forgive myself if anything happened to you."

"Nothing *did* happen to me."

"But something *could*. They know that you were there. You're a witness."

This is the first time that this has occurred to her and it makes her pause, hold her breath, stare at the floor—filthy gray carpeting, wadded ball of paper next to the waste basket, toppled stack of books against a wall: a Henry Miller, a Rush Limbaugh, a philosophy textbook, others she does not recognize. Hank is at Rain's. The image in her mind is the height of cliché: her son running and laughing with Patrick Henry, hair rustling in slow motion as he moves toward a football thrown too short. The fat oaf in his rebel flag hat, cruising a large pickup through the Summertree parking lot. In all likelihood, though, Hank and Patrick Henry are inside at this moment avoiding the upper-90s temperatures, drawing or creating some sort of pretend world of coexisting plastic army soldiers, cowboys, Indians, and dinosaurs. She looks into William's eyes and when she speaks, her words are measured: "That's as much a reason as any. We can't let that bastard do this. If he terrorizes us and we don't fight back, then he's just hurting us again and again. It'll never stop because we'll always be afraid."

While William is in the examining room, Jan flips through a science magazine to steady her nerves in the brightly lit waiting room, reads about subatomic particles—protons, electrons, neutrons, quarks. Quarks were named after a line from Joyce's *Finnegans Wake*. Appropriate, since much of the article resembles the gibberish she remembers from her failed attempt at that book. Still, she is fascinated by this idea of a world, her world, composed of trillions of tiny worlds. She remembers her high school chemistry teacher Mrs. Chiles's sketch of an atom, a chalk sphere of nucleus surrounded by a circle with a small dot running its circumference—an electron. The drawing looked like a tiny Saturn, moon circling it, and Jan wondered, staring at her hand, how many of these orbiting things it would take to make a person. Mrs. Chiles caught Jan staring at her raised hand. "Do you have a question, Ms. Pender?" Jan clutched her palm tightly as if she were hiding something.

She imagines all the atoms making up William's body, what they must go through when they connect with a fist or boot, the chaos as those worlds concuss. Dr. Hanson comes into the waiting room then and says, "Ms. Pender? Could you come in for a second?" Hanson is a short, stocky man with a little pony tail and an intense smile. His intensity is infectious: Jan jumps, magazine flopping to the floor, and does not bother to pick it up as she hurries after him, purse banging her hip. William sits on the examination table, futilely trying to button his shirt with his broken hand. She quickly steps close and buttons it for him, sees a flash of William's stomach where the guy must have punched him, the skin dark red, like the blood has collected just below the surface. She fights the urge to part his shirt and stare, knows it will only make her feel worse. Instead, she smiles into his face and he grins back. The doctor is talking: "Here is a prescription for Tylenol #3. Take two every six hours as needed." He places a slip of paper on the table next to William. The doctor gives Jan that concrete smile. "Make this guy stay home. He shouldn't be walking around—anywhere—for at least another week. Can you, or someone else, stay with him for the next two, three, days?"

"He's staying at my house. I'll watch him."

William opens his mouth, but Jan just nods once, and he shuts it without saying anything.

Dr. Hanson points to the x-ray glowing on the wall. "The lung looks okay, and there's no sign of internal bleeding. He's just going to have one hell of a bruise." He looks at William and smiles. "Call me in a few days if you don't feel better. You should be fine."

In Jan's car outside, William closes his eyes and says, "God, I'm so tired. I feel like I could sleep for twenty-four hours."

Jan stares at the car keys in her hand for a long time, so long she can see him out of the corner of her eyes looking at her, waiting. "I think we should go to the police station and file a report," she says, finally turning.

He shakes his head. "Jan, I'm so tired. I just want to go home."

"No. If you don't do it now, you're not going to."

"Don't be silly. I'll do it tomorrow."

"No, you're going to sleep for twenty-four hours. And when you wake up you'll decide that things will be better if you ignore it."

He stares at the dash. "Don't tell me what I'll do," he says through barely open lips. "You have no idea what this is like."

She traces the steering wheel, takes a breath. "I was raped." He jerks back as if she has taken a swing. But she is not looking at him now. She is staring out the window, gripping the steering wheel with the intensity of a driver on a wet and winding road who needs her concentration. The convertible directly in front has been backed into its space so that she can read the personalized license plate: SPOILT 1. The wind is blowing a flyer across the parking lot directly behind the convertible—a white paper rectangle flat against the black pavement. It floats up, back and forth, and then flat again.

Jan closes her eyes and speaks in a monotone: "It's been almost five years. I knew the guy who raped me and I was scared he would hurt me if I pressed charges, but Ray persuaded me to. When he was out on bail I kept getting phone calls. The caller was always silent, but I knew it had to be Clarence, even though I suppose it could have been anyone, or no one. It scared the hell out of me. Without really making a conscious decision, I just didn't show up in court on the day of the trial. The case fell apart. Clarence insisted the sex was consensual and since I wasn't there, the evidence seemed to point this out. The hospital exam showed his sperm in me, but the only sign of struggle was a fat lip I had where his forehead hit me." Jan opens her eyes and looks at William, feels a crooked smile without humor on her face. It occurs to her that, to an outsider, they could be lovers discussing weekend plans. She stares at a smashed bug on the windshield. "I *didn't* struggle. I was scared. I guess I thought if I didn't struggle it would be over quicker." In her peripheral vision, she sees William reaching for her. "No, don't." She sniffles loudly in the tiny car, leans against the window and licks the salty taste from her lips. "Only a few people know about this: Ray, Rain. Now you. My parents don't even know. I thought it was easier to keep it to myself." She looks down at her jeans, scratches at a spot of dirt. "I'm less and less sure." She wipes her cheeks and eyes with the back of a hand. "Billy, when I was younger, I didn't used to be so afraid." She sighs. "I've always regretted not showing up in court that day. *Always*. He was black. Sometimes, I'll see a large black man at the grocery store or on the street and I'll just freeze. My skin gets cold, I've even had trouble breathing. It just makes me feel sick, like I'm a racist." She closes her eyes and takes several deep breaths as if she is trying to conquer the nausea, and then opens them again, even smiles, if somewhat sadly. "I wonder if Clarence had been punished for what he did, if I might feel a little less scared in the world. Know what I mean?" He nods. "Normal people don't go out and get revenge. I guess that's what I'm saying if nothing else: It's the only way you have of getting even with those guys for what they did to you." Jan touches William's face, the stitches, bruises, the cracked lip. "It makes me so fucking mad."

The next few hours are full of activity. Jan and William go to the police station, file a report. William removes his shirt so that an officer can photograph his stomach which is now an oval-shaped dark shade of purple. Jan forces herself to watch, chewing a hang-nail. Afterward, this same cop, an amiable, chubby fellow with shockingly tiny teeth, follows them to Book Purgatory and makes William's truck filthy with white powder to look for fingerprints. It appears a meaningless mess, but the officer manages to find what he says looks like "a promising thumb" on the underside of the dash near the exposed wires. By the time this is all taken care of, Jan's shift is long over and it is time to pick Hank up from Rain's. "I need to go home and sleep," William says, swaying on his feet, eyes barely open, one of the pain pills already in his system.

Jan squeezes his shoulder as the cop pulls off. "I was serious about you staying over."

William smiles, closes his eyes. "I'll be fine."

Jan leans into him, puts her arms around his waist, sniffs the light scent of sweat in his T-shirt. She has always been uncomfortable expressing affection at the bookstore, even when they were going out. She and William can be seen from the large Book Purgatory windows, but she does not care. "I'd like you to. Hank would too—he likes you, you know. It's like you said, we could be in danger. We could protect each other, and I could look after you. Just for tonight." She leans back so that she can see him, hands on his waist, smiles. "Maybe tomorrow too. We can play it by ear."

He opens his mouth, closes it, says, "I need to feed my dog and cat."

"I'll drop you at my place. When I go get Hank, I'll run by your apartment and feed Flann and pick Harry up, bring him with me." She winks. "Everything's going to be fine."

At Jan's house, William refuses help walking. "I'm not that bad," he says, shuffling around the side to the kitchen door.

"Whatever, Gramps."

"Ha, ha, ha," he says following her inside. "Would you get me a glass of water so I can take another couple pills? The pain's bad." He moves slowly from the kitchen, arms out from his body, as if he is in so much pain he cannot bear to touch himself. Jan fills a glass and goes down the hallway to her bedroom, but he is not there. Standing in the doorway, she stares around the room as if a six-foot-two man covered in tattoos could be hiding somewhere. She finds him, eyes closed, on the living room couch, an arm stretched above him, the one in the cast against his belly. He is too tall for the couch, feet—in old, white socks, a big toe sticking through a hole—hanging off the edge. "Hey," Jan says, sitting on the coffee table.

"Hey," he responds without opening his eyes.

She shakes two pills into her hand. "Here."

He opens his eyes, props himself on an elbow, takes the pills, drinks a few gulps of water, hands the glass back. "Thanks." He lies back.

"You can sleep in my bed."

"I'm comfortable." He runs a hand across his buzzed hair and smiles. "I don't know if I'm going to sleep. My mind is racing."

"With what?"

"Stuff."

They sit in silence for a long time, Jan listening to him breathe. She feels stuck there, afraid to move. Finally, she leans forward and takes his glasses off. He does not open his eyes. "You should try to sleep," she whispers.

"I will," he whispers back.

She cannot resist touching the bruises and cuts again, but gently, to avoid giving him pain. She finds the puffiness over his eye particularly compelling, keeps coming back to it until she is caressing that spot. There is something about the swelling, the marring of his left eye, rough ridges of black stitching, which is sensuous. William's eyes open, and he puts his hand against Jan's back, rough fingers grazing the skin where her shirt rides up. She feels her eyes welling again, smiles and wipes her fingers quickly across her eyelashes. Touching his lip, she glides her finger across two fake bridge teeth, bends to lightly kiss his puffy lips. Her fingers are gentle on his bruised cheek, and she cannot resist letting her tongue slide between his teeth. His lips work slowly with hers, and his hand moves from her back to her waist to her ass.

She helps him off with his jeans, slowly, because every movement seems to cause new pain. She whispers, "Are you sure you want to do this?" and is surprised by how hard his dick is, and then she is slipping off her shorts and underwear, and climbing carefully on top, his mouth in-between grimace and grin. He says, "Gentle, gentle," and Jan is saying, "Sorry, sorry," feeling clumsy. She is so wet, he slides in with ease, both sighing together, room peaty with sex. There is the quiet, moist sound of them moving together, breathing, a motorcycle revving somewhere out in the day and diminishing. He pulls up her shirt, fingers sliding under her bra, pulling it down, directing her nipples to his mouth, her back arching, fingers gliding along his rib cage with its cracked ribs. She knows she is about to come, can feel it burgeoning, thighs tight and slick against his. But before this happens, the kitchen door bursts open and there is the pounding of shoes against linoleum coming toward them. Jan gasps, sits upright, hands covering her breasts, and she stares into the shocked faces of Hank and Patrick Henry. "Oh shit," she says, and "Fuck," William mutters.

Rain comes in smiling, already speaking: "We were out for a walk and didn't expect to...see you..." She puts a hand to her mouth, says, "Oh, my god." But she recovers quickly, brightly saying, "Boys, let's go to Hank's room for a bit." Her hands on the two boys' heads, she hustles them from the room, arching an eyebrow at Jan. William nods toward the pile of clothes, and Jan nods back, getting off him, pulling her shorts on, handing him his jeans in brisk, efficient movements. There is the sound of the refrigerator opening and closing and then Art comes in with an open beer, does a cartoonish double-take, and sits in the rocking chair, a mock serious expression on his face. "Tsk, tsk, tsk," he says, shaking his head.

"I'm really, *really* sorry about this, "Jan says, tying her ponytail with a rubber band, kicking her panties under the couch.

Art loses the mock seriousness and breaks into a grin. "Don't worry about it, baby. Sex is good." In the dusk light, his white teeth take on such stark contrast to his ebony skin that his smile is Cheshire-cat-like and Jan has to grin back although she is horrified that her son has just caught her fucking a man.

As Jan helps William struggle on his pants, Rain comes back into the room. "Do you think you could give them a minute?"

Skinny legs crossed, flip-flop hanging, Art shakes his head. "Nah, they're all right."

"*Come,*" she says, "*here,*" crooking a finger, eyes wider.

"All *right,*" he says, getting up and following her down the hall.

William gets into Jan's bed and almost immediately falls asleep. She throws some pasta in a pot and sautés vegetables while Rain makes a salad and Art drives to William's apartment to get Harry and feed Flann. When he comes back, he has got a bottle of wine, a loaf of bread, a video, and a bouquet of flowers which he arranges in a vase on the table. At dinner, Art makes an eloquent blessing, thanking God for allowing their two families to come together at unexpected moments like these. Jan opens her eyes, sees Hank staring, and gives an embarrassed wink. Art has rented a Kurosawa film and, although Jan likes the director, she is not in the mood for black-and-white scenes of samurais and dialogue she has to read. While he watches the movie stretched out on the floor in front of the little TV, a pillow bunched under one armpit, and the boys and Harry play outside in the last of the summer light, she and Rain sit at the dining room table drinking the rest of the wine. She smokes two cigarettes with Rain and only feels a little guilty.

"So," Rain says, "what's going on?" She raises that eyebrow again, the left corner of her mouth turned up.

Jan smiles, taps a nail against the wooden table. "I don't know."

"Be careful." She nods slowly, drags on her cigarette and blows the smoke at the ceiling. "He's not going to be hurt forever. You might ask yourself if you're going to want him when he doesn't need you."

"I know, I know." Jan squeezes her hand. "Thanks. I want to make smarter choices. I'm tired of just letting things happen."

"I'm just trying to keep you real."

Rain's got that wine glaze in her eye and Jan grins. "You goddamned beautiful chick. You know I love you?"

Rain throws back her wine. "You have to. Who else would put up with your shit?"

"No one, babe." Jan closes her eyes, likes the slight dizziness coming over her.

The phone rings, and she jumps to get it before the second one. It is the cop with the tiny teeth. She listens for a few moments, says, "Oh, thank you so much for calling. That's such a relief." She goes quickly down the hallway to her bedroom. William is sleeping on his back, loudly snoring, and she slides in next to him, listening to his rough breathing and watching his silhouette in the light coming from the hallway. "William," she says, lips inches from his ear. She has to repeat his name once more and nudge him lightly before he will come awake, snorting and trying to sit up. "No, no, it's okay." She nudges him back down. "I just wanted to tell you that that cop called and they picked up the guy. He's in jail. The cop says he thinks the judge won't give him bail after this, but if he does he'll let us know."

"Mmmm," William says, licking his lips.

Jan waits for more, but William's breathing has evened out and he is already back asleep. She leans in to kiss his stubbly cheek and says, "Good night."

"Good night," he says. At the door, he whispers, "Thank you." She stands there listening for a moment and then goes back down the hallway.

Patrick Henry climbs onto Rain's lap just as Jan gets back to the dining room, hangs on her neck, bending her forward. "Hey, hey, you're too big for that," Rain says. She kisses him on the head, squeezing him back.

Jan caresses his cheek, marvels at his beautiful olive-brown skin, in-between his father's dark pigment and his mother's porcelain complexion. "Are you sick of playing with Hank, P.H.?" she asks, sitting.

"I don't know, I guess. I'm sick of swinging. That's all he wants to do. I say, 'You want to play Parcheesi? You want to play Nintendo?' He just says 'Nah,' keeps swinging."

"Let me see if I can talk some sense into him." Jan kisses the boy on his curly head.

Hank is just a dark shadow swinging back and forth on the rusty set at the far end of the lawn. Jan switches on the backyard light, projecting thick shadows over the unmowed grass. There is an eerie stillness to the night compounded by the rhythmic squeak of swing chain and the sky is a dull yellow as if a tornado is coming. Harry lies next to the swing set with his snout on his front paws, and Jan kneels to stroke his back and behind the ears. The dog barely moves, tail flicking against the overlong grass, tongue emerging slowly to lick her hand. "You've tired this dog out, buddy." The swing's chains squeak five more times and Jan says, "How are you doing, honey?"

"Fine." He does not return her glance, rhythmically kicks his legs.

Jan sits in the other swing and pushes back off the dirt, having to raise her knees to keep her feet from dragging. "Are you tired?"

"No."

"Are you sick of playing with Patrick Henry?"

"I don't know. Maybe."

"Are you bothered about seeing me and William this afternoon?"

He kicks, leaning back, pulling on the swing's chains. After a couple more swings, he says, "I don't know. I don't think so."

"Do you know what we were doing?"

"You were having sex." He is staring ahead at the house, kicking.

"Right."

Their two swings are squeaking at different intervals now, filling the otherwise quiet night with a strange syncopation. "Do you love William?" he asks after a few more swings.

The question takes her by surprise and she flies forward and backward several times, the sweat breaking on her forehead and under her arms, and then says, "Yes." She is surprised that she can answer this, pleased too because she senses that if the answer had been "No," Hank would have been disappointed in her. They kick and bend their knees, leaning back and staring at the yellow night in silence for a long time, chains squeaking their slow, steady rhythm. Sometimes the two swings squeak together and this sound fills Jan with a joy so profound it is almost like pain.

11

Jan kicks the potter's flywheel which makes a sound like ball bearings on a flat surface. The art building is empty, blissfully cavernous. This is her last semester. She will graduate with a degree in history, emphasis American South. She will not teach history, will not go to graduate school, will probably never *do* anything with her degree. But she will have it and for now that is enough. With the days counting down toward graduation, she feels she does not have time to do all she wants. The shelf she has been allocated for her ceramics class seems woefully empty of satisfying work: cups with wonky mouths, bloated bowls. Both William and Rain, who has her MFA (and who, Jan often thinks, should know better) tell her that they are beautiful. Sometimes, when the afternoon sun is right, when the overhead fluorescents are extinguished and the air is still, she believes them: there *is* something delicate, almost like poetry to them, their rough, earthy exteriors, Popsicle stick incisions, slip coatings, unpredictable glazes. But she does not want to make poetry, she wants bowls and plates and cups which people will actually use.

Except for William's dog, Harry, who sleeps on the concrete floor nearby, Jan is alone in the studio. Hank has been with William all day. They were supposed to go to a matinee and lunch and William said he might take Hank to Book Purgatory to look for *Spider-Man* comics, Hank's new obsession. It has taken a while, but Jan is realizing that she trusts Hank with William and, if she is honest, she will admit that in some ways he connects with her son better than she does. They live in the moment and think about things, long and deeply, slipping into contemplations which seem like sleep. They both approach tasks—from the banal, like sweeping the floor, to the complex like drawing a picture or learning a song—with baffling concentration and patience. In fact, Hank says that William is teaching him to play a song on the guitar, "a surprise song" he says, which he is learning for her birthday in two months.

Yon Hall's air conditioning ticks, and Jan feels the wet clay building on her hands, over the dry, cracking clay beneath it. Clay dust is powdery on her tongue. A curl loose from her ponytail brushes lightly against her cheek each time she kicks the flywheel. The sun coming through the large picture windows warms her face and neck. On most Mondays, the immaculate green lawns running between the buildings of the Fine Arts Complex would offer her a scene of constant activity: people lounging on the stone wall rimming Yon Hall, a group of crunchy guys playing hacky sack, the occasional street preacher predicting hellfire for young people. But it is spring break and the bright day seems almost unsettling in its stillness. A professor walks by stroking his beard, muttering at the ground; a group of East Asian students pass talking and gesturing with animation; but Jan will work for over an hour at a time without seeing another person out these windows.

She leans back on her stool and looks at the tall cup perched in the center of the wheel. It seems perfect. But she knows she will discover flaws if she looks long enough, so cuts the cup from the wheel with her wire and places it on her ware board without another glance. She bends to tear another chunk of clay off the moist mound in the dirty white bucket at her feet. It makes a satisfyingly heavy smack against the wheel. The studio is equipped with electric wheels also, but she likes the feel of control she gets from kicking, the light sweat it causes, the slight rasp. She runs her fingers around the circumference of the lump of clay and pulls its walls up. The chunk of reddish wet earth in her hands makes a sibilant squish. It looks like magic the way it spirals up from the wheel. She has been throwing for nearly a year and is still amazed with the sudden, fragile transformation of a lump of mud. The fragility of each piece, the balance of this task, sometimes makes her forget to breathe.

"You're a good boy, aren't you?" she asks Harry. He raises his snout and gives one "yip," thumps his tail a couple times. He *is* a good boy. At first, when she started bringing him to the studio, he would wander off. And she let him. But she learned her lesson after she caught him peeing in a corner. She shouted at him then, but immediately felt guilty when he slunk away with his tail between his legs. That is probably why the art department has a no-pets policy. She has learned that pets, dogs especially, are like children in many ways. They do not always tell you what they want. Sometimes, you have to anticipate their needs. She has gotten better at taking him outside for bathroom breaks and to throw the ball. Even though she has found it easy to get lost in her work, to forget to eat, she has learned to remember Harry.

Jan kicks the wheel twice more and runs a damp sponge up the inside wall of the cup, wiping the moisture so it will not crack. She has learned clay has memory and sometimes, no matter how much she cajoles it with careful hands, it shifts back to earlier mistakes, ingrained flaws. Taking a breath, she grins at Harry. "This one's going to be beautiful," she promises the dog and he thumps his tail once more, not raising his snout this time.

All her mugs are really cups because she hasn't managed to make a good handle. She hums, lets her eyes close for a moment. Although many of her artist friends, Rain among them, like to play music while they work, Jan prefers silence, the sound of working and her own thoughts. She loves the gentle kicks, that first pull of clay like drawing in space, the unconscious movements, more like dancing than any sort of *work*. As it gets dark outside, she can hear the sound of crickets if she holds her breath. The dishware she has made today and not destroyed—a couple plates, several bowls, cups—are spaced out on the table beside her, a dull red and brown under the ceiling lights.

Clay draws her to form round shapes. She pictures the rings radiating from her sinking car two years ago in Lake Walters. Circles on the surface where the bubbles from Hank's lungs had rushed to escape to the surface. The round mouth of that lake opening to swallow them. Of course, she knows the real reason she makes round shapes is because curves conform to the movement of the potter's wheel, to the curve of a lip drinking water.

Jan loves thinking of herself as a potter, loves that she carries evidence of her work with her when she leaves the studio. When she grocery shops or takes Hank to the park and she is wearing her clothes smeared with dried clay or slip splatters, she tells the world she is an artist. When she was in high school, she hungered to be like her artist friends whose clothes were always a palette of old paint, hands filthy with charcoal. Jan could not create the realistic imitations of nature her friend Dru could so she thought she was a failure, and no one rushed to disagree. When she discovered poetry, she began to call herself a poet, deliberately broke pens so her fingers would be smeared with ink. Still, deep down she knew she was a fraud, knew her poems were not any good. Although she often questions the quality of her pottery, she knows she is getting her hands dirty because she is really doing work and not just pretending like when she was a teenager and half-heartedly cut herself with a stolen X-Acto or worked to hate her innocuous parents because that was the way she imagined poets were. She can feel the clay beneath her fingernails so she knows that it is real.

Sometime later, Jan pushes a ware cart with a couple trays of her work out to the kiln yard. Pieces she made days ago, the clay bone-dry, is hopefully sturdy enough now to face the kiln's heat. She loads the dishware, stoneware ghostly white in the dim light of the yard, onto the shelves in one of the gas kilns, and turns it on. Tomorrow evening she will cut the heat and when she looks through the spy hole, her work will glow a whitish orange like banked coals. She will glaze it and then fire it once again. Feeling the heat from the firebrick radiating against her face—almost two thousand degrees in there—she thinks it is amazing anything can pass through that temperature in one piece. She gingerly touches her right cheek, remembering the reddish hue in the mirror this morning like a mild sunburn—only on the right side of her face, the side she usually keeps to the kiln when working, what Rain calls "kiln burn."

Using an overturned bucket as a stepladder, she climbs on top of one of the squat kilns not in use and then hops up on the cinderblock wall rimming the yard. She walks a few feet, hands at her sides like a tightrope walker. Then, sitting, she swings her legs over the other side, facing the shadowy lawn surrounding the Fine Arts Complex, the landscape dipping and rising like an artist's rendering of a nighttime sea. She would smoke now if she still did that. Instead, she chews a hangnail, occasionally speaking to Harry who crouches and pants on the pavement below. But mostly she just stares at nothing. Other than the hum of cars on 13th and buzz of crickets, the night is silent. The stillness in the air is exhilarating, delicious, as if she might drink the dark. And then she realizes with a shock that there is no fear. The dark feels safe—it is hard to believe that there were serial killings just a few miles from here less than two years ago. Her thoughts shift, gingerly approach the night of the rape years before that, the weight of her rapist, and then she brings her mind back to the now. She concentrates on the kiln blaze slipping into her peripheral vision, warm on her cheeks, in her retina, caressing her body, dwarfed by all this functional, modernist architecture. It is a pleasing, safe feeling and she tries to remain as still as possible, slows her breathing to a shallow susurration. She loves being here by herself, is greedy for the solitude and that makes her feel guilty, though she does not know why. There is not much time. Soon school will be back in session and the buildings will vibrate with activity and bodies. And then the semester will be over and she will not belong here. There is a possible job: At the end of the semester, Rain is leaving her position as a pottery instructor at the children's museum and has said she will put in a good word for her. Jan feels unqualified for the job, assumes she will not get it, but when she imagines teaching kids to make a bowl, cup, or whatever shapes appeal to them there is a tickle of excitement in her throat which threatens to turn into real giddiness. Also, at the end of the semester, Hank is going back to South Carolina, this time for Ray's wedding.

Jan has trouble thinking of the marriage without bitterness. In her twenties, she had ached for Ray to propose. She could not even imagine anything beyond: house, yard, dog, children, life placid like water. There was no future, clichéd or not, beyond the moment of him asking, with or without a ring—just Ray next to her on the couch. She could not imagine him kneeling. He would look into her eyes without wavering and those guitarist's fingers, unclipped nails on the picking hand, would lightly touch her hand. He would not rush, would not be nervous, no hesitation in his blue eyes which would not blink. His soft mouth would move slowly to form the words: "Jan, please marry me." She would know he was serious, that he really wanted to spend the rest of his life with her, that he was not doing this simply because she was pregnant. Her fantasy never went beyond that moment, not even to where Jan said yes, although she knew she would. She would have married him in a courthouse, without even a single family member or friend present. His asking seemed more important than the actual marriage. Later, after Hank was born, when her hints became less subtle, when they fought about marriage, she realized that he would neither marry nor dump her. And then, in the months after the rape, Jan could see in his eyes—that fear, that hesitation to speak the fear—that he *would* marry her if she brought it up again. But she would not. The fantasy of the two of them on the couch seemed ludicrous and naïve by then, a young girl's fairy tale. Jan loved Ray—if she is honest, she will admit that she loves him still, some part of her at any rate. But when she was raped, it was like something inside her was mutilated. Like her rapist stuck his gigantic hand into her and scooped out some vitality, his big, stupid clumsy hand crushing it to a pulp and wiping it on the leg of his jeans without a thought. With that part gone, Jan no longer cared enough about her relationship with Ray to ignore his infidelities and kicked him out. She does not mind that Ray is getting married to Julie, in fact, hopes he will finally be happy. There is a lump in the center of her chest as she thinks of all the trouble they have been through. Sitting on that wall at the art building, she takes a deep breath and lets it out slowly. She wants to think that they all deserve happiness now, but is afraid to even let the words form in her head.

She jumps, the impact of her sneakers against pavement jarring her shins, puts her cheek close to the kiln, almost too hot to bear. Eyes closing, her lips move silently as if praying. She visualizes what her pieces will look like when she takes them from the kiln in two days, after their final firing. Harry licks her calf, but she does not open her eyes. Every time she fires a batch she feels as if she is getting closer to some basic truth. She feels as if, just in the act of holding such essential matter as food and water, these things she makes are perfect, that there is no meaning outside them. But she has also made enough pottery to know that if she examines her work, she will see a lack of symmetry in the cups, or maybe a conventionality to the plates. She will have a sudden urge to destroy the work—throw it against the pavement, that satisfying crash of shattering. There would be a thrill in the excess of the act. She has done it before. But part of her always feels there is something perverse in destroying it. Promising herself she won't smash these pieces, at least for a week, Jan thinks of the designs Rain adorns her own work with: dancing devils, cartoon Jesuses, Mother Mary with a power fist. Jan wants to paint her own designs, she is not sure of what, but something. She has not painted since high school and already knows the child-like images she would produce. Maybe she should let a real child paint her work. Hank loves to paint, is not bowed down by other people's expectations. She imagines Hank in the studio with her the coming weekend, painting her work with overglaze while she throws other bowls and cups. They would talk some, occasionally take Harry for a walk. Her fellow artists would stop to compliment Hank on his painting, but she and her son would be mostly silent except for her bare foot on the wheel.

Harry whimpers, that quiet growl he makes when he has been ignored for too long. Jan kneels so he can nuzzle her behind the ear, snuffling in her hair the way he likes, breath hot and ticklish. "You're just a big, needy baby, aren't you? Aren't you?" she asks, and his tail bangs against her thigh. "Come on, baby, come on. Let's go home." She stands so suddenly her head spins and she stares at her shadow on the red brick wall, gigantic and wiry and powerful-looking in the night and appearing so suddenly it could be anyone's. There was a time when a moment like this would terrify her, make her afraid to bike home alone even though she would know the shadow was hers, that she was alone. Now she sees it for what it is: the proof that she is standing between the light hanging from the ceiling and the back wall. Nothing more. She has been through enough to earn her fear and she is not sure why she is not afraid now. The lack of fear is frightening in itself. She wraps Harry's leash around her hand as she walks through the empty building, turning off lights as she goes. "Come on, baby, come on," she says to the dog. "Let's go home." She repeats this phrase so many times as she heads outside to the bike rack that, after a while, it turns into a little song.

Acknowledgments

The first chapter of *The World Out There* appeared in *Berkeley Fiction Review* in 2003 under the title, "Breathe."

The line quoted on p. 47 is from the poem "Winter's Asperity Mollifies" by Donald Hall (*The Museum of Clear Ideas*, Houghton Mifflin, 1994).

The following institutions and organizations have supported my writing process with money, time, and/or space to work: Queensborough Community College, PSC-CUNY, University of Nebraska-Lincoln Department of English, Virginia Center for the Creative Arts, and the Lower Manhattan Cultural Council. Their support is greatly appreciated.

Many thanks to family, friends, and colleagues who have been generous in their support, feedback, and encouragement over the years it took me to write this novel. I would particularly like to thank Allen Wier, Marilyn Kallet, Erin Flanagan, Ladette Randolph, Liz Ahl, Jon Ritz, Sherrie Flick, Steve Werkmeister, Tyrone Jaeger, Curt Rode, Wheeler Dixon, Leslie Kerby, Jason Andrew, Sean Scott, and Micki Skudlarczyk. My friend and mentor Gerry Shapiro offered encouragement and constructive criticism in the early drafting of this novel. I am sad that he did not live to see it in print, but know that he would have been proud of me. And finally, although this novel is a work of fiction, like Hank, I was raised by a single mother. Jo Talbird died in 2018 after a long struggle with Parkinson's disease. This novel is dedicated to her. And as always, thank you to my precious wife, Melinda Yale, who gives the struggle meaning and inspires me to get out of bed in the morning—to write and to do so many other things

About the Author

John Talbird is the author of the chapbook, *A Modicum of Mankind* (Norte Maar). His fiction and essays have appeared in *Ploughshares*, *Grain*, *Juked*, *The Literary Review*, *Ambit*, *Potomac Review* and many others. He is on the Editorial Board of *Green Hills Literary Lantern* and a frequent contributor to *Film International*. An English professor at Queensborough Community College-CUNY, he lives in New York City with his wife, Melinda Yale.

www.ingramcontent.com/pod-product-compliance
Lightning Source LLC
Chambersburg PA
CBHW030543040726
47497CB00008B/2570